KU-486-909

THE
KREMLIN
LETTER

A chilling novel of master spies in
merciless competition

by

NOEL BEHN

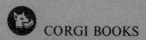

CORGI BOOKS

A DIVISION OF TRANSWORLD PUBLISHERS

THE KREMLIN LETTER

A CORGI BOOK 552 07872 7

Originally published in Great Britain
by W. H. Allen & Company

PRINTING HISTORY
W. H. Allen Edition published 1966
Corgi Edition published 1968

Copyright © Noel Behn 1966

Condition of sale – this book is sold subject to the
condition that it shall not, by way of trade *or otherwise,*
be lent, re-sold, hired out or otherwise *circulated*
without the publisher's prior consent in any form of
binding or cover other than that in which it is published
*and without a similar condition including this condition
being imposed on the subsequent purchaser.*

This book is set in 10pt. Times Roman

Corgi Books are published by Transworld Publishers Ltd.,
Bashley Road, London, N.W.10

Printed Web Offset in England
by Petty and Sons Limited, Leeds.

CONTENTS

Prologue

To Dad.

Happy Very late
Birthday.

James
xxxx

"IMPOSSIBLE TO PUT DOWN...
SUSPENSEFUL THROUGHOUT...
AN INGENIOUS, BRUTAL ENDING."
True Magazine.

*"Remember Zeiff?" he heard Ward say.
"Remember how you forced acid down his
throat? Not enough to kill him, but enough to
make him scream. You like to make people
scream, Colonel. Well, I've got a little
something for you . . ."*

THE KREMLIN LETTER is about deceit
and betrayal; about men and women who act
courageously from base motives; about the
use of sex, drugs, violence and cunning as
weapons in a special arena of the Cold War,
where there are no enemies and no friends –
only colleagues and competitors.
THE KREMLIN LETTER is about . . . a
letter. Its contents are political dynamite;
it has the explosive potential of a nuclear
warhead; it is priced at several million
pounds – and it is worth any number of lives,
their own included, to the ruthless agents of
East and West who struggle to possess it.

"A BEAUTY!" raved the *Chicago Tribune*
in a front-page review.

PROLOGUE

THE PEPPER POT IS BROKEN

COLONEL Vladimir Ilyich Kosnov walked silently down the prison hallway and entered cell number 108. The two green-uniformed men in front of the cot moved to one side so that he could examine the body. Polakov was lying on his back, his eyes wide open. His left hand was clenched to his mouth.

"I watched him all the time, comrade Colonel – every minute. I watched him through the Judas hole," the guard explained nervously, standing to attention, his hands at his red-piped trouser seams.

"I know these men," interjected the prison commandant. "They are all reliable. If he says he watched the prisoner every minute then you can be sure he did."

Colonel Kosnov heard nothing. He reached down and wrenched the hand from the dead man's mouth. He held Polakov's fingers in his own and examined them. The nail on the thumb had been bitten through. It was cracked as a piece of plastic might crack. He leaned over and sniffed the dead thumb. The faint smell of almonds stung his nostrils gently.

"It would be impossible for him to conceal anything on his person," said the commandant. "We searched him thoroughly. There is no way he could have done it."

Kosnov looked at the commandant impassively. "Then I must assume he is still alive," he said.

The commandant sighed and glanced at the body, as if the colonel's words might miraculously infuse it with life.

Kosnov took a last look at Polakov. He thought he detected a slight smile on the dead man's lips. Before he could restrain himself he smiled back. He turned on his heel and left the cell. The guard and commandant followed. At the end of the corridor, he walked quickly through the steel door, slamming it in the face of the two men following him. He climbed the stairs to the next floor, where his adjutant waited in front of a cell.

"How are they, Grodin?" asked the colonel.

"Khorosho," answered the lieutenant.

Kosnov peered through the Judas hole. Polakov's young wife was asleep. In the next cell his mother and sister sat on the floor, their eyes closed, holding each other's hand. He looked back to the sleeping face of the wife. She was quite lovely. I should have married, he told himself.

Straightening, the colonel motioned to the cell in which the two older women dozed. "Kill them," he ordered. Then, dismissing the adjutant, he opened the door of the widow's cell and stepped in.

Five hours later Uncle Morris sent a cablegram to Sweet Alice. It began:

THE PEPPER POT IS BROKEN

SECTION ONE

CHAPTER ONE

THE DEFECTOR

LIEUTENANT Commander Charles Rone, USN, Regional Director – Systems, of the Office of Naval Intelligence, woke at precisely six A.M., brushed his teeth and completed his Royal Canadian Air Force exercises in four minutes and twenty-eight seconds. He shaved, showered and began dressing in front of the floor-length mirror. His trousers had been pressed slightly off the crease. He changed to another uniform, pinched his tie to perfection, buttoned his jacket and buffed his shoes to a high black gloss with the electric polisher. He picked up his briefcase, tucked his copy of the *Wall Street Journal* under his arm and started out for the Officers' Mess.

He finished half a grapefruit, two poached eggs and one slice of rye toast before pouring his third cup of black coffee, neatly folding back the newspaper to the closing stock-market prices, taking a deep breath and beginning to read.

He was counting his losses when the door flew open. He didn't have to look up to recognise the rasping voice of Captain Felson.

"Rone! The plane is waiting. Where the hell are all your things?"

"What plane? What things?"

"The seaplane. Your civilian things. Your kit. Everything. Where are they?"

"In my quarters. Where else?"

"Don't sit there, Commander. Get them."

"Why?"

"Ask the admiral."

From behind a long oak desk, devoid of antiquity or character, the admiral watched Rone approach. He did not bother to return the salute, but simply said, in an angry and official tone, "Lieutenant Commander Charles E. Rone, you are hereby informed that as of 1400 hours today, October 10th, you will no longer be under the jurisdiction of the Department of the Navy."

"Excuse me, sir?" Rone said in disbelief.

"You are further informed," continued the admiral, "that as of 1400 hours, October 10, your commission as an officer in the Navy of the United States will be suspended, and concurrent with said suspension all rights and benefits accruing to you in the past or due to you in the future, as either an officer in the Naval Establishment or a member of the Armed Forces of the United States, will forthwith and forever be revoked and cancelled – not that it makes a goddam bit of difference to you, I suppose?"

"But sir—" Rone began.

"And you will no longer address me as 'Sir.' "

"But I prefer calling you 'Sir.' "

"And I prefer that you don't."

"Under what authority have I been separated?" he demanded.

"It is proper and binding," the admiral replied.

"Under the Uniform Code of Military Justice I demand to know exactly the circumstances under which this order was given. To my knowledge there is no possible way an officer can be discharged without either his knowledge or consent."

"I'm sure your new friends in Washington can explain."

"*What* friends?"

"Rone," the admiral said, ignoring his question, "I suppose in this day and age your behaviour is called initiative. I also suppose that people who get what they want, regardless of the method or cost, are to be congratulated. Well, I'm old-fashioned, mister, and I call what you did plain and simple insubordination. No, there's a better word for it, a word that your former colleagues like to use – defection."

"I have not defected or deceived or done anything else."

"I know of no other word for a breach of loyalty," the admiral snapped back, "and in this case you had at least two such loyalties to betray, the Naval Establishment on the one hand and your own intelligence organisation on the other. A good many Regular Army and Navy officers are damned sorry that CIC or ONI were ever formed – they seem to believe that intelligence personnel develop stronger loyalties to their own organisations than they do to either the Army or Navy. Well, Mr. Rone, you've gone them one better, you've proved that a really good intelligence officer won't even stand by his own kind. Why aren't you in civilian clothes?"

"No one told me to change."

"Only officers in the United States Navy are entitled to wear that uniform. Once upon a time, legend has it, some men even died for it. When you've changed, my car will take you to the airport – as is expected in cases like this. Dismissed – *Mr*. Rone."

A thin, silent young man in a Brooks Brothers suit moved in behind Rone as he waited for his baggage at the Washington Airport.

"Mr. Rone," he half whispered, "you will please follow me."

"My Valpac hasn't come down yet," Rone answered.

"It's already in the car." He led Rone quickly through the crowd to a limousine, in which two very similar young men were waiting.

"You're late," one of them said as the car moved off towards the city.

"The plane was late," Rone explained.

"We may miss the train."

"They'll hold it for us," the driver said firmly.

The car turned a sharp corner and sped over the Chesapeake Bridge.

"Where are we going?" Rone asked.

"To the station."

"Can any of you explain how I could be discharged without my consent?"

"Ask the man on the train."

The three young men hurried Rone along the train corridor.

"In there," said one of them, motioning to a partially opened drawing-room door. The trio continued on alone to the next carriage – still carrying Rone's Valpac.

A short, sunburned man in dark-green slacks and an

open-necked Hawaiian sportshirt stood in the middle of the compartment.

"You're late, Mr. Rone," he said.

"The plane was late."

"Then you should have taken an earlier flight."

"This was the one I was put on."

"Then the admiral is at fault." The man walked to the window and sat down. "The admiral will have to answer for it. Someone always has to answer in these matters."

Rone remained standing. "By what jurisdiction was my commission revoked?" he demanded.

"You can have it back if you want."

Rone had no answer.

"That choice is up to you," the man continued. "However, after reading your record I have the impression that my clients might be able to offer you something quite interesting."

"Such as?"

"Money."

"To do what?"

"To do the second thing your record claims you crave for – to live dangerously," the man said with a smirk.

"I don't find this amusing," Rone said firmly.

"How do you find one hundred and twenty-five thousand dollars? Tax-free dollars, I might add. That's only the retainer, of course. If you're selected there could be more."

"Selected?"

"My people will have to see if you work out. But the minimum, whether you're used or not, is still one hundres and twenty-five thousand dollars."

"And what's the maximum?"

"At least another hundred and twenty-five thousand . . . if you survive. Under certain conditions it could be double or triple that."

"And what do I have to do?" asked Rone.

"First of all, agree to give up your commission in the Navy," the man said apathetically.

"Then what?"

"Then I'll tell you what we have in store for you."

"You mean *after* I've agreed to do it?"

"Come now, Commander; originally we were going to

12

take away your citizenship as well."

"No deal."

"Whatever you say," the man said without concern. "The train stops in about ten minutes. You can get off then and your commission will be restored. They told you about the quarantine, of course?"

"What quarantine?"

"You'll be detained for at least six months."

"For what?" Rone asked indignantly.

"Why, for this meeting, what else? Security in matters like this is slightly sticky."

Rone stood glowering at the man.

"You've probably made a wise choice. There are always certain risks involved in these projects – you'll be much safer back in the Navy."

Rone remained standing near the door. He could feel himself flush.

"All right," he heard himself saying, "when do I begin?"

"Read these." The man shoved a thin manila folder along the seat. Then he yawned and took off his tinted glasses.

"Shall I read it standing up or can I sit down?" Rone asked casually.

"You can read it standing on your head if it helps," the man replied indifferently. "Just read it." He turned and stared out of the window.

Rone sat down and looked at the folder. On the outside was printed "The Highwayman."

"I've already read it," he said.

"Read what?" said the man, still looking out of the window.

"'The Highwayman,'" answered Rone.

"The road was a ribbon of moonlight over the
purple moor,
And the highwayman came riding –
Riding – riding –
The highwayman came riding, up to the old inn-door."

The man turned slowly towards Rone. He had a square bronzed face with an aquiline nose. His silver-white hair was crew-cut. His eyes were green, coldly green. He

13

studied Rone a moment or two, then turned back to the window.

Rone opened the folder and found himself looking at two teletyped messages pasted on the top and bottom of a sheet of paper. They appeared to be cablegrams, but he couldn't be sure since all four margins had been neatly trimmed to eliminate any identifying printing or marks. In addition, the address in the top left corner of each message had been covered with a typewritten identification sticker which listed the subject of the message, who sent it, who received it, and the exhibit or filing number. He began reading:

```
EXHIBIT:    1              DATE: SEPTEMBER 18
SUBJECT:  PEPPER POTS
TO:          SWEET ALICE
FROM:       UNCLE MORRIS
             THE PEPPER POT IS BROKEN. THE
             CUPBOARD IS BARE. WHAT DOES
             THE A&P HAVE ON ITS SHELVES?
```

```
EXHIBIT:    2              DATE: SEPTEMBER 18
SUBJECT:  PEPPER POTS
TO:          UNCLE MORRIS
FROM:       SWEET ALICE
             ONLY STANDARD BRANDS IN
             STOCK. WHAT'S NEW WITH THE
             COMMON MARKET?
```

Rone noticed that neither the pages nor the messages had been stamped top secret, secret, or any other classification. He held his place and looked at the front of the folder. No restrictions were there, either, yet he felt instinctively that this was secret information or higher. He turned the page. This was the last sheet of paper in the file and only one message was pasted on it.

```
EXHIBIT:   3              DATE: SEPTEMBER 19
SUBJECT:   PEPPER POTS
TO:        SWEET ALICE
FROM:      UNCLE MORRIS
           COMMON MARKET QUALITY
           UNACCEPTABLE. THE STEW IS
           COOLING. HAVE YOU READ ANY
           GOOD POEMS LATELY? IF SO SEND
           VOLUMES.
```

Rone closed the folder.

"What do you make of them?" asked the man, still not bothering to look at him.

"They're antiques," answered Rone. "The type of communications that were used twenty, thirty years ago."

"Never mind that. Do you understand them?"

"I think so."

"Let's hear."

Rone opened the folder and turned to the first page of messages. "Sweet Alice is American since she's the A&P. Uncle Morris is most likely British. He is not a member of the Common Market and these messages were sent in English. I can't tell yet whether they are intelligence agencies or individual agents.

"The Pepper Pot is an agent – or was an agent. I must assume a very good agent. Pepper is a condiment. Something that is used in every corner of the world. Therefore a pepper pot could be found in every corner of the world as well. No matter what the city, country or continent there is nothing unusual or suspicious about seeing a pepper pot. So we know this agent is just like that. He's at home anywhere and he goes any place without evoking suspicion. He would be one hell of a hard man to replace – and that's exactly what the problem is. He *must* be replaced. 'The Pepper Pot is broken,' says the message. That means he is either injured, captured or dead. I assume he is dead.

"Uncle Morris, our friend from England, looks around for a replacement in his own country – but 'the cupboard is bare.' So he contacts Sweet Alice to see what the

A&P has on its shelves, or if America has an agent with the qualifications to replace him. But we don't have anyone, we have 'only standard brands in stock.' Sweet Alice asks 'what's new with the Common Market,' suggesting that England try finding someone in Europe.

"In the last message Uncle Morris says that he has already tried Europe and found nothing. He warns Sweet Alice that 'the stew is cooling': If someone isn't found soon, either the United States or England, I'm not sure which, will probably compromise a very important case."

"Is that all?" asked the man, still looking out of the window.

"That's all I'm sure of," replied Rone. "Uncle Morris asks Alice about poems. This undoubtedly means another approach to the subject, but I can't tell what."

"Maybe this will help." The man had turned long enough to push another few pages of message towards Rone. Rone picked them up and began reading.

EXHIBIT: 4   DATE: SEPTEMBER 19
SUBJECT: POEMS
TO: UNCLE MORRIS
FROM: SWEET ALICE
               THE LIBRARY HAS FEW VOLUMES LEFT. COULD SEND FOLLOWING: ANNABEL LEE, J. ALFRED PRUFROCK, CREMATION OF SAM MCGEE, HIAWATHA.

Rone saw that the "subject" had changed. He read the second message on the page.

EXHIBIT: 5   DATE: SEPTEMBER 20
SUBJECT: POEMS
TO: SWEET ALICE
FROM: UNCLE MORRIS
               INTERESTED IN SAM MCGEE. DO YOU HAVE A THIRD EDITION?

Rone turned to the next and last page he had been handed. It contained only one message.

```
EXHIBIT:    6              DATE: SEPTEMBER 20
SUBJECT:    POEMS
TO:         UNCLE MORRIS
FROM:       SWEET ALICE
            SAM ONLY IN FIVE EDITIONS. THIRD
            ONE MISSING.
```

Rone thought for a moment. Then he went back over the preceding two pages.

The man had closed his eyes but when he heard Rone stir he said, "Let's hear these."

"First of all, I made a slight mistake," Rone began. "I assumed that the A&P represented all American agencies. I now see that it is only one. And I don't know which one it is. But the library is another agency. Uncle Morris first asked what the A&P had on its shelves, or what agents it had available, next he asked what the library or librarian had in the way of poems. So the library is the second agency and poems are a specific type of agent they must have. But I'm not sure what 'poems' or these particular titles signify."

"Try and figure it out."

Rone paused. "The library probably carries novels, plays and nonfiction as well as poems. On that assumption I would say poems or poetry are specialised agents, individualists of some kind. And perhaps these agents are slightly outdated or old-fashioned – the titles mentioned are mostly standard, things that have been around a long time. Possibly agents out of the OSS days; maybe not. I'm not sure."

"What would the names represent?"

"I'm not sure of that either," Rone began. "Annabel Lee lives near the sea or ocean – in a kingdom by the sea. Maybe she's associated with naval affairs or possibly islands."

"Or invasions?"

"Yes, maybe invasions," Rone concurred. "J. Alfred

Prufrock? Well, once again I'm not sure. Perhaps it has something to do with prostitutes?"

"Or possibly the author?"

Rone thought a moment. "An American living in England? Of course. An American agent who passes as an Englishman!"

"And Sam McGee?"

Rone began to recite:

"Now Sam McGee was from Tennessee, where the
*   cotton blooms and blows,*
Why he left his home in the South to roam
*   'round the Pole, God only knows.*

"The poles – the North pole. The far north. Both Sam McGee and the author spent time in the Yukon or the far north. Our man operates or did operate in far northern areas. That's his speciality. But he couldn't speak the right language – the 'third edition.' Each edition represents a certain strategic language. The language of a far northern country. A country that could be approached from, or borders on, the far north. That could be China or Manchuria – or Russia."

Rone was suddenly aware that he spoke both Chinese and Russian.

For the first time since Charles Rone had started reading, the man turned and looked at him. "Let's get something to eat," he said, rising.

CHAPTER TWO

TOOTHLESS TONY AND FEATHERLESS FRED

ONLY single seats were available in the dining car. The man joined a table at the far end. Rone was placed with an elderly couple and their grandson.

Rone's lost commission and his session with the admiral were almost forgotten. The three young men, who must still be wandering down a corridor somewhere or other, really didn't matter. It was the sunburned man and the cablegrams that held his attention. Everything he had seen today was a travesty of established intelligence procedure as he knew it. The last straw was the quiet man at the end of the dining car. And the messages which were not even classified.

When they had left the compartment the man had thrown the folders on the seat and left the door unlocked. Rone had pointed out that anyone could walk in and take them, and anything else for that matter. The man had simply answered, "Let them." Rone volunteered to stay behind and guard the room. The man was quite emphatic about not eating alone, so off to the dining car both of them went. Rone had concluded that obviously the three young men were in the vicinity and would be watching the compartment.

The elderly couple and the child left the table just as the train was reaching the Charlotte station. The waiter placed a cup and a silver coffeepot in front of Rone and left before he could ask for cream. His mind drifted back to the messages. He felt something was wrong, that he had overlooked something quite obvious. He looked out on the slow, swirling crowd of people on the floodlit platform below and saw his three escorts passing by with his Valpac. They weaved through the masses and disappeared into the station.

"Something wrong?"

He turned back to the table. The man was seated opposite him smoking a thin cigar and pouring a cup from Rone's coffeepot.

"My luggage just got off the train."

"I'll give you some of my stuff."

"And now no one is guarding the compartment."

"Have some coffee. Is there any cream?"

Rone didn't answer. He held his cup as the man poured in the tepid black fluid.

"You did very well with those messages. Better than I thought you would."

"I spent some time in crypts."

"I know."

"Something still doesn't fit."

"You got most of it."

"But not all. Uncle Morris and Sweet Alice still don't make sense."

"Why worry about it?"

"Why not?" asked Rone. The man was silent. "Something's wrong with Sweet Alice and Uncle Morris."

"Let's get back to the compartment." The man threw down some money and got up.

When they returned to the compartment the beds had been made up and Rone found the entire contents of his Valpac neatly out on the blankets. Beside them was a small suitcase which was obviously meant to replace his bag. He noticed that a black metal box which he hadn't seen before was sitting on the man's bunk.

"I think I know what it is that's wrong," Rone suddenly said.

"Let me hear."

"At first I thought Sweet Alice and Uncle Morris were part of an established organisation. They could have been code names for a department or even an agent in that organisation. The main reason for this was that their names did not correspond with the others in the messages. In other words, names such as Pepper Pot, Annabel Lee and Sam McGee are all descriptive of what that person is. They tell us about his function or speciality. But Sweet Alice and Uncle Morris do not. That's why I assumed that they were special departments or networks of major agencies. They were like a telephone exchange, not a number. In fact I was sure they were not even people.

"But several factors made me realise that they could not be agencies or even agency-controlled. First of all, these are original copies of cablegrams."

"They could be interdepartmental memos."

"But they're not. They're the originals. If they were memos they'd be marked 'top secret' or have some other classification. But none of this material is classified. Yet this is obviously a top-secret case – or even higher. Not only the body of the messages points to that, but the whole method of bringing me here is evidence of great urgency and great secrecy. Classifications such as secret or confidential or top secret or their equivalents are used by every major intelligence operation I've ever heard of. In any of those operations there are so many people involved that you have to specify who will see what. But in this instance no one seems worried about that – because they know just who *will* see it. They don't have the bureaucracy of the major operation. I must therefore assume they are independent of them."

"That's a nice assumption. But I don't think a lack of classification can really justify your conclusions."

"That's only part of it," Rone continued. "The use of cablegrams in the first place is rather unusual. Most major organisations have their own communication facilities. And they are restricted facilities. They're also quite capable of handling both domestic and international traffic. If these organisations were involved why would they bother to risk the faulty security of commerical communications? I don't think they would. These messages are more like two men communicating than two agencies – and they are talking about a highly sensitive case. At times I have the feeling they don't want the major agencies to know anything about it."

"But there's a third thing that convinces me this is not a standard agency procedure. The messages were not in code. The meaning is obscure, but not crypt. Now, on the assumption we are talking about a very big case, a standard organisation would send everything in code and the messages would be decoded and classified. The method of communication used in these messages suggests an individual agent who might not have the time or the knowledge to code his message."

"Did it ever occur to you that the case might not be as important as it seems?"

"I thought of that," Rone admitted. "But I had to

21

eliminate it on two or three specific counts. First my own discharge. From what I gather, a source above both the Navy and possibly the Defence Department arranged it, and that kind of power is seldom used on routine cases. Why they want me I don't know, but the method by which I was secured is rather revealing."

"Another indication of the importance of the case is that whoever Sweet Alice and Uncle Morris are, they think nothing of swooping down and grabbing personnel from whatever organisation they choose. We see that quite plainly in the case of the A&P and the library. If those groups had anybody these two wanted I bet they would have had them with no questions asked.

"The third thing that points to this being an important case are the dates on the messages. Six messages were sent from September 18 to September 20, six messages that required hundreds of hours of research and paperwork. Under ordinary situations this much work would take ten days or, at the least, a week. But this was done in three days. No, when Uncle Morris and Sweet Alice get into the picture things start to happen. And when Uncle Morris tells us that 'the stew is cooling' I have the feeling something very serious is happening."

"Then you think that Sweet Alice and Uncle Morris are individual agents?"

"I'm not exactly sure," replied Rone. "They are either part of a small, powerful organisation that behaves very much like an individual agent, or they are individual agents who have the strength and connections of a powerful organisation."

"Why not continue your homework?" said the man, holding out another folder.

Rone opened it.

```
EXHIBIT:    7              DATE: SEPTEMBER 21
SUBJECT:  POEMS
TO:          SWEET ALICE
FROM:      UNCLE MORRIS
              STEW IS FREEZING. CAN YOU BRING
              OUT THE HIGHWAYMAN?
```

Rone saw that the situation was getting worse. He turned the page.

```
EXHIBIT:    8           DATE: SEPTEMBER 22
SUBJECT:    POEMS
TO:         UNCLE MORRIS
FROM:       SWEET ALICE
            BOOK BANNED IN BOSTON. DOUBT
            IF CENSORS WILL GIVE IN.
```

The Highwayman was taboo. He wondered who the censors were. Apparently there were forces more powerful than Sweet Alice and Uncle Morris. He turned the page.

```
EXHIBIT:    9           DATE: SEPTEMBER 22
SUBJECT:    HIGHWAYMAN
TO:         SWEET ALICE
FROM:       UNCLE MORRIS
            VOLUME A NECESSITY.
```

Rone noticed that the subject had changed. He also felt that Uncle Morris had made up his mind.

```
EXHIBIT:    10          DATE: SEPTEMBER 23
SUBJECT:    HIGHWAYMAN
TO:         UNCLE MORRIS
FROM:       SWEET ALICE
            CENSORS CLAIM HIGHWAYMAN
            BURNED. A&P PRO.
```

Rone stopped. The censors had said the Highwayman was "burned". He wasn't sure whether that meant dead, lost or forbidden. He had no idea what "A&P PRO" meant.

```
EXHIBIT:   11            DATE: SEPTEMBER 23
SUBJECT:  HIGHWAYMAN
TO:        SWEET ALICE
FROM:      UNCLE MORRIS
           LATEST INFORMATION ESTABLISHES
           HIGHWAYMAN STILL IN PRINT.
           REQUEST VOLUME BE SENT
           IMMEDIATELY.
```

He concluded that the censors had claimed the Highwayman was dead, but Uncle Morris could prove that he wasn't. He was calling their bluff. He was officially asking for the Highwayman. Rone wondered why Uncle Morris would know that he was alive, but Sweet Alice wouldn't.

```
EXHIBIT:   12            DATE: SEPTEMBER 24
SUBJECT:  HIGHWAYMAN
TO:        UNCLE MORRIS
FROM:      SWEET ALICE
           CENSORS CLAIM YOU ARE
           MISINFORMED. ALSO STATE THAT
           THREE LIBRARIES WOULD NOT
           CARRY VOLUME ON THEIR SHELVES.
```

The censors were holding to their story. They still claimed the Highwayman was dead. They also let it be known that even if he was alive three libraries would have nothing to do with him. Three, Rone thought to himself. Three major agencies? CIA, CIC and FBI? That could explain it. But then who are the censors?

```
EXHIBIT:   13            DATE: SEPTEMBER 24
SUBJECT:  HIGHWAYMAN
TO:        SWEET ALICE
FROM:      UNCLE MORRIS
           CAN YOU TAKE FEATHERLESS FRED
           TO TEA?
```

Rone had no idea what this meant. He looked over at
the man. He was asleep. He turned to the next page of
messages.

```
EXHIBIT:   14            DATE: SEPTEMBER 25
SUBJECT:  HIGHWAYMAN
TO:        UNCLE MORRIS
FROM:      SWEET ALICE
           NO EYES FOR ME. THE CENSORS
           ARE CLIMBING ON HIS BONES.
           DOES TOOTHLESS TONY HAVE A
           GUITAR?
```

Rone read the message over, then turned back to the
previous page and re-read that one as well. Featherless
Fred seemed to be the last resort, but either he wouldn't
listen to Sweet Alice or Sweet Alice had no way of getting to him. The censors were blocking the way. They
were "climbing on his bones" or seducing him. Sweet
Alice felt that only Toothless Tony could convince him.
But he had no idea who Toothless Tony was, and Featherless Fred was equally obscure.

```
EXHIBIT:   15            DATE: SEPTEMBER 25
SUBJECT:  HIGHWAYMAN
TO:        SWEET ALICE
FROM:      UNCLE MORRIS
           TOOTHLESS TONY IN GOOD VOICE.
           WILL SERENADE TONIGHT.
```

Toothless Tony was ready, whoever he was. Rone turned the page. There was only one message on it – and it was not a cablegram.

TOP SECRET   TOP SECRET

THE WHITE HOUSE

DATE: SEPTEMBER 26

██████████████████████████
██████████████████████████
██████████████████████████
██████████████████████████

DEAR ████████████████

IT HAS COME TO ████████████████████
ATTENTION THAT YOU AND CERTAIN OF YOUR
ASSOCIATES ARE AT ODDS WITH OUR BRITISH
FRIENDS. I AM SURE THAT YOU HOLD ONLY
THE BEST INTEREST OF OUR NATIONAL
SECURITY IN MIND WHATEVER THE POSITION
YOU MAY TAKE. AS ALWAYS IN THE PAST
████████████ AND I WILL ABIDE BY YOUR
ULTIMATE DECISION. I AM SURE YOU AND
YOUR ASSOCIATES WILL TAKE IN MIND OUR
POLICY OF MAXIMUM COOPERATION WITH OUR
BRITISH FRIENDS IN MATTERS OF THIS SORT
BEFORE FINALISING YOUR VERDICT.
████████████ WOULD IN NO WAY WISH FOR
YOU TO JEOPARDIZE OUR INTERNAL SECURITY
– IF THAT'S WHAT IS INVOLVED. I HOPE YOU
CAN REACH SOME CONCLUSION AS SOON
AS POSSIBLE.

YOUR MOST ADMIRING FRIEND,

████████████████████████

TOP SECRET   TOP SECRET

For reasons of national pride. Rone was somewhat reluctant to establish the identity of Featherless Fred. If it wasn't who he thought it was, he was certainly very close to him. Rone noticed that the letter was classified top secret. This meant that at least one person, maybe more, from a major agency saw it. If Rone's hunch was right then censors were with the agencies or, more likely, over them. But they were definitely not part of the Sweet Alice and Uncle Morris operation. What confused Rone most was that this letter was written to someone at one of the agencies, since it was classified. He wondered what their top-secret material was doing in with Sweet Alice and Uncle Morris information. The major agencies might give up or loan out an agent, but seldom if ever did they like giving out classified documents – especially when they came from the White House. Rone didn't have to guess what was on the next page as he began to turn.

```
EXHIBIT:    16            DATE: SEPTEMBER 27
SUBJECT: HIGHWAYMAN
TO:         UNCLE MORRIS
FROM:       SWEET ALICE
            HIGHWAYMAN SUDDENLY BACK IN
            PRINT. LIBRARIAN DOES NOT HAVE
            VOLUME ON SHELF, BUT CAN
            LOCATE. CONDITION UNKNOWN.
            CENSORS APOLOGISE FOR SLIGHT
            MISUNDERSTANDING – HOW ODD.
```

So, Rone thought to himself, Sweet Alice does have a sense of humour. Uncle Morris was right in assuming the Highwayman was still alive, but he was no longer at the library – no longer with his old agency. The main problem now was to find him and see if he was still capable of replacing the Pepper Pot.

```
EXHIBIT:    17            DATE: SEPTEMBER 28
SUBJECT: HIGHWAYMAN
TO:         UNCLE MORRIS
FROM:       SWEET ALICE
            LAWYER REPRESENTING VOLUME
            SLAMMED DOOR IN LIBRARIAN'S
            FACE. SAYS VOLUME WILL NEVER
            GO BACK ON SHELF.
```

Rone smiled to himself.

EXHIBIT: 18   DATE: SEPTEMBER 29
SUBJECT: HIGHWAYMAN
TO: SWEET ALICE
FROM: UNCLE MORRIS
          SUGGEST YOU SEE LAWYER
          YOURSELF.

EXHIBIT: 19   DATE: SEPTEMBER 29
SUBJECT: HIGHWAYMAN
TO: UNCLE MORRIS
FROM: SWEET ALICE
          OWNER INTERESTED IN SELLING
          VOLUME TO PRIVATE COLLECTION.
          HAS MANY CONDITIONS — BUT
          MUST SETTLE PRICE FIRST. WILL
          ESTABLISH VALUE ON THE 1ST.

Rone could not see that the Highwayman was earning his name. Whatever he was before, he was a mercenary now. He wondered what the other conditions were.

EXHIBIT: 20   DATE: OCTOBER 1
SUBJECT: HIGHWAYMAN
TO: UNCLE MORRIS
FROM: SWEET ALICE
          VALUE UNHEARD OF. LIBRARIAN
          REFUSES TO DISCUSS MATTER ANY
          FURTHER. HOW MANY ARE COMING
          FOR TEA?

Rone now saw that the librarian paid the bills for Sweet Alice, or at least he had to pay for the agents they took. Since the librarian was only one agency he assumed that any agency that provided personnel to Sweet Alice had to pick up the bill themselves. He knew that the question "How many are coming for tea?" established the price, but he still couldn't work out how much that was.

```
EXHIBIT:    21              DATE: OCTOBER 1
SUBJECT:    HIGHWAYMAN
TO:         SWEET ALICE
FROM:       UNCLE MORRIS
            STEW IS COLD. MY GUEST PREFERS
            DEMITASSE.
```

Rone knew that Uncle Morris had offered to help financially. He could afford a demitasse – half a cup of coffee – but the message before stated tea. Uncle Morris wasn't offering tea – he was offering only the price of half a cup of coffee. So tea represented one figure, thousands, tens of thousands, or higher, and coffee represented another. Rone realised this wouldn't work. If tea was a hundred thousand dollars and coffee represented ten thousand, then half of that would be five thousand. Uncle Morris wouldn't offer only five thousand dollars on a hundred-thousand-dollar agent. No. Rone concluded that tea and coffee represented the same amount.

```
EXHIBIT:    22              DATE: OCTOBER 1
SUBJECT:    HIGHWAYMAN
TO:         UNCLE MORRIS
FROM:       SWEET ALICE
            CENSORS BACK UP LIBRARIAN. DID
            YOU BUY TOOTHLESS TONY A
            BANJO?
```

Rone now saw that the instrument Toothless Tony played determined who he talked to. In a previous telegram Sweet Alice had asked, "Does Toothless Tony have a guitar?" In exhibit 22 Sweet Alice asked, "Did you buy Toothless Tony a banjo?" In both cases a stringed instrument was used and in both cases a question was asked. Either the stringed instrument or asking a question was the clue to have Toothless Tony contact Featherless Fred. Rone already knew what was on the next page before he turned to it.

TOP SECRET   TOP SECRET

THE WHITE HOUSE

OCTOBER 2

�────────────

�────────────

�────────────

DEAR ▅▅▅▅▅▅▅▅

▅▅▅▅▅▅▅▅▅▅ AND I WERE DELIGHTED TO LEARN OF THE COOPERATIVE ATTITUDE YOU AND YOUR ASSOCIATES HAD TAKEN TOWARD OUR BRITISH FRIENDS. SINCE YOU WERE COMPLETELY FREE IN REACHING THIS DECISION WE UNDERSTAND HOW IMPORTANT THIS MATTER MUST BE TO YOU. THAT IS WHY I AM DROPPING YOU THIS NOTE.

IT HAS COME TO MY ATTENTION THAT A SLIGHT MISUNDERSTANDING HAS ARISEN AND IT SEEMS OBVIOUS TO ME THAT OUR BRITISH FRIENDS ARE AT FAULT. UNLIKE OURSELVES THEY COMMUNICATE IN THE LANGUAGE OF INTERNATIONAL DIPLOMACY WHICH INTERPRETS THE STATEMENT "COMPLETE COOPERATION" TO MEAN BOTH TECHNICAL AND FINANCIAL. WE IN THIS COUNTRY, ON THE OTHER HAND, OFTEN DIFFERENTIATE BETWEEN THE TWO. I HAVE NOT BROUGHT THE MATTER TO THE ATTENTION OF ▅▅▅▅▅▅▅▅ SINCE IT IS SO NEGLIGIBLE. I KNOW YOU WILL DO WHAT IS BEST FOR THE SECURITY OF THIS COUNTRY. PLEASE KEEP ME POSTED AS TO THE PROGRESS OF THIS MOST URGENT CASE.

YOUR ADMIRING FRIEND

▅▅▅▅▅▅▅▅▅▅▅▅

```
EXHIBIT:   23          DATE: OCTOBER 3
SUBJECT:   HIGHWAYMAN
TO:        UNCLE MORRIS
FROM:      SWEET ALICE
           LIBRARIAN DELIGHTED TO COME TO
           TEA. AM ON MY WAY TO SEE
           LAWYER.
```

Rone smiled to himself.

```
EXHIBIT:   24          DATE: OCTOBER 4
SUBJECT:   HIGHWAYMAN
TO:        UNCLE MORRIS
FROM:      SWEET ALICE
           LAWYER SAYS CLIENT WILL NOT
           EAT AT AUTOMAT OR PUB. INSISTS
           ON EATING AT HOME. INSISTS ON
           CHARGING SHOPPING LIST TO US.
```

Rone studied the message carefully. The Highwayman
wanted independence. He refused to work out of or
through the automat or pub. Rone concluded that those
must be the American and English agencies. He would
do his own shopping – find his own men and facilities –
but Sweet Alice and Uncle Morris would have to pay
for it.

```
EXHIBIT:   25          DATE: OCTOBER 4
SUBJECT:   HIGHWAYMAN
TO:        SWEET ALICE
FROM:      UNCLE MORRIS
           RENT THE HOUSE.
```

```
EXHIBIT:     26              DATE: OCTOBER 4
SUBJECT:  HIGHWAYMAN
TO:          UNCLE MORRIS
FROM:       SWEET ALICE
             FOR DESSERT LAWYER HAS
             ORDERED ALL – REPEAT ALL – BABY
             PICTURES OF HIS CLIENT.
```

Rone concluded that the Highwayman had made his
final demand. He wasn't sure what it was, but he thought
the baby pictures represented past history – that would
mean the Highwayman wanted all classified files on himself. If that was the case there would be no mention of
him anywhere in intelligence records. To the world of
intelligence, a world of endless amassing and recording
of information, this was by far the most trying demand –
and the greatest affront. For the first time, Rone felt that
the Highwayman had overplayed his hand. He turned
the page.

```
EXHIBIT:     27              DATE: OCTOBER 5
SUBJECT:  HIGHWAYMAN
TO:          SWEET ALICE
FROM:       UNCLE MORRIS
             THE STEW MUST NOT FREEZE. GIVE
             THEM TO HIM.
```

There was only one page left in the file, but Rone
didn't bother to read it now. He put the open folder on
the floor and began undressing. He turned off the overhead light, lit a cigarette and lay down on top of the
blankets.

"Did you finish?" asked the voice from the other bed.

"All but the last page. Do you want to hear it?"

"Why not?"

"The Highwayman has everything he wants," Rone
began. "He has money, he has complete autonomy –
and he has privacy. He bought back his past. There will

be no printed word on him in any file of any agency. I wonder how that would feel?"

"What do you mean by autonomy?"

"Independence," Rone explained. "He can work completely on his own without answering to any agency. They'll give him what he wants, when he wants it, with no questions asked. He is his own master. He'll form his own organisation and operate it in his own way. I would say the Highwayman had done rather well for himself."

"And what do you mean by privacy?"

"All the files on him are to be handed over."

"Are you sure of that?"

"Quite sure," Rone replied. "What you gave me to read is a perfect example. Original cables from both Sweet Alice and Uncle Morris in the same file? Why would that be? Ordinarily each one would keep the other originals and place a copy of his own message in a file for reference. That isn't the case here. All the originals are together. Not only that, but two top-secret messages from the White House are included. No, I'd say these are part of the original files the Highwayman was asking for – and right now we're on our way to deliver them."

"Is there anything else?"

"Yes," Rone replied.

"What's that?"

"You're Sweet Alice."

"Why not read the final page? And then catch some sleep."

Rone picked up the folder and turned to the last sheet. It was marked with yesterday's date.

```
EXHIBIT:   28              DATE: OCTOBER 9
SUBJECT:  HIGHWAYMAN
TO:       UNCLE MORRIS
FROM:     SWEET ALICE
          SCOOTER BROKEN. SENDING IN
          THE VIRGIN.
```

"What's a virgin?" Rone asked.

"You are."

CHAPTER THREE

STURDEVANT

RONE awoke at six-thirty sharp. Sweet Alice was still sleeping. Two square black suitcases had been set in the middle of the floor. He washed and shaved in the tiny compartment sink, took out fresh socks, underwear and a clean shirt. He had almost finished dressing when a waiter, carrying breakfast, arrived at the door. Sweet Alice was stirring. The waiter set up a small table in the middle of the compartment and uncovered a tray of eggs, griddlecakes and Canadian bacon. Sweet Alice managed to struggle into a pair of rust-coloured slacks and a fresh Hawaiian shirt.

"Better eat fast. You get off soon," he told Rone.

"Alone?"

"Yes," replied Sweet Alice, searching the table. "They never have cream on these damn trains. You'd think they had something against cows."

"You're quite a writer," Rone said, lifting a napkin and unveiling a silver cream pitcher.

"Think so?"

"Who is Uncle Morris?"

"My sister," said Sweet Alice, sipping his coffee.

"Why do you use cablegrams? Why not the transatlantic telephone?"

"We move around a lot. I'm never sure where Uncle will be and Uncle's never sure where to find me. Telegraph offices are always there. A message can wait two or three hours. Can't waste your day sitting in front of a phone. Anyway, it's better to have a record of what you said – just in case."

"Why am I a virgin?"

"You just *are*. Someone who's uninitiated."

"I've been in intelligence twelve years."

"Where you're going, you were just *born*."

"Then why take me?"

"I wouldn't know. Ask the Highwayman."

They finished breakfast in silence. Sweet Alice seldom

34

looked up from his plate. He poured a final cup of coffee, lit a small cigar, looked at his watch and then stared out of the window.

"You don't seem to like the Highwayman," Rone said, avoiding discussing his destination.

"Can't say. Never met him."

"The messages sounded as if you knew him quite well."

Sweet Alice turned back to the table and absently stirred his coffee. He studied Rone as a father might study his young son before telling him the facts of life.

"I knew Sturdevant," he said. "That was enough. I suppose you've heard of Sturdevant?"

"No," answered Rone. "Who is he?"

"Was, is the correct tense. He's dead now and good riddance."

Rone detected a note of ambivalence in Sweet Alice's voice. "What was his connection to the Highwayman?"

"Sturdevant trained him – and a lot more of the people you'll be meeting. If my guess is right you'll be right in the middle of Sturdevant's little club – and if that's the case you really are a virgin. Did you ever hear the phrase 'cross-reference boys'?"

"No," Rone said. "No, I don't think so."

"You might in the next few months. It was a term Sturdevant coined to describe the modern intelligence agents – it refers to the computers we use today." Sweet Alice took a long drag on his cigar and settled back in his chair.

"When the war in Germany was ending, another one was just beginning, an internal war in this country and England as well. I suppose it could be called the intelligence revolution, the struggle within the intelligence organisations between the old and the new, between modernisation and status quo. It's hard to be sure what was really involved on either side, but in most cases the issue was between the personal and the impersonal – a battle royal between mechanisation and individuality. This country walked into World War II about as sophisticated in intelligence matters as a naked five-year-old. We had a handful of agents, almost no facilities and an inveterate dislike of espionage. But when we walked out of the war not only had we learned – we were already changing what was established procedure for fifty years.

Out of necessity we had developed mass-production intelligence."

"You mean our present approach?" asked Rone.

"More or less," said Sweet Alice. "Before World War II, intelligence operations had been predicated on the availability of highly trained agents. Men who had specialised in this type of work most of their lives. The professional spy, if you like. This was true for most of the major powers with one exception, the United States. As I said before, we have always had a national antipathy for this type of operation, so whereas England or Germany or Russia had the career intelligence agent, we had nothing. But the war created its own demands, and we did what we could. We organised OSS and the beginning of CIC, to operate at an international level, and at home the FBI revamped itself to handle internal security. We did a pretty damn good job of it, too. We turned out some of the best operatives in the world – and Sturdevant was one of them.

"But you can't achieve in five years what other countries have been developing for fifty. You can train hundreds or even thousands of agents in a short period of time, but you can't give them experience. Only a handful got that – and they did well, as I said before. We simply did not have enough seasoned men. So we did what this country has always done – we mechanised.

"We realised that one veteran agent could get more out of an interrogation or interview than twenty freshly trained men. He could detect the flaw, the contradiction, the clue by instinct and experience. We attempted to do it by electronics. We used fifty agents asking the same questions! Then we took our fifty interviews, put them in an electronic computer, and let the machine cross-reference the material and come up with the inconsistencies.

"If an enemy agent with a lisp infiltrated one of our war plants, then we investigated every lisping man, woman and child in every sensitive position in every war plant, office or military base, and we filed them on IBM cards. If that agent showed up at an atomic plant where twenty-one other people had a lisp, we could just run the cards through the machine, eliminate twenty-one suspects, and shoot the twenty-second."

"It's not quite that simple," Rone interjected.

"Would you rather give the explanations?"

"Sorry," Rone said, reminding himself to keep his mouth shut.

"On one hand," Sweet Alice continued, "our specialised agents were working on specific cases, and on the other, our inexperienced men were gathering up every bit of information on everything and everybody and feeding them into the computers. The two limbs of the same tree grew and expanded – but the mechanised limb, as usual, grew much faster and began bending the tree in its direction. It was the intelligence, as Sturdevant called it, of cross-reference."

Sweet Alice sat back and lit another cigar.

"But intelligence is based on both the individual agent and mechanical techniques," Rone said cautiously. "Where does the conflict come in?"

"It's a matter of balance," began Sweet Alice. "The mechanisation required tremendous expansion in men, machines and techniques – and by the time we had developed our own individual agents, the whole complex of intelligence work was starting to turn towards cross-reference. I suppose the ultimate dream of a truly technological agent would be to run a security check on everyone in the world."

"I still don't see the conflict," insisted Rone.

"It came in the structure of the organisations," Sweet Alice replied. "The mechanics of running one of these operations became increasingly more involved. There were no longer *twenty* operatives in the field, but maybe two or three *thousand,* at all levels of security. Certain protocol had to be established, and certain restrictions were bound to be placed on the agent to co-ordinate his activities with the rest. In the minds of many old-time agents, bureaucracy was replacing free will."

"And Sturdevant couldn't function under such restrictions?" Rone asked.

Sweet Alice shook his head emphatically. "No, not at all. Just the opposite. No one functioned better under this new system than Sturdevant. He was the perfect example of the individual brilliant agent who could utilise every modern technological advance. He thrived on it. But a great many other agents found the changes intolerable,

37

and they in turn began the internal war. Sturdevant got involved later."

"You're losing me."

"Robert Sturdevant, for all his skill, was uncontrollable. He had no morality, no emotions and no conscience. He would use anything or do anything to get his results. To me, he was a brutal, sadistic assassin. During World War II we fought fire with fire – or at least that is what we told ourselves, to justify Sturdevant's activities. We needed him, and I thanked God he was fighting on our side, but at times I felt he would have been just as happy working for the Germans or Russians – at times I felt his only loyalty was to destruction. They used to say, 'Point him in the direction of the enemy – then duck.' What brought matters to a head was that he began forming his own group, his own cadre. His attitude was infectious; where at the beginning there was only one depraved agent, by the end of the war there were thirty – we called them the SS.

"It was during the cold war that things became intolerable. By now American intelligence had grown so important that it had *diplomatic* implications. And in turn it had to bend to State Department policy. Sturdevant would not, or could not, change his ways. He was still the unpredictable cobra. He would act on the spur of the moment, policy or no.

"By the mid-fifties even the conflicting intelligence powers had established certain ground rules. Captured agents were quietly exchanged, certain methods of interrogation were forbidden, and so on. Sturdevant would have none of this. It was at about this time that the agencies began putting pressure on him, and it was also at this time that the old-time agents began their last-ditch stand. Sturdevant became the logical leader for the malcontents, and the battle began. Understand, he wasn't without strong support in Washington. A great many intelligence experts sided with him – and he came very close to winning. But he didn't. Once he had lost, every major agency turned its back on him and his group.

"Some of his political friends arranged an independent operation for him in the Far East, which would have continued his income and provided a pension, but he turned it down. Instead he and a few of his men became mercenaries in the Middle East for a while, but apparently his spirit had finally been beaten down – he disbanded his men and dropped out of sight. Then in 1954, Sturdevant was reported dead in Istanbul."

"How did he die?"

"He committed suicide." Sweet Alice was staring out of the window again.

"And the Highwayman was with him through all of this?"

"To the end. Supposedly he handed him the gun and watched him blow his brains out. You've picked yourself some nice playmates."

The conductor stuck his head through the door and announced that the train would be stopping in five minutes as requested. Rone quickly put his things in the grip. Sweet Alice opened one of the black suitcases and put in the file Rone had read the night before. He closed it and moved both suitcases to the door.

"You'll deliver these to the Highwayman," he told him.

Rone and Sweet Alice went to the end of the carriage. The conductor opened the door and stood on the bottom step as the train began to lose speed.

As the train stopped, Rone jumped off. The conductor handed him down the two black suitcases and the grip and then whistled to the engineer. The train began to move.

Rone picked up the bags and turned towards the station. He had no idea what town or even state he was in.

CHAPTER FOUR

THE HIGHWAYMAN

THE sign hanging from the roof of the white wooden station house read: Gethsemane, Ga., Pop. 487. He entered a spotlessly clean waiting-room with a highly polished potbellied stove in the middle of the floor. The ticket window was shuttered, and a neatly printed cardboard sign announced: "Closed for funeral. Please buy tickets on train." Rone crossed the room and stepped out onto a small porch.

At the far end of a large square with a bronze Civil War soldier in its centre stood a small Greek Revival church. A small party of mourners stood in front of it. Rone watched as they turned to look at him. Then one of the women bent down and whispered something to a boy beside her. The child nodded obediently and ran into the church. A moment later he reappeared with an elderly man and pointed in Rone's direction. The man squinted, nodded and pulled the boy back inside the church with him.

Several seconds later the two reappeared with a third man in a black gown. Once again the boy pointed towards Rone. The man in the gown began running down the steps. Organ music rose from within the church. When the man reached the statue he stopped and waved his arms. Rone pointed to himself. The figure impatiently beckoned him forward. Rone picked up the suitcases and crossed the square. By the time he had reached the statue, the man had gone back into the church. The organ music stopped. There was a sound of scraping feet and coughing.

Rone passed the parked hearse, and pushed through the heavy wooden doors. He stood, baggage in hand, at the head of a single aisle which led down through the pews to a flower-decked casket resting several feet in front of the altar. Every head in the tiny church turned quietly towards him and gave a sympathetic nod.

"Will the bereaved please come forward."

To the left of the altar Rone saw the deacon, standing in an elevated pulpit.

"Dear Nephew Charlie," he said, looking directly at Rone, "your seat is waiting at the front."

Rone was motionless. Someone quietly stepped up behind him and said, "Just go right down and take your seat, Nephew Charlie. And for God's sake try to look sad."

Rone still did not move.

"You can leave your luggage with Mr. Ward," the deacon called out.

Rone hesitated. Reluctantly he handed the suitcases to the man behind him and started down through the gallery of upturned, saddened faces. He walked slowly to the coffin and cautiously peered in.

He had never seen the man who was lying peacefully inside. He stepped back to the first-row aisle, as the deacon had indicated, and uncomfortably took a seat. Throughout the service he kept looking at the face in the coffin. He listened attentively as the wispy silver-haired deacon spoke of "Uncle Raymond's" unblemished soul and sinless ways.

After what seemed an eternity the sermon ended. Rone rose on cue and placed the flowers which were handed to him beside the coffin. He leaned over body just far enough to convince the congregation he had kissed his "uncle." Gently, he closed the coffin. The deacon wept.

Organ music began and the mourners sang the final hymn. After the benediction Rone took his place with the other pallbearers and began the long lift up the aisle. As they cautiously moved through the door Mr. Ward moved up beside him. "Attaboy, Nephew Charlie," he whispered, "attaboy – if you don't go to other people's funerals, they'll never come to yours."

The casket was lifted onto the black-draped vehicle. It was unseasonably hot; they drove slowly under a scorching noon sun, and by the time they reached the open grave Rone and most of the mourners were covered with a mixture of dry, powdery clay and rising perspiration.

Rone stood opposite Mr. Ward as they began to lower Uncle Raymond into the earth. He estimated that Ward was between fifty and fifty-five. He had a broad face with a flat, rectangular forehead and a strong, square lantern

41

jaw. His cheekbones were almost Indian, his thin firm lips betrayed a slight but perpetual grin. The nose was thick and flat; Rone guessed that it had been broken on more than one occasion. Bushy eyebrows pushed down on his grey deepset eyes.

After Uncle Raymond reached the bottom of his final resting place Ward stood upright. He was taller than Rone had first thought – although he walked with a slouch he was over six feet. He had a thick neck and his large, strong shoulders bulged under the dark clerical gown. Rone threw dust on the grave and turned to receive the condolences of the congregation.

"If they ask," Ward whispered, "you can tell them you're from anywhere at all except Philadelphia. Uncle Raymond hated Philadelphia. He did a little time there."

Don't think about anything, Rone had to remind himself as he inspected the two suitcases beside his bed. He went down to the bathroom at the end of the hall and ran water into the black four-legged iron bath. There was something about Ward that troubled him. Something about his face – about his features. He bathed, changed into clean Daks and a fresh white shirt, and went downstairs to the kitchen. Ward was bent over the sink washing.

"Well, Nephew Charlie," he said to Rone, cupping water in his hand and splashing it on the back of his neck, "you did right well in church today."

"Thanks," answered Rone.

Ward straightened up, reached for a towel and began patting his face dry. "I suppose you're all hot and anxious to meet the Highwayman?"

"Whenever you say."

"In a few minutes." He turned towards Rone. His mouth flashed into a wide, toothy grin. "Bet for a minute you thought I was him. Well, I'm not." Ward stretched into a faded denim shirt. "Now how about those questions? You look like a man steaming over with questions."

"Who was Uncle Raymond?" It was the skin on Ward's face that bothered Rone. He tried not to stare.

"Good old Uncle Raymond was your predecessor – the scooter on the shopping list. Sweet Alice told you about the shopping list, didn't he?"

"No."

"Why that rascal." Ward strained forward over the sink and peered into the mirror as he ran a coarse-toothed comb through his hair. "You're Uncle Raymond's back-up man, his replacement. Sort of like football. Each man on the first string has gotta have a substitute. He upped and died. So off the bench you come. Get the idea?"

"I think so," answered Rone.

Ward turned from the sink. "Sorry we had to call you out so unexpected, but ole Uncle Raymond didn't give us much notice."

"And the simplest way to get me into town was for the funeral?"

"Trot right up to the head of the class." Ward stopped abruptly and grinned at Rone. "Nephew Charlie, you wouldn't take it unkindly if I sorta offered you little odds and ends of advice every now and again, would you?"

Rone hesitated. "No. Not at all."

"Well, if you're going to look me over, don't be so damn obvious."

"Look you over?" Rone was embarrassed. "What gives you that idea?"

"I've always gone in for the direct approach – so I'd say look me straight in the face and don't shift your eyes around so much. Course, there's always two schools of thought about things like this, but I'd say that when I'm sitting in a room with only one other fellow, and he's less than two feet away from me, and we're talking, and he ain't looking at me – when all those things happen – I might start wondering if something ain't wrong. There's nothing less suspicious than being obvious."

"Thanks."

"No trouble at all," Ward said. "You see, Nephew Charlie, we may be going up against some pretty fancy fellows. Boys that know all the tricks and then some. Not that you're not as smart as they are, because you're a pretty slick one yourself – at least that's what your record shows." Ward paused. "You're one of them computer men, ain't you?"

"I've done other things."

"Nothing wrong with machines, I guess. A little cumbersome if you're travelling light, though." Ward and Rone stared at one another for an exaggerated moment. "Anyway, getting back to the point. It's not a matter of you not being as smart as the opponents, 'cause you are, otherwise you wouldn't be with us – it's just that you might not be as fast."

"I'm not sure I understand," said Rone.

"Well, take my face, for instance. You worked out it's been fixed over, grafted, but you worked it out here, in the kitchen, and just a few minutes ago. You should have known it back at the graveyard."

"I couldn't tell. You were covered in dust."

"That should have made it easier, not harder. I was sweating right through the back of my shirt and the silly gown I was wearing, so there should have been sweat on my face too. Sweat collects in pores – like ink does on a fingerprint – so if you couldn't spot any lines through the dust you had only two choices – either the skin was pulled too tight to show them up or my face just wasn't perspiring. Any way you look at it something was wrong."

"Thanks again," Rone said half-heartedly. Nonetheless, he was impressed.

"My pleasure. Who knows, if my adding machine breaks down you may be able to give me some hints. Come on, it's time to meet the man."

Rone followed Ward through the back door and out along the path. They entered the church through the oak doors. Ward secured them from inside with a crossbar and led him down the aisle. The deacon emerged from a side entrance behind the pulpit. His dark trousers and collarless shirt hung limp in the close church humidity. He approached Rone cautiously and almost with disdain. Finally he extended his hand. "We had expected you earlier," he said.

"It was out of his control," Ward stated flatly.

"I see." He stood back and studied Rone. "You are an expert on electrical machines, I'm told."

"Computers," Rone clarified.

"He does other things," Ward interjected.

"You're taller than I thought," he said, more in confusion than displeasure.

"He'll do," Ward said firmly.

44

"I hope you're right," the Highwayman answered without dropping his gaze from Rone. "Size could be a factor here."

"He'll do just fine. The Puppet Maker will work it out."

"I hope so." He turned to Ward. "Was everything in the suitcases?"

"I'll check them out after dinner. No need rushing." Rone noticed a patient, almost gentle tone in his voice.

The Highwayman seemed perplexed. He nodded and turned back to Rone. "Ward is absolutely right. There is no need to rush. I seem to have developed the tendency to hurry in my twilight years – as if I want to get on with it. Ward knows better. You listen to him. Each of us can still learn a great amount from Ward. It's been very heartening to see you. Yes, it has been very heartening." The Highwayman turned and walked back through the door. Ward was already up the aisle and out of the church.

Rone caught up to him as they neared the square.

"You left the church open," he reminded him.

"No one will go very far with it." Ward sat down on a cement bench facing the statue. He took an apple out of his back pocket and began paring it with a penknife. The sun had begun to set. A somewhat cooler, more arid breeze drifted across the grass.

"Well, what do you think of him?" asked Ward.

"I couldn't tell. He didn't say very much."

"You're disappointed, aren't you? Disappointed and worried. Everything was all rah-rah until you met the hero of the game, eh?"

"I didn't say that."

"I don't see you gushing with enthusiasm."

"He wasn't what I had expected."

"I'll tell you something, Nephew: stop expecting. It's better that way. It cuts down on the rate of disappointment."

"You seem more worried about him than I do."

"There's a big blue ocean between worry and concern – I'm not worried. He's getting old. That in itself doesn't amount to a hill of beans – but he *knows* he's getting old, that's all that's bugging him. He's starting to think about time. He'll get over it."

"You don't sound too sure."

Ward looked up at him with a broad grin. "I'm sure, Nephew – I'm *very* sure. There's not much difference between him and a boxer. Ever see them jokers just before the fight? They're trembling like a leaf. Wait till the bell sounds."

"Nothing seems wrong with *you*," Rone said without wanting to.

"I fight a different kind of war. He knows what he's doing. He'll get us through okay."

"You've been with him a long time, haven't you?"

"Long enough."

"Then you must have known Sturdevant."

"I knew him." Ward was slicing the peeled apple into eighths.

"It sounds like you didn't like him."

"Look, if I give you all the answers at once – Can we call the quiz show off?"

"If that's the way you want it."

"Sturdevant was a fraud. He was none of the things people said about him. He wasn't a cold-blooded, sadistic killer. He was two things – a great con man and an incurable *de*generate. He had the knack of getting other people to do everything for him. He wasn't a bad strategist, but a one-man crusade he wasn't. He was also a coward. Yes sir, Nephew Charlie, a *real* coward. And he knew it. He stayed way behind the lines – if he was up front he'd've shattered like glass – so he kept out of action and built up his own legends. He peddled more bullshit in World War II than Goebbels. His boys were good – damn good – and he gets a given degree of credit for that. But for the rest, that man in there did most of the work – he was Sturdevant's operations chief all the way through. He was the tactical brain. Sturdevant was nothing."

"Then why all the reverence?"

"Because in war men need a cause – not a motto like 'The War to End All Wars' or 'Vee for Victory'; that's fine back home or in training camps, but when you're on the line you need something more immediate than that – your own kind of personal hero or motto. At one time flags and, standards used to be enough. Later bagpipers and buglers led the charge. Sometimes it's a banner, sometimes it's a shout. In this particular case what was needed was a man. The man was Sturdevant."

"Do you believe he killed himself?"

"Are you asking if I believe he's dead?"

"No. Do you think he committed suicide?"

"That's what he'd like everyone to think. Only he didn't even have backbone enough to do that by himself. He made the man you just met pull the trigger."

"What about the other stories – about the brutality?"

"I told you he was a DG, a queer, everything else that went along with it. When he wasn't plundering I suppose he was raping. He was more a dog with a hard-on than a man with a mission."

"It sounds like you had a run-in with him."

"Not a chance. We each knew where the other lived. He kept his distance. I spent five years looking for an excuse to cut his liver out and he knew it. You seem mighty fascinated by him."

Rone was aware of this. He also knew he was wandering further from the answers he wanted.

"What was the Pepper Pot after?"

"I'll tell you when the time comes."

"But we're going in where he left off, aren't we?"

"You read the messages – draw your own conclusions."

Rone decided to press his luck. "Why was I picked?"

"It's like I told you before, you were the back-up man for Uncle Raymond."

"But why me? Why someone new? Why not one of your own men? Why not someone you've worked with before?"

Ward popped a section of apple into his mouth. He chewed with slow deliberation. He answered before he had completely swallowed. "There aren't that many of us left. We're getting old, you know."

Rone's fears began to rise. "But why me in particular? You apparently had the pick of anyone you wanted for a given job. I'm interested in why you decided on me. What were the aptitudes you were looking for? What was it I had?"

Ward spit out several seeds. He broke into his familiar grin. "You're afraid we're going to stick you back on computers, aren't you?

"Now I ask you, Nephew Charlie, do we look like the kinda guys that would have any use at all for them contraptions? No, you don't have to worry about that. As to the rest, well, I don't exactly know what an aptitude is, but you did have a few abilities we found kinda useful. I don't want to go into all of them now, but among other things we kinda got the impression you could let someone else die in your place without giving a good goddam. Now that ain't easy to come by!"

After dinner, the two black suitcases were brought to the kitchen. Ward picked one up, placed it on the breakfast table, took out a key and opened it. When he swung the top Rone could see that it was divided into three metal-topped sections. Ward opened the first. It was filled with files. He looked through them rapidly, stopped at one, pulled it out and threw it to Rone.

"You might find this interesting," he said.

Rone looked down at the manila envelope stamped "top secret"; there was a sticker on it with typed words: "Security Investigations and Clearance – CIC for ONI." Below it he read, "Subject: Rone Charles Evans."

If there was one major taboo in modern intelligence organisations, it was an agent examining his own investigation.

Rone looked up. Ward had already closed the first suitcase and was busy opening the second. It was crammed full with packs of money. Ward threw a couple at Rone and said, "Start counting."

Rone counted the old twenty-dollar bills. There were ten thousand dollars in each bundle. Within half an hour he had counted an additional one hundred and ninety thousand in tens and twenties. He had no idea how much Ward had counted. He handed Ward the paper with his additions and then helped him put the money back in the suitcase.

"You better get some sleep, Nephew," Ward said. "You may be getting an early call."

Rone started for the stairs.

"Hey, don't you want this?" Ward called, holding up the security clearance.

Rone walked over, took it and went upstairs to his room.

Later, as he lay upon the starched sheets he began reading it:

TOP SECRET

SECURITY INVESTIGATION FOR TOP SECRET CLEARANCE

FOR

CHARLES EVANS RONE

COMPILED BY THE COUNTER-INTELLIGENCE CORPS
FOR
OFFICE OF NAVAL INTELLIGENCE

INDEX OF MATERIAL COVERED

NAME: RONE   CHARLES   EVANS
AKA: NONE
   HEIGHT: 6' 1½"
   WEIGHT: 13 st. 8 lbs.
   EYES: BROWN
HAIR: LIGHT BROWN
MARKS: NONE
DATE OF BIRTH: 9 JANUARY 1929
PLACE OF BIRTH: RAWLINS, WYOMING
FATHER'S NAME: CHARLES LAWRENCE RONE
FATHER'S OCCUPATION: DOCTOR--RANCHER
FATHER'S ADDRESS: P.O. BOX 12, RAWLINS,
   WYOMING
LIVING OR DEAD: DECEASED 6/6/39
MOTHER'S NAME: (MAIDEN) ELSIE EVANS
MOTHER'S ADDRESS: NOT APPLICABLE
LIVING OR DEAD: DECEASED 6/6/39
BROTHERS OR SISTERS: EVAN--DECEASED
   6/6/39

EDUCATION:
   GRAMMAR SCHOOL: RAWLINS GRAMMAR SCHOOL,
      RAWLINS, WYO. GRAD. 1942
   HIGH SCHOOL: RAWLINS HIGH SCHOOL,
      RAWLINS, WYO. GRAD. 1946
   COLLEGE OR UNIVERSITY: LELAND STAN-
      FORD U., PALO ALTO, CALIF. GRAD.
      1950
      YALE UNIVERSITY LAW SCHOOL, NEW H.
      GRAD. 1953
MILITARY SERVICE: NROTC STANFORD
                      UNIVERSITY ENLISTED
                      USN 5 JULY 1953

```
OCCUPATIONS:       HUNTING GUIDE--JACKSON
                   HOLE, WYOMING 1941-1946
                   (SUMMERS)
                   AUTOMOBILE MECHANIC-
                   RAWLINS, WYO.
                   1942-1944 (PT)
                   RIDING INSTRUCTOR--PALO
                   ALTO, CALIF. 1946-1948 (PT)
                   SKI INSTRUCTOR--YOSEMITE
                   N.P. 1948-1950 (PT)
                   LANGUAGE TUTOR--NEW
                   HAVEN, CONN. 1951-1952
                   (PT)
SPORTS:        FOOTBALL--STANFORD 1946-1950
               (NOMINATED FOR ALL AMERICAN,
               NAMED ALL COAST)
               RIFLE TEAM--STANFORD 1946-1950
               (PLACED THIRD IN NAT. COMP.)
               ALPINE CLUB--STANFORD
               1947-1948
```

LIST OF REFERENCES:

Rone turned the page.

CIC

AGENCY REPORT

```
SUBJECT:   RONE, CHARLES EVANS
AGENCY:    FEDERAL BUREAU OF INVESTIGATION
OFFICE:    NEW HAVEN, CONN.
           NEW HAVEN FBI REPORTS THAT
           BOTH LOCAL AND NATIONAL OFFICE
           FIND NO DEROGATORY INFORMATION
           CONCERNING SUBJECT.

                           T. STEIN
                           FIELD AGENT
                           CIC
```

CIC

SUBJECT: RONE, CHARLES EVANS
AGENCY: ATTORNEY GENERAL'S OFFICE
ADDRESS: JUSTICE DEPARTMENT
           NO DEROGATORY INFORMATION
           CONCERNING SUBJECT.

CIC

AGENCY REPORT

CASE NO:
SUBJECT: RONE, CHARLES EVANS
AGENCY: STATE POLICE
OFFICE: NATION-WIDE
           ALL FORTY-NINE STATES
           RESPONDED, NEGATIVE INFORMA-
           TION WITH THESE EXCEPTIONS:
ARIZONA--KINGMAN, 16 JUNE 1949--SUBJECT
           ARRESTED FOR SPEEDING ALONG
           ROUTE 66. ACCUSED OF DOING
           90 MPH IN 60-MPH ZONE.
           NO DRIVER'S LICENCE. (WYOMING
           REQUIRES NO LICENCE.) FINED
           TWENTY-FIVE DOLLARS ($25.00)
           AND RELEASED.
CALIFORNIA--LOS ALTOS, 21 SEPTEMBER 1946--
           ARRESTED SPEEDING, 50 MPH
           IN 20-MPH ZONE. FINED
           FIFTEEN DOLLARS ($15.00).
           LOS ALTOS, 4 MAY 1950--
           ARRESTED SPEEDING, 50 MPH IN
           20-MPH ZONE. FINED FIFTEEN
           DOLLARS ($15.00).

MENLO PARK, 23 AUGUST 1946--
ARRESTED NOT STOPPING AT
STOP SIGN. FINED FIVE
DOLLARS ($5.00).
PALO ALTO, 17 OCTOBER 1946--
ARRESTED FOR THE FOLLOWING:
        DRIVING ON WRONG
        SIDE OF STREET.
        DRIVING ON SIDE-
        WALK.
        DRIVING AT NIGHT
        WITHOUT LIGHTS.
        DRIVING ACROSS
        CITY PARK.
        CHASING FOOT
        PATROLMAN ACROSS
        CITY PARK IN AUTO.
        DRUNKEN DRIVING.*

        *NOTE: SUBJECT WAS
            CLEARED OF
            DRUNKEN
            DRIVING. HE
            WAS FOUND
            GUILTY OF
            ALL OTHER
            CHARGES
            WITH SUS-
            PENDED
            FINES.
            APPARENTLY
            STANFORD
            UNIVERSITY
            HAD WON
            FIRST FOOT-
            BALL GAME

IN TWO
SEASONS.
RONE SCORED
WINNING
TOUCHDOWN.
JUDGE'S SON
ON TEAM
ALSO.
ATTEMPTING TO BACK
CAR INTO S. PACIFIC
R.R. ST.
TYING FEMALE
UNDERGARMENT TO
CAR AERIAL.
OVERLOADING CAR
(9 PERSONS).
SQUEEZING TOOTH-
PASTE IN ARREST-
ING OFFICER'S
POCKET.
PALO ALTO, 5 AUGUST 1947--
ARRESTED SPEEDING, 60 MPH IN
25-MPH ZONE. FOUND GUILTY--
SUSPENDED FINE.**
**NOTE: SAME JUDGE AS ABOVE.
PALO ALTO, 25 JANUARY 1949--
ACCIDENT REPORT:
AT ONE-FIFTEEN
A.M. RONE'S CAR
WAS TRAVELLING
SOUTH AT ESTI-
MATED 60 MPH
(LEGAL SPEED) ON
HIGHWAY 101 (A
THREE-LANE #HIGH-
WAY WITH A CENTRE
LANE FOR PASSING).

SUBJECT MADE
CORRECT SIGNAL TO
PASS TRUCK IN
FRONT OF HIM. HE
MOVED HIS CAR
INTO CENTRE LANE
AND ACCELERATED
FOR PURPOSE OF PASS-
ING. APPARENTLY
AT SAME TIME CAR
APPROACHING FROM
OPPOSITE DIRECTION
ALSO DECIDED TO
PASS TRUCK HEADING
NORTH. CARS MET
HEAD--ON AT ESTI-
MATED 70 MPH. ALL
PASSENGERS IN
APPROACHING CAR
(FATHER, MOTHER,
THREE CHILDREN)
WERE KILLED
INSTANTLY. GIRL
SITTING BESIDE
SUBJECT WAS
THROWN THROUGH
WINDSHIELD AND
KILLED--SUBJECT
APPARENTLY HAD
TRIED TO SAVE HER
AT LAST MINUTE BY
THROWING SELF IN
FRONT OF HER, BUT
HIS HEAD SMASHED
AGAINST WIND-
SHIELD, BREAKING
JAW AND NOSE BUT

SAVING HIS LIFE
(SEE MEDICAL
REPORT). TRUCKS
WERE UNHARMED.
INVESTIGATION
ESTABLISHED THAT
ONCOMING CAR HAD
NOT SIGNALLED
CORRECTLY
(ATTESTED TO BY
BOTH TRUCK
DRIVERS) AND THAT
CAR ALSO HAD WEAK
LIGHTS. SUBJECT
WAS CLEARED OF ALL
RESPONSIBILITY FOR
ACCIDENT. SUBJECT
HAD RECENTLY BEEN
ENGAGED TO GIRL
KILLED WITH HIM
(SEE INTERVIEWS
RW 3, 8, 14, 24,
25, 37).

PALO ALTO, 30 JANUARY 1949--
ARRESTED SPEEDING, 65 MPH IN
30-MPH ZONE. FINED TWENTY-FIVE
DOLLARS ($25.00).
NOTE: SINCE SUBJECT'S
FIANCEE HAD BEEN KILLED
ONLY FIVE DAYS EARLIER
THIS INVESTIGATOR TOOK
INTO CONSIDERATION THE
CHANCE OF EMOTIONAL
STRAIN OR EXCESSIVE
DRINKING. APPARENTLY
NEITHER WAS THE CASE.
SUBJECT BORROWED CAR

AND HAD DATE. ARREST-
ING OFFICER BELIEVES
HE STOPPED SUBJECT AT
3:30 A.M. AND AS HE
REMEMBERS FEMALE COM-
PANION'S CLOTHING WAS
NOT ALL ON).*
*See special investiga-
tion on page 72.

Rone turned to page 72.

SECRET

SUBJECT: REQUEST FOR SPECIAL INVESTIGA-
          TION
TO: CHIEF, DIVISION OF SECURITY
          INVESTIGATION
FROM: CHAIRMAN, BOARD OF REVIEW

AFTER EXAMINING AND ANALYSING
THE INFORMATION SUBMITTED IN
THE SECURITY INVESTIGATION
OF LT. J.G. CHARLES EVANS RONE
(CASE ONI #1687-224-3588) THE
BOARD OF REVIEW FINDS ITSELF
UNABLE TO RECOMMEND OR NOT
RECOMMEND THE ISSUANCE OF A
SECURITY CLEARANCE TO SUBJECT.

IN ALL, SUBJECT'S RECORD IS
EXCELLENT BUT CERTAIN SPECIFIC
INCIDENTS HAVE BEEN UNCOVERED
THAT RAISE THE POSSIBILITY OF
OVERT COWARDICE OR POSSIBLY
SOME TYPE OF MENTAL DISTURB-
ANCE. EVEN THOUGH THESE EVENTS
OCCURRED WHEN SUBJECT WAS

BETWEEN THE AGES OF SEVENTEEN
(17) AND EIGHTEEN (18) AND
EVEN THOUGH THERE HAS BEEN NO
SUBSEQUENT SIMILAR EVENT, IT IS
STILL FELT THAT A SERIOUS
DOUBT AS TO SUBJECT'S ACCEPTA-
BILITY HAS BEEN RAISED.

WE THEREFORE REQUEST PER-
MISSION TO ESTABLISH A SPECIAL
BOARD OF INVESTIGATION, COM-
POSED OF THREE PSYCHIATRISTS
AND THREE SENIOR INVESTIGATING
OFFICERS, TO SECURE AND REVIEW
ADDITIONAL AND MORE SPECIFIC
INFORMATION. WE ALSO REQUEST
THAT SUBJECT BE ASKED TO SUB-
MIT TO CERTAIN PSYCHOLOGICAL
AND PSYCHIATRIC EXAMINATIONS.

THE REASONS FOR THIS REQUEST
ARE HEREIN SUMMARISED FROM
MATERIAL PROVIDED IN HIS IN-
VESTIGATION. REFERENCE TO
ORIGINAL REPORTS ARE INCLUDED:
1. In summer of 1945
    subject was employed
    as hunting guide Grand
    Teton Lodge, Jackson
    Hole, Wyo. On June 19
    of that year he led a
    party of four hunters
    up into the Teton
    Mountain Range in
    search of Kodiak bear.
    At approximately eight
    thousand feet they

spotted a wounded bear
on the ledge above
them. Subject led
party above prey and
then dropped down on
ledge to trap him.
However one of
party slipped giving
bear advance warning
and when they dropped
onto ledge bear had
moved and was now
blocking their escape
route. Also bear was
on thin ledge which
meant only one man
could get to him.
Although subject was
not only guide and
responsible he was an
excellent hunter-and-
climber--yet he let
another man go in his
place. Man was
severely mauled by
animal and even though
knocked to lower ledge
was not killed. He
eventually lost arm.
Only after man was
mauled did subject
finally act and kill
bear. Man and party
sued hotel but suit
finally dropped.
Inhabitants of Jackson
Hole accused subject

of cowardice. (SEE:
INSTITUTIONAL CHECKS #
12, PERSONAL INTER-
VIEWS # 5, 6, 7, 8.)

2. In August of 1947
   subject was fishing at
   Jenny Lake, Moran,
   Wyoming (four miles
   from Jackson Hole),
   when a flash storm
   occurred, trapping a
   boat with several
   persons far out in the
   lake. Subject who is
   strong swimmer started
   out to their rescue.
   When subject saw
   another boat also go
   to assistance of
   floundering people he
   turned around and swam
   to shore. The towns-
   people of Jackson Hole
   accused subject of
   cowardice. (SEE
   PERSONAL INTERVIEWS
   #11, 12, 17, 18, 22.)

WE FEEL THAT THESE TWO
INCIDENTS ALONE WARRANT
FURTHER INVESTIGATION ON THE
ISSUE OF COWARDICE AND POS-
SIBLE MENTAL TROUBLE. THERE
IS ANOTHER INCIDENT WHICH THE
PSYCHIATRIC REPORT POINTS TO
AS RATHER UNUSUAL.

3. In late January 1949
subject was involved
in head-on auto colli-
sion in which he was
driver of one car.
Occupants of other car
were killed and so was
subject's fiancee, who
was sitting beside him.
Yet five days later he
was found in a com-
promising position with
another woman. (SEE
AGENCY REPORT--STATE
POLICE: Page 15)

THE PSYCHIATRISTS FEEL THIS
REACTION TO TRAGEDY PLUS A
RECURRENT DREAM SUBJECT VOLUN-
TEERED HE HAD AS CHILD MIGHT
INDICATE SOME PERSONALITY
WEAKNESS.

TOP SECRET

SUBJECT: REQUEST FOR SPECIAL INVESTIGA-
TION
FROM: CHIEF, DIVISION OF INVESTIGA-
TION
TO: REVIEW BOARD

REQUEST FOR EXTENDED INVESTI-
GATION IN CASE OF LT. J.G.
CHARLES EVANS RONE (#ONI
1687-224-3588) IS GRANTED.

REPORT ON SPECIAL INVESTIGATION
as requested by:
BOARD OF REVIEW ------ CIC

SPECIAL INVESTIGATION BOARD

DR. MYRON ZIEFF (PSYCHIATRIST)	MAJ. RICHARD B. STEEN CIC
DR. JULES R. JAYLIN (PSYCHIATRIST)	MAJ. SAMUEL L. AYER CIC
DR. JAMES D. TEE (NEUROLOGIST)	CAPT. WEBB L. BURR ONI

INTRODUCTION: On 17 February 1954 the Chief, Board of Review, directed that a special body of the above-named men be formed to further examine and investigate Lt. J.G. Charles Evans Rone (subject) in light of possible derogatory information found during the course of his security clearance. . . .

FINDINGS: The three doctors concur that the ''hunting incident'' and the ''boat incident'' (IC# 12, PI# 5, 6, 7, 8, and PI# 11, 12, 17, 18, 22) are related directly to a traumatic experience subject suffered on June 6, 1939. On this date subject was out in small boat in Yellowstone National Park with his mother, father and elder brother. The boat was approximately a thousand yards from shore when a flash storm common to that area, suddenly hit. Somehow the boat was capsized. The subject and his mother did not know how to swim. The subject's elder brother swam subject to shore, then returned to rough water in attempt to assist subject's father, who was having difficulty bringing subject's mother to shore. As the storm increased in intensity subject stood on shore and watched mother, father and elder brother drown.

In the opinion of the examining doctors this event created serious and spectacular personality change in subject. Prior to this tragedy subject had been a rather restrained ''indoor boy.'' He preferred studying to athletics or other outdoor activities. After the tragedy the subject was adopted by his uncle (mother's brother), who was a successful rancher. Subject made immediate transition to athletics. He became an excellent swimmer, hunter, mountain climber, etc. He diligently overcame any phobias he might have, as in the case of moun-tain climbing. Uncle reports as a boy he would place lit matches and cigarettes to hand until he became impervious to their burning.

Although this is only a summary of our findings (a complete report is attached), we are also in agreement on the probable motivation for this transition. The subject undoubtedly blamed self for death of his parents and his brother. . . .

His almost maniacal attempt to remedy these two weaknesses (i.e., lack of responsibilities and lack of ability) led not only to compensation, but to overcompensation. As he overcompensated physically so did he overcompensate in responsibility. He feels that anyone or anything in danger is his own private responsibility. After the tragedy he proved time and time again his ability to function well in dangerous situations. The hunting and second boating incidents were caused by one factor--he had so overcompensated in this sense of responsibility, that he absolutely refused to let anyone else help. Should someone try to assist him, he would withdraw and quit--not from fear but from rage.

Further investigation of the hunting incident seems to support this opinion of the doctors. On re-interviewing, it was found subject did immediately move in to kill bear, but that man who had chartered the hunting trip wanted to do it himself.

The incident of the floundering boat in Jenny Lake is another example of his attitude in danger. When he saw the rescue boat approaching and had no way to tell them to go back he washed his hands of the matter (once again in rage) and swam back to shore. Later that

night he had a fight with the
rescuers, saying they had actually
endangered the stranded boaters. A
fight resulted, in which the subject
badly beat up all three rescuers.
This may have coloured feelings of
local residents towards him.

The third event, his seeming
indifference to his fiancee's death,
is a further indication of his overcompensation. As he overcame actual
pain, so he may have overcome the
fear of death. As pain has become
meaningless to him, so has death.
Thus, in the auto accident, he did
everything within his power to
prevent it, and then simply accepted
the fact of death, and forgot it.

The fourth and final phase of the
investigation dealt with a recurrent
nightmare subject supposedly had as
a child. When he was eight he went
to a motion picture called ''The
Invisible Man.'' In the film the
invisible man walks into the room
with his head in bandages, wearing a
hat, dark glasses, scarf and rain-
coat, but underneath audience knew
there was nothing--that he was
invisible. Subject's apparent
fright began when the man took off
his glasses and there was nothing
there. Subject remembers that he
could not sleep for almost two weeks
after seeing this film. He required
the light in his room to be on and
the door left ajar. He said he

could not stop thinking about the eyeless eyes. He was fascinated with the concept of being invisible.

As of this writing, the subject is still a physical and emotional stoic. He has created such a high threshold of pain and grief reaction that few things can affect him. The subject realises better than anyone that his attempted monopoly on responsibility is detrimental to himself and others. Although he still has the same deep-seated feelings, he has learned not only to accept the aid of others but to do so graciously--but his preference remains to do it alone.

RECOMMENDATION: The findings of this special board have led to a unanimous decision in favour of subject. Although his basic attitudes and conflicts could interfere with his function in normal society, he has consciously or unconsciously sought out a society where they fit his role. He has the makings of an excellent intelligence officer, capable of the most difficult and trying work. His major shortcoming would be a tendency to seek out danger when it is not necessary.

Rone closed the folder, turned out the light and went to sleep.

CHAPTER FIVE

RONALD V. NEPHEW

THE doorknob turned and Rone awoke. It was still dark.

"Shag your bones, Nephew Charlie," Ward called out, "and gather up your doodads. You'll be leaving soon."

"What time is it?" Rone asked.

"About four. Hurry up. We'll be waiting downstairs."

Rone entered the kitchen ten minutes later. Ward and the Highwayman stood over the breakfast table. It was stacked high with files. They were looking down at two photographs.

"I'm not sure," the Highwayman was saying, "on second thought this other man does have two sons – perhaps we should—"

"They're too old," Ward interrupted. "Daughters work better anyway. Let's stick with Potkin. I think that's our best shot."

Rone glanced down at the photograph Ward was tapping with his fingers. It pictured a short, powerful man with a fat oblong face.

"Believe me," Ward reassured him, "the butcherboy is for us."

"Yes, I suppose you're right," the Highwayman conceded indecisively. "But then again . . ." He looked up to Ward blankly. "If only we had more time to think this out. We – we may be overlooking something."

"You've covered it all," Ward said. "You've covered every detail well. You're right in choosing the fat man. We can hold the other one in reserve. We don't have that much time."

The Highwayman plucked at his fingernails and nodded. He looked over at Rone. "Then we should send the Virgin south?" he asked, turning back to Ward.

"That's right," Ward agreed. "We had better start with the Whore."

"I've never really liked him."

"He does his job," Ward told him. Then he turned and

threw his arm around Rone. "Nephew Charlie, grab up your pack. The fun and fury is just beginning."

Ward drove the '48 Ford pickup truck slowly through the town, out beyond the cemetery, and on to a wide clay road.

"Well, Nephew," said Ward, "I hope you ain't averse to travelling."

"Not at all."

"Good. Good. That's good to hear. By the by, how do you stand on Mexican feeding? Tortillas and all that kinda crap?"

"I like it."

"You sure are easy to live with," Ward beamed. "Nephew, if there's one thing that does my aching old heart good it's two things. First is seeing a city fella dragging his ass outa bed at four in the morning and the second is knowing he likes Mexican chop suey."

"Then I'm going to Mexico?"

"Colotepec. Or to be more exact, a little coastal town called Tavolato halfways between Colotepec and Poggutia. You can figure out how to get there from Mexico City – if there's some flat land around, rent yourself a plane."

"Who am I after?" Rone asked.

"Lord Ashford's Whore." Ward opened the lunch-pail beside him, reached inside and handed Rone a booklet. It was an English passport. A photograph of a distin-guished-looking moustached man was pasted inside. Rone thumbed through it and found it complete, except that no name was printed in it.

"What's his name?" he asked Ward.

"Beats the hell outa me. By this time it could be any one of fifty. Here's a list of the last dozen he's used." He handed Rone a small envelope. "You'll also find some more photographs of him, some with the moustache taken off and some with a beard sketched on, in case he went caveman." Ward handed Rone a small cigarette case. "You'll find a stamp – rubber letters – and some ink in here. The type face and the ink are the same as the British use. When you decide on a name for him just print it in."

"Anything else?" asked Rone.

69

"Nephew Charlie, we're just beginning to play grab-bag." Ward passed him an American passport and a wallet. "Here's yours. I don't think you'll need it, but it's good to have it just in case. How do you like your new monicker?"

Rone opened the passport and saw a recent picture of himself and then his name: Ronald V. Nephew. He opened the wallet. It contained a complete set of credit cards in Nephew's name. Plus three thousand-dollar bills, ten hundreds, assorted fifties and tens.

"Are fives out of style this year?"

"They take up too much space."

"What cover story do I use?" Twice before in ONI Rone had gone undercover, once as a doctor, once as a tree surgeon. In both cases he was trained in a new identity for almost three weeks.

"What's that you asked?"

"What cover story should I use?"

"Nephew Charlie, you're just taking a little hop down to Mexico – you ain't sneaking into Peking. Tell 'em anything you like. Tell 'em you're a wetback heading in the wrong direction, for all I care. I got a feeling you ain't gonna bump into the Gestapo down there."

Rone felt anger rise. Don't say anything, he told himself. Just keep your mouth shut.

Ward reached into the lunch-pail again. "Now, when you find the Whore, you just tell him that the Tillinger Fund is planning a little expedition. Tell him he gets twenty-five down, a hundred on finishing and another hundred and twenty-five if he's asked in swimming. Here's his down payment." Ward handed Rone a thick package of bills.

Rone weighed it in his hand. "Twenty-five thousand?" he asked.

"Twenty-five thousand, just like I said. And here's an extra ten you can use for trouble money. Exchange a couple of hundred in your wallet for pesos at the airport. Keep the rest outta sight. Got that?"

"Yes."

"Now if the Whore gives you any trouble – for some reason he doesn't want to come - you get him either to Oaxaca or Acapulco. This stuff should help calm him." Rone was handed a small bottle with a clear fluid in it.

"Two or three drops will freeze him for about twenty hours. An extra drop or two will maybe give you another ten hours. If you go over six drops call an undertaker. Now assuming you do have to bring him out that way, go to either one of these two addresses." He gave Rone two cards. "This one is Acapulco and this is Oaxaca. I know Oaxaca is closer to where you'll be, but you'll get faster service in Acapulco."

"What will they do?"

"Fly him into the States. Five thousand is the standard rate per person. They'll want to dump you around El Paso but you insist on getting up to Nogales. Then drive him up to Tucson and turn him over to this man." He handed Rone another card with a Tucson address. "If he really gets out of hand once you're in the States, identify yourself and have him arrested for border jumping. We'll take it from there. But make sure that's a last resort."

"What shall I identify myself as?"

"Now that is a problem," Ward said with a scowl. He reached back into the bucket, beamed and held up two identification cases. "Take your pick."

Rone didn't care for the joke. He chose the folder on the left. It was FBI credentials for Ronald V. Nephew, complete with Rone's photograph.

"It's no counterfeit," Ward explained, "but just don't let a Bureau boy find you with it – they're a little touchy about these things." He looked down at the neat pile that had accumulated in Rone's lap. "Nephew Charlie, you should have brought a shopping bag for all them goodies."

"Is that all?"

"Just about," Ward answered, handing Rone a final typewritten card. "Not that I mean to rush you – but be back at this address in seventy-two hours. The Puppet Maker will be expecting you."

Rone read the card. It was an address in Minneapolis, Minnesota. "With the Whore?" he asked.

"That's right. Unless like I said before you gotta lock him up – then just come on by yourself. Well, that's it. You remember everything I told you?"

"Yes."

"That's a mighty lucky thing, Nephew Charlie – 'cause I sure the hell don't." Then for some inexplicable reason

71

Ward began to hum "The Road to Mandalay."

They continued down the clay road for another half mile and then turned onto a double-laned asphalt highway. It was near dawn. The truck travelled the new road for three miles before Ward pulled into an abandoned gas station. A grey '63 Buick was waiting. Its sole occupant was the driver.

"There's your ride to town — see you in three days," Ward said, letting Rone out.

As Rone got into the car Ward threw out one final instruction. "And remember, whatever you do, try not to kill him."

CHAPTER SIX

LORD ASHFORD'S WHORE

"THERE it is." The pilot motioned with his head.

Rone looked out of the window. He saw bleached white patches of beach stretching along the coast, steep jungle-covered cliffs rising from the glittering Pacific – but he did not see a city or even a village.

"On the ledges," the pilot called, dipping the monoplane sharply. "Look on the mountain ledges."

Rone now saw that the cliff was stepped with protruding shelves that had been cleared of jungle. Small primitive huts were clustered on each of the ledges. A network of vine-covered paths wove down the face of the rock connecting one shelf with another. At the base of the cliff was a wide beach and a small cove.

The plane climbed over the top of the cliff and landed in a clearing about half a mile from the village. Within the hour Rone and the pilot had made their way down the narrow paths to the cantina beside the cove. The pilot acted as interpreter. On Rone's instruction he handed the proprietor a photograph of Lord Ashford's Whore.

"*Si, si,*" the proprietor said immediately. Then he spat in disgust and began a long diatribe during which he kept pointing at Rone.

"He wants to know," the pilot said, "if you are his long-expected brother. It seems that Señor Janis – that is what he calls the doctor – doesn't pay his bills."

The explanation was interrupted by another explosion of vehemence from the proprietor, who had placed a thick stack of bills on the counter.

"Señor Janis arrived here two years ago by ship," the pilot continued. "Or possibly he was thrown off the ship. Anyway, it sailed the next morning without him. He has been charging ever since and has never paid one peso. He keeps saying he is expecting his brother, who will pay the bills. Many men have come to see him – but none have been his brother, none have paid the bills."

73

"Ask him what men have come to see him," Rone instructed the pilot.

After another exchange of Spanish during which the proprietor grew even more agitated the pilot turned back to Rone. "He remembers at least four. None spoke English. One may have spoken French. He says Señor Janis is a pig."

"Ask him if the men came together or at different times."

After another discussion the pilot answered Rone. "They came at different times. The last was about two months ago. He says Señor Janis is the greatest pig that ever lived."

"Did Janis ever leave here with any of the men?"

The pilot and the proprietor exchanged sharp words. "He does not feel like talking about pigs," the pilot informed Rone.

"How much is his bill?" Rone asked.

"Sixteen thousand pesos," said the proprietor, suddenly discovering English. "He owes sixteen thousand pesos, but I will settle for ten thousand, or even better I will take five hundred in gringo – I mean American dollars."

Rone counted out a thousand dollars and laid them in a neat pile on the counter. He then placed one hand on them and leaned over towards the proprietor. "Did he ever leave with any of the men?"

"No, no, Señor. He has never left since the day the ship sailed without him."

"Who were the men who came to see him?"

"One was French, one may have been German, the other two were foreign – not English or United States, but I swear I do not know what."

"What has Señor Janis done with his time? How does he spend his days?"

"How does anyone here spend his days? They drink soup and have women. These people are Indian. I am not; I come from the north of Mexico City itself. But these people are Indian. They make soup from cactus roots and drink it. That is why they cannot work. That is why they cannot pay bills. They just drink the soup – it makes them numb."

"Peyote? Cacao?"

"Not in this area. But it is the same kind of thing. They just drink it and have the women. They are shameless. They are all pigs." He continued to eye the money nervously.

"And Señor Janis – is he a pig too?" Rone stared coldly at the weakening man.

The proprietor hesitated, then broke into a wide grin. "Everyone is a pig – but Señor Janis, ah, he is a magnificent pig."

Rone picked up the stack of bills and handed half of it to the sweating proprietor. "I am his brother. He will be leaving here with me. When he leaves you will get the rest of your money."

The proprietor stuffed the bills into his shirt.

"Where can I find him?" Rone demanded.

"Up there on the third ledge – at the house of the bitches."

The pilot waited at the cantina while Rone climbed the path towards the third ledge. As he approached he heard the voices of arguing women. The tension grew. Screams and hisses erupted. He reached the ledge in time to see a large bronze-faced Indian woman rush from the hut and throw herself on two smaller girls sitting near a cauldron. The three rolled in the dust, kicking, scratching and screaming. Within minutes two other Indian girls joined the melee. The cauldron was overturned, a thin reed chair was smashed, dresses were ripped, eyes were gouged, hair was pulled, faces were hit, naked butts were kicked, and one magnificently exposed tanned breast was bitten.

"*Brava – brava – magnifico!*" Rone heard a masculine voice laugh out. "*Olé, olé,* and all of that rot."

There, at the far end of the ledge, stood a tall copper-faced man with snow-white hair and beard. He wore only a pair of brightly coloured native shorts. His lean, muscular body looked like that of a twenty-year-old Olympic swimmer. But he was twice or perhaps three times that age. When he saw Rone he flashed a brilliant smile. "I'll bet fifty pounds on the fat one," he shouted. "Fifty pounds says she'll take the lot. Are you on?"

"I'll take the fat one for a hundred," Rone called back.

"Is my credit good?" the white-bearded man shouted.

"It's good."

75

"Then you have yourself a bet!"

"Nite! Suba! The crotch! Hit that big cow in the crotch! Will you listen? Will you listen to me? Blast her in the box!"

The woman turned and twisted and rolled. One of the smaller girls freed herself and crawled a few feet away. She stood up and looked over to the man.

"In the *cojones*," he roared at her, pointing to his own anatomy.

The girl nodded and picked up a crude wooden ladle that had fallen from the cauldron. She cautiously approached the thrashing pile, raised her weapon high above her head, waited for the right moment, and brought it crashing down between the fat woman's legs. There was an agonised shout. Rone's entry doubled up and rolled helplessly out of the pile. She lay there immobile as the other women got to their feet.

"Not a bad act," said the man, crossing to Rone. "I'm thinking of taking it to Honduras. Say, chap, you do have that hundred on your person, don't you?"

Rone handed the man six fifty-dollar bills.

"They can fight again in an hour if you like." He walked over to the motionless body on the ground. "Sorry old cow, maybe this will take away the ache." He dropped two of the bills in front of her. The fat woman was in too much pain to do anything but stare at them blankly. The four women had not bothered to dress. They stood silently near the hut, wiping the blood and dirt from their naked bodies. The man handed each a fifty-dollar bill. They exploded like children at a birthday party, covering him with kisses and hugs. Then they ran to the crumpled body and cheerfully dragged her inside.

The man sat down in a frayed wicker rocking chair at the far end of the ledge and motioned to Rone.

"Well, you've seen the lot of them, take your pick. Between you and me, chappie, that fat cow is *magnifico*. Absolutely *magnifico*. She can do things to you no other woman you will ever meet can equal. Her muscular control is sheer artistry." He rocked back in the chair and examined Rone's reaction. "But you're an American, aren't you?" He frowned. "I forgot. You fellows are only interested in faces. Then you'd better take one of the others. They are all superb. Trained them myself. They'll even put their clothes back on if you find that more enticing. It's a shame about your state of mind, though – the fat cow is brilliant, but you'll never know how to enjoy her, will you?"

The man looked dejected for a moment, then the smile returned. "Why worry about national fetishes at a time like this? Absolution is at hand. Take your pick. For twenty dollars any one of them is yours. For thirty you can have two. For fifty take the entire stable."

"The Tillinger Fund is planning an expedition," Rone said.

"Bully for the Tillinger Fund. The business at hand is more important. For *forty* dollars you can have them all."

"The Highwayman expects you."

"Of course he does, chappie. I'm the best there is – in my line." He leaned towards Rone and spoke confidentially. "I'll toss you double or nothing. Eighty dollars or the whole batch for free. Now what about that for fair play?"

"I have a plane waiting," said Rone.

"Dammit, man," bellowed Janis. "Where's your sense of proportion? You're talking business and I'm offering aesthetics. Are you or are you not going to flip a coin?"

"The plane's waiting," Rone repeated.

"Then let it wait," Janis burst out in anger. He regained his composure quickly and studied Rone for a moment. "Am I to assume that if I don't wish to go, you have to make me?"

"Something like that."

"Can you?"

"Yes."

"Without killing me?"

"Yes."

Janis winked at Rone. "Would you like to bet on it, chappie? Say, five hundred pounds – fifteen hundred dollars, that is?"

"Can you cover it?"

"I would trust that my credit is still good?"

"Not for this."

"Oh," Janis said, with visible disappointment. "That complicates matters."

"And if I don't bring you out," Rone reminded him, "they will send someone else who can."

77

"Why should I do anything for them? After all, they let me rot for five years."

"They've all rotted for five years – most of them even longer."

Janis was silent for a moment. "I owe nothing to the Highwayman. If it were Sturdevant, then things would be different."

"Sturdevant is dead."

Janis roared with laughter. "Good God, don't tell me they have you believing that whore's cry too. Look, chappie, I *know* Sturdevant. And I tell you he never could or would take his own life."

"Then where is he?"

"He's waiting, my boy. Somewhere, some place he's waiting, like a lion in the thicket. He'll be out when the time is right. You mark my words, chappie, he's waiting."

"You sound very sure."

"I am very sure. He's too competitive to stay out much longer. I knew him better than any living man. I know what makes him tick. You see, he's a gambler at heart. Just as I am, except that he is slightly better. He has more patience than any man I know. That's what a great gambler needs above all other traits. You must learn to sit on your hands. You must learn not to move until the time is propitious. You wait until either the odds are in your favour or the stakes are so high you cannot refuse. When either one of those things occurs, Sturdevant will show his face."

"I've heard that he was a coward."

"You'll hear many things. That he was frightened, perverted, sadistic. No matter who you talk to there will be a different story. Remember just one thing. You will only hear what Sturdevant wants you to hear. He thrives on confusion. But you see he's the last of the great hunters. He needs an even fight. In this day and age that isn't easy to find. So he's developed a thousand little devices to keep him out of meaningless skirmishes. Very few people can understand this. Since time began very few people have been able to understand the brave man, and almost *none* have understood the just man."

"I still have to bring you with me," Rone reminded him.

"And I don't think I care to go," Janis stated. "It isn't

78

as much to do with the Highwayman as you think. You see, there's a basic law of physics which states that at one time or another all bodies within this atmosphere must come to rest. I think I have come to rest here. Like Sturdevant I desire a fair fight and I have found it here. I'm a sensualist, old man. I trade in human weakness – usually sexual.

"Man's self-indulgence and animalism is my stock in trade. As long as one male is left on earth who bothers to look up a skirt other than his wife's, I will prevail. As long as one woman eyes another and gets some inexplicable physical reaction, I thrive. Fetish and taboo are my creed. Take away religion and law, kill conscience, revert to what we really are – and I no longer exist. That's why this place fascinates me. These Indians are completely devoid of inhibition. They are totally amoral. There isn't one physical impulse that they won't explore with the innocence and intensity of a child. What little twinge of morality they might have contracted from progress is eliminated by that mushroom soup they drink.

"I ask you, what can be a greater challenge to a man like myself than something like this? You could say that I am dedicated to corruption, ultimate corruption. But to me, ultimate corruption is simply elevating man to his natural state – that of the sensual animal. Where do you begin if he has already lived by his impulses for five hundred years? Good God, chappie, I've been trying to run a bordello here, but how is that possible when the entire population is giving away what I'm selling? No, my unenlightened friend, they are smarter than you and I. They fascinate me. They are completely incorruptible, since there is nothing there to corrupt. I am transfixed, hypnotised. I am their pupil. My loyalty is here. I shall remain."

"Money is involved," said Rone.

Janis paused. His eyes twinkled. The broad grin reappeared as he shook his head from side to side. "No, I've changed. This is where I belong."

"A great deal of money," Rone emphasised.

"You simply refuse to understand, chappie. A change has occurred within these perverted bones. A religious phenomenon has transpired."

Rone dropped a package of bills on the ground. He

saw Janis' eyes widen. "This is just the beginning," he informed Lord Ashford's Whore. Rone picked up the pack and began counting."

"It has taken me most of my life to develop principles," Janis protested staring at the money. "I will not be shaken."

"Twenty-five thousand here and now," Rone said as he continued counting.

"I have found my niche."

"Twenty-five thousand now," Rone continued, "and another hundred thousand on completion."

"One hundred and twenty-five thousand?"

"One hundred and twenty-five thousand dollars," Rone repeated.

"This must be a rather interesting case." Janis caught himself at the brink. "No. Money can't budge me. Not any more. To begin with, I'm too old. The Whore of yesterday is dead."

"Plus," said Rone, "one hundred and twenty-five thousand more if you go on the expedition."

"Two hundred and fifty thousand?"

"A quarter of a million dollars," Rone said. He finished counting and tossed the stack of bills towards Janis.

"It must be a very important case. Very, very important." His eyes were frozen on the money but he didn't move.

Rone waited several seconds and then reached out to take the money back. "It is a very important case. I'm sorry the Whore of yesterday couldn't make it."

"He's dead," Janis mumbled dejectedly. He watched as Rone started to put the money back in his coat, then reached out and stopped him.

A grin crossed his face. "Old man, welcome to the resurrection."

SECTION TWO

CHAPTER SEVEN

THE DELEGATE FROM THE U.N.

THE short man with long arms and stooped, rounded shoulders was led from the incoming Aeroflot jet to a private office at the Moscow airport. He turned open the cover of his Russian diplomatic passport and handed it to the waiting officer. The name read: Mikhail Potkin.

"United Nations?" the inspector commented politely.

Potkin nodded.

The officer compared the photograph with the man standing opposite him. The balding, oblong skull, the thick nose and lips and the small ears, flat against the head, were the same. The black, slightly Oriental eyes could not be mistaken. He stamped the passport and handed it back. The leather grip was tagged without being opened. The briefcase and package Potkin held in his hands were ignored.

"A driver is waiting for you," the inspector told him.

"I must make a telephone call first."

"Of course." The officer swung back the door to an adjoining office. A telephone sat on the desk.

"A private call," Potkin stated.

"Of course." The officer left the room, carefully closing the door behind him.

Potkin patted the perspiration from his forehead. A voice in the receiver said hello.

"I've j-just arrived," Potkin said.

"Welcome home. How is your wife?" asked Aleksei I. Bresnavitch.

"Quite well."

"And your daughters?"

"Also well."

"Good. Will you be with us long?"

"I plan to return tomorrow."

"Ah, then it is a very important meeting after all. When does it begin?"

"A driver is waiting for me now," Potkin answered impatiently.

"I understand. I'm having a few people in tonight. Drop over when you have finished. Don't worry about the time. This letter business may keep you there quite late."

"Thank you."

"Did you bring the package?"

"Yes."

"Ah, good. I will expect you later."

He heard the click of the receiver. Potkin did not like the idea of going to a party. He did not like being met by Colonel Kosnov's private limousine. He had never liked returning to Moscow at such short notice. Potkin followed the driver through the terminal. He wondered what Bresnavitch had meant by "this letter business".

Captain Mikhail Potkin, division director of United States counter-intelligence activities for Colonel Kosnov's powerful Third Department, got in the back seat and the black Zim started for Moscow. He pulled the briefcase to his lap and began reviewing the reports. He knew he must concentrate. The meeting was extremely important. Many questions would be asked, details would be challenged, conclusions would be analysed. He was not good at meetings; he became nervous, he stuttered. He was embarrassed when he stuttered. He was a field man, not an administrator. He could lead operations, but he could not necessarily explain them. He produced results; that should be enough.

It was important that he concentrate, but his mind drifted back to Kosnov and Bresnavitch. Even if he did not admit it, he was aware of their feud. He was in the middle. Kosnov was his direct superior, the benevolent dictator, the understanding tyrant. But Bresnavitch was his patron, his benefactor. It was Bresnavitch who had rescued him after the Hungarian fiasco. It was Bresnavitch, the influential friend from the Kremlin, the man earmarked for the Central Committee, who had obtained him a position with Kosnov in the first place. Now they were at each other's throats and he was in the middle.

It's this damnable case, he told himself, turning back to the first file, to the memorandum delivered by courier less than eight weeks before. Everything about this project has been trouble, he thought.

He re-read the message initiating Series Five. At the time the request had simply asked for the names and locations of CIA personnel in the United States who had recently been reassigned. Potkin had pointed out to the courier that a surveillance team recorded the comings and goings of agents at the CIA central headquarters in Washington. He felt this was a good indication of who might be briefed for new missions. Since his observers knew the regular staff, any new visitors might be considered as potential special operatives. Potkin had confided that he did have sources within the headquarters itself, but he felt it too risky to use them for what appeared to be standard cataloguing. The next day Moscow had concurred, and he had begun assembling the information for transmission.

Potkin turned through his reports. Everything had gone smoothly until mid-September, until the first rumours of Khrushchev's rift with the Central Committee had begun filtering back. A message arrived saying that his system was too inaccurate; more specific information was needed. Potkin's reports covered only thirty per cent of CIA agent movement. Ninety per cent was now needed. Never in the past had such a demand been made. The most important evaluations had never requested more than a sixty per cent mark. Potkin had contacted Moscow directly for verification.

"We are no longer interested in percentages," he was told. "We must know the location and assignment of every CIA agent who has set foot in the United States over the last four months. The other divisions will worry about the agents in their areas. You must cover the United States. Percentages are no longer applicable. We must anticipate *who* they may send into Russia to replace Polakov."

Potkin had protested. There was no way of getting such complete information without seriously jeopardising his contacts within the organisation. He had spent years developing them. Even if they were successful he doubted whether they could obtain *total* information.

"Jeopardise them," he was ordered. "Do whatever is necessary to get it."

Potkin looked up from his records. The driver was honking the horn. Hundreds of young girls in tight orange gymnasium uniforms were forming in columns along the road. He thought of his daughters. If he were living in Moscow they would be marching today. Gymnastics would be good for them. They led too sedentary a life in New York.

He read the notes of September 20. Another courier had arrived demanding the same type of information on the Army's CIC that he was compiling on CIA. Once again Potkin contacted Moscow directly in protest. He pointed out that three bars and restaurants adjacent to CIC headquarters and training centre at Fort Holabird, outside Baltimore, were operated by his network. They knew most of the soldiers who had received training there over the last five years, but they did not have information concerning their assignments.

"Why not?" he was asked.

"Be-be-cause no one has ev-ever requested it," he remembered answering in anger.

"We are now," he was told.

Potkin had pointed out that he did not have enough manpower to cover both CIA and CIC in such detail. Where were his men? Working on other cases. "Take them off," he was ordered.

Potkin had pleaded he had only two reliable agents within Fort Holabird itself. One was a double agent, a captain in the review section. The other was an army private who was being trained as a CIC agent. Outside of the risk involved, Potkin had argued, their chances of even getting near the restricted information required were almost non-existent.

"Use them," he was ordered.

As improbable as it had appeared at the beginning, Potkin had obtained the information.

What bothered him was the ease with which he got it. Everything seemed to fall into place too easily. Secret files seemed too available. Security seemed too lax.

He set his copies of the CIC and CIA reports to the side.

"Too easy," he repeated to himself. "Much too easy."

84

Not that his men had just walked in and taken what they wanted. They hadn't. They took great risks entering areas where they did not work. They could have been caught at any moment. They hadn't been. Perhaps they had been lucky? Perhaps they were more skilful than Potkin had realised? Perhaps something else was involved? Potkin had relayed his material to Moscow. Kosnov had been pleased.

Two days later another emissary had arrived. He too congratulated Potkin and then informed him that the FBI end of Series Five had been transferred to his department. Potkin had blanched. He had never dealt with the FBI. That was Rudman's operation.

"The colonel is not pleased with Rudman's progress. Everything is turned over to you," he was told.

Potkin read the message he had sent to Kosnov warning that with such short notice and so little progress up to date he might have to buy the FBI information from other countries.

"Do what you have to do," the reply had come.

He had explained that it would cost a great deal of money. A great deal of money in American currency. "Do what you have to do."

Potkin pulled out the receipts and thumbed through them. A total of $432,850 had been spread among eleven Iron Curtain and Middle Eastern countries before he had secured a list of language-aptitude scores for FBI agents working in the United States. From this he had been able to deduce those who might be capable of undertaking a Russian mission. The only thing was, he had had no way to evaluate the accuracy of his information – any of it. The material had been sent to Moscow with the receipts. Kosnov had also been dubious but had expressed his gratitude for something to work from. He had relaxed. The worst was over. Four weeks had passed since Series Five had been initiated.

Potkin turned to the most infuriating memorandum of them all. It conveyed Kosnov's congratulations on the FBI information and informed Potkin that the same type of information was now being requested on ONI, OAI, Congressional investigating committees, the Attorney General's investigating staff, union-investigating groups, industrial investigators, newspapermen, radio and television men – in short, anybody capable of carrying out a mission in Russia.

Potkin flushed as he re-read it. He patted the perspiration from his face. He turned to the memos on the conversation with Kosnov. He had claimed it would be absolutely impossible. He didn't have the men, money or contacts to attempt such a project under expeditious conditions. He would have the men and money, he had been told. Even so, he had protested, the project was inconceivable. He had suggested a compromise. Use the language-aptitude approach that had finally proved acceptable in the FBI survey. A compromise had been reached. Complete investigations were to be run on Navy and Air Force intelligence personnel. The language survey could be used on the remaining groups. The currency had arrived. Agents Potkin never knew existed, many of them covert for ten or fifteen years, had appeared.

Now, $1,800,000 later, his final reports were in Kosnov's hands. There had been no immediate response. No pleasure or displeasure. No congratulations. He had waited three days. Then, yesterday, he had been ordered to Moscow.

Colonel Kosnov's limousine drove slowly through the side streets. Potkin put the files back into the briefcase with the exception of the ONI and OAI records. He assumed these would be their main concern at the meeting. He tried to read them but his concentration was elsewhere.

Why the investigation in the first place? he asked himself. The information had covered only overt operatives. What about the undercover agents that nobody knew about? Kosnov was too old an intelligence hand to assume he had canvassed the entire field. What had suddenly become important enough about Polakov's successor to initiate such expense and danger for something that was incomplete? What did Series Five have to do with the Bresnavitch-Kosnov feud? What did Bresnavitch mean by "this letter business"? What would happen at that damned meeting?

It is bad coming back to Russia at short notice, Potkin told himself, putting the last two reports back into the briefcase. He turned and watched the crowds walking happily towards Red Square. His daughters had always loved the parades. He must bring them back soon to see one.

The crowds grew larger. Workers, athletes, soldiers, women and children, many dressed in the regional costumes of the Ukraine, Latvia, Georgia and a dozen other Soviet domains, swarmed along the streets. The sound of band music could now be heard. They were less than five minutes from Third Department headquarters. Potkin reached into his pocket and took out the typewritten list his wife had given him:

```
                    IMPORTANT
APARTMENT:   1. Give Anna's winter coat
                (in box under her bed)
                to war widows' fund.
             2. Bring back Sonia's diary.
                (Hidden in bottom of her
                bird cage--and don't read
                it.)
             3. Make sure kitchen window
                is repaired.
             4. Make sure blinds are
                pulled down and tacked
                before leaving.
             5. Before leaving turn
                electricity off in base-
                ment rather than in hall-
                way.
             6. Don't forget to lock
                door when leaving.
MESSAGES:    1. See my mother.
             2. See Zora's mother
                and father (if time
                permits).
             3. Call Petrov and tell him
                Sonia hasn't forgotten
                him even if she doesn't
                write.
```

```
            4. Call Ilya Manilow
               (General Grudin's grand-
               son) and explain that
               Anna's school does not
               allow girls to study
               mechanics but that she
               wants to be a pilot.
PURCHASE:   1. Buy caviar (as much as
               possible).
            2. Don't buy vodka. #
```

The car came to a sudden stop. Potkin looked up. The street was jammed with people heading to the parade. Two *militsioneryi* stood in front of the limousine. The driver jumped out and talked with them. He returned to the car and opened the back door.

"I'm sorry, comrade, but the street is closed," he explained. "I'm afraid you'll have to walk from here."

"Tha-tha-that's all right," Potkin replied, unperturbed. He gathered up his briefcase and the package for Bresnavitch. The driver helped him out.

"I'm afraid you'll be late," the driver told him apologetically.

Potkin shrugged. He took a look at the jubilant crowd, lowered his head and began walking.

Colonel Kosnov also ignored the parade. He stood in the operations room, his back to the other officers, and looked out of the window. Below him lay Red Square. The October winds already warned of another long, arduous Russian winter, but tens of thousands of marching Muscovites behaved as if spring had just arrived. Kosnov did not need to look at them. He had seen it all before. It was always the same, no matter what the occasion. The tight columns of marching soldiers, the mobile equipment, the rockets, the endless legions of workers and the signs they carried – Long Live the Glorious Communist Party Founded by Lenin, Long Live the Soviet People, Builders of Communism. It was always the same.

Today, however, one thing was different. On top of the Lenin Mausoleum stood a single line of men: Khrushchev was no longer among them. Kosnov stared

88

at them and at the cosmonauts in whose honour the parade was being held: Colonel Komarov, Dr. Yegorov and the scientist Feoktistov. The trio had orbited the earth in one rocket. A major triumph on any other day. Today the exploit was secondary. The eyes of the world were on those who stood beside them: Leonid I. Brezhnev, the new first secretary at the Communist Party, and Aleksei N. Kosygin, the new premier of the USSR.

His private telephone rang. He crossed the room and answered it. Communications Security informed him of the conversation between Potkin and Bresnavitch. He nodded and hung up. He looked at his staff seated around the table. Lieutenant Grodin sat to his left. He was Bresnavitch's son-in-law. Potkin and he would go into the Bresnavitch camp. They knew about the letter. Grodin had undoubtedly told his father-in-law. Captain Meyeroff and Captain Mirsk sat opposite each other. They must be counted with Kosygin. He doubted how much they knew about it. The same was true for Colonel Targen and Lieutenant Bulov. They were Brezhnev's contingent. Captain Petrovsky leaned towards Suslov. Major Maslin still sided with Khrushchev, but he would get over that.

The conference phone rang. Lieutenant Grodin picked it up.

"Captain Potkin is on his way up," he told the others.

"I regret being late."

Potkin stood at the door. He walked to the conference table, took his appointed seat, lifted his briefcase in front of him, folded his hands over it, and stared straight ahead. A thin ring of perspiration rose on his brow.

"Captain Potkin," Kosnov began.

Potkin sat tensely straight. His emotionless face turned mechanically towards the colonel.

"Let me commend you and your department on an extraordinary accomplishment. We had asked for the impossible and you have come quite close to fulfilling that request."

Potkin stiffened. What does he mean by quite close? he asked himself.

"If the other international offices were as efficient as yours we would indeed have a magnificent organisation."

Potkin withdrew his hands from the briefcase. He smiled rigidly. He was safe.

Kosnov continued. "We have studied your reports with great interest. Understandably, questions have arisen. That is why we asked you here."

Potkin nodded.

"Let us start with the CIA. Your report shows that only ten new assignments were given over the last six weeks, and none of them, according to you, appear relevant. How do you arrive at this conclusion?"

Potkin relaxed. "Th-the standard briefing time for ordinary cases is under two weeks. Mo-mo-most usually a-a we-we-week or less."

"Are you sure of this?" asked Kosnov.

"It has been true in the past," Potkin managed.

"And these ten briefings were all under two weeks?" asked an officer whom Potkin had never seen before.

"Ah-ah-all were under one week. And all men were sent to standard operating offices."

"All but one," Kosnov interjected. "A Mr. Lyman Smith." He looked in the file. "According to your report, Mr. Smith was to be sent to Cairo as an architectural consultant to a housing project. That is correct, isn't it?"

Potkin thumbed through his report. He found the pages.

"Th-th-that is correct."

"He never arrived in Cairo," stated Grodin.

Potkin stiffened.

"However," said the man Potkin did not know, "on the day Mr. Lyman Smith was supposed to arrive in Cairo, a Mr. Theodore Webber arrived in Budapest – as an industrial consultant. We have a photograph of Mr. Webber sent to us from Budapest." The man pushed it across the table to Potkin. "It bears a strange resemblance to the photograph you provided of Mr. Lyman Smith."

Potkin compared the picture with the one in his file. It was the same man. Webber? Smith? He opened his briefcase and thumbed through it. Webber? Smith? He remembered something about Smith. What was it? He knew the men at the table were watching him.

"When did you say Webber arrived in Budapest?" Potkin asked without a stutter. He seldom stuttered under real pressure.

"On September 12," replied his assailant.

"And when had I stated he was due in Cairo?"

"On September 12."

Potkin shuffled through some more papers. He found the one he wanted. "Here is my master report. 'Arrival due between September 12 and September 20.'"

His adversary looked down at his own report. "Mine says only September 12."

"Have you the actual report or a summary?" Kosnov asked.

"A summary," the man answered. "But it makes no difference. Even if the date was between the 12th and the 20th. The man still turned up in Budapest, not Cairo."

Potkin relaxed. "He delivered a cake."

"He did what?"

"He delivered a cake." Potkin repeated. "An angelfood cake with vanilla frosting. Sprinkled with red candy dots. It was a birthday cake for a Mr. William Novak. Mr. Novak's mother, who is a close friend of the director of the CIA, baked a cake for her son. At the last minute Mr. Smith was asked if he would deliver it on his way to Cairo. He did so. Then he went on to his assignment. If you will check you will find he is now in Egypt."

"Then why weren't we notified?" demanded the man.

"Be-because he arrived in Cairo on the 18th. Well within the t-t-time limit we specified."

"He could have been delivering a message in Hungary. Something could have been in that cake."

"I was only asked wh-where he was going and when. Not what he was going to do on the way."

"That is understood," said Kosnov. "But what percentage of operatives have you now investigated? Let us forget about the cake."

"Approximately eighty-five per cent of the agents. We are still working on the remainder."

"Not at all bad," replied Kosnov. "Were you able to bring the data on recent discharges and retirements? This has a low-priority potential rating, but it is still worth having in the machines."

In the week before Potkin's trip to Moscow, Kosnov had requested information on agents who had retired, been discharged or were on leave. Only names had been asked for. No records. That would come later.

"I have re-re-retirement and discharge." Potkin opened his briefcase and passed copies around the table. The list contained one hundred and thirty-three names. They decided to initiate investigation on those who had left the service after Polakov's death. This left fifty-nine. The forty-second name read: Rone, Charles Evans. USN (ONI), Lt. Comd., Disch. Oct. 10, 1964.

Colonel Kosnov left the party at precisely nine o'clock. Potkin remained. He had spent the first part of the evening trying to find Bresnavitch. He finally gave the package to Bresnavitch's son-in-law, Captain Grodin. Potkin tasted the food sparingly. He drank two glasses of vodka. He did not see Brezhnev or Kosygin. Potkin had been told they would be there. Perhaps they hadn't arrived. Perhaps they had left. Mikoyan was there. Suslov was not. Suslov was sick, it was said. Could one believe it? There were a few other notable absences. Khrushchev, of course. The Chinese, naturally. Potkin idly wondered if Maya and the children were all right. He had been backed against the wall by a bearded Cuban, with a large cigar and an impossible Spanish accent to his rudimentary Russian, when Grodin summoned him. He followed him up the marble staircase and into the library. It was a warm, wood-panelled room with a carved stone fireplace. Logs were burning. Bresnavitch was standing beside the desk examining the contents of the package Potkin had brought him. It was a small oil painting. There was an expression of reserved ecstasy on his face.

"Superior, is it not?" Bresnavitch called out to Potkin.

"Yes."

"Come closer. Come closer. You can hardly make it out from that distance."

Potkin did as he was ordered. He stood studying the picture. He did not like art. He did not understand it. He slept at the ballet.

"*Now* what is your opinion?"

"It is very pretty."

"It is more than that. It is one of his best. It is superior. Wouldn't you agree?"

"Yes."

"Did you know that you were carrying a Klee?" Bresnavitch asked.

"No."

"What did you think was given you then?"

"Just a package."

Bresnavitch was glowing with pleasure at his new acquisition. He played with Potkin. "Just a package?"

"Yes."

"Not even a picture?"

"No."

"You must have felt the frame? You must have wondered what it was?"

"I have carried too many packages for too many people to begin wondering what is inside. This time it was something of beauty. On other occasions it might have been otherwise."

Bresnavitch laughed. "That is our Potkin. The eternal logician. If it had been me, I would have looked. I cannot bear not knowing everything that is going on."

Bresnavitch put down the painting, led Potkin to a deep leather chair beside the fireplace and seated himself opposite him.

He leaned towards Potkin. "Tell me, comrade, which one do you think it will be?"

"What?"

"Who will be the victor? Brezhnev or Kosygin?"

"Ah – ah – ah – I have no – no – idea."

"Come. Comrade Potkin," coaxed Bresnavitch. "you must have discussed it with someone. Your wife, perhaps?"

"No. No one."

Bresnavitch displayed a long and practised frown. "Comrade Potkin, this is 1964. Lenin and Stalin are dead. Beria is gone. The Soviet Union is no longer a dictatorship. We are now powerful, prosperous, educated. Our strength has always been our ability to adjust – to the worst as well as the best. Comrade Suslov is still a Stalinist. He is heard. We reject his ideas rather than eliminate the man. The Central Committee rules the country. It is many men with many opinions. They do not have to be in agreement. But they cannot be ignored. Comrade Khrushchev found this out the difficult way."

"I still ha-ha-haven't thought about it."

"Of course you've thought about it, just as every Russian, European, American and Oriental has thought about it. Just as Brezhnev and Kosygin themselves have thought about it. We delude no one. It takes no dialectics to prove that only one man can rule, be it communism, capitalism or monarchy. History has been quite specific on this point. We are all speculating on the ultimate victor. It has become the national Russian pastime. The way things stand now, I say it will be Suslov. What about you, Grodin?"

"I would say Kosygin."

Bresnavitch made a long face and turned to Potkin. "And you, comrade, what is your guess?"

"Ah – ah – I haven't given it any thought. You – you must believe me. I have no opinion."

"But you are a Russian. This is your country and your future," Bresnavitch said sternly. "What is more, you're a member of the Communist Party."

"Ah – ah – I have been working. I haven't had time to do anything else."

"It is exactly what you have been working on that could seriously alter the situation in the Kremlin."

"I don't understand," Potkin said.

"What do you think Kosnov is up to? What do you think the real motive is for Series Five?"

"Ah – ah – I would ra-ra-rather not talk about it."

"But you will talk about it, my dear comrade, that is exactly why you are here. I am asking you again: what do you think is behind this mania Colonel Kosnov has developed for Series Five?"

Potkin grew calm as he turned to subjects that were within his own realm of competence. "I think it can be of great value."

"In what way?"

"Complete knowledge of enemy agents and their locations makes all counter-espionage work much more easy."

"Is that what Colonel Kosnov is interested in? Making counter-espionage work easier?"

"I would suppose so."

"Suppose, Comrade Potkin?"

"I am not informed of all of his plans. I only do what is asked of me."

Bresnavitch smiled condescendingly. "Comrade Pot-kin, your department has spent almost thirteen million roubles in the last two months. Whether I am supposed to know that or not, I do. The information did not come to me through my son-in-law here. It is immaterial if you believe that or not. Doesn't thirteen million roubles seem rather excessive just to make work a little easier?"

Potkin had no answer.

Bresnavitch sat back and folded his hands under his chin. "What do you know about the letter?"

"Wh-wh-what letter?"

Bresnavitch and Grodin exchanged looks.

"What do you think Kosnov is after?"

"Polakov's replacement," answered Potkin.

"Why should that be so important?" Bresnavitch leaned towards Potkin. "Why should it be worth thirteen million roubles in just your department alone?"

"Ah – ah – I don't know."

"But it does seem that this case is more important to Kosnov than any other he has handled?"

Potkin thought. "It seems im-important."

"Do you know what Polakov was doing in Moscow?"

"No."

"He was delivering a letter. A letter from the British. We have reason to believe that it was meant for a high Soviet official. Possibly as high as the Central Committee."

"Wh-what kind of letter?"

"We believe it was an agreement."

"I don't understand."

"At least four major groups attempted to depose Khrushchev and take up his mantle. Each in its own way attempted to gather support within the Kremlin and the Central Committee. Every ploy was played, every lure offered to entice potential allies. As the competition mounted, risks were taken, grave risks – and sometimes foolish ones. As we all know, manoeuvrings in such situa-tions are always open to misinterpretation – and misinter-pretation often borders on, shall we say, 'treason'?"

Bresnavitch moved across the room, picked up the carafe and returned to his seat.

"One of the contending groups obviously tried to muster support from the pro-Western elements of the government. They apparently entered into some type of arrangement with the West. A *written* arrangement."

"The letter?" asked Potkin.

"Exactly." Bresnavitch poured himself a vodka. "The letter was proof of the agreement. Material evidence to gain support. We are not exactly sure what was in it, but it was a guarantee."

Potkin shook his head slowly. "This is the first I have heard of this," he assured them. He analysed what he had been told. "Then Colonel Kosnov is after the holder of the letter."

"It would appear so, wouldn't it?" Bresnavitch sipped his drink contentedly. "But Comrade Potkin, the letter was never delivered."

"Wh-what?"

"Polakov was apprehended before he could make delivery; apprehended by Kosnov."

"Then where is the letter?"

"Where would you think?"

Potkin hesitated. "Colonel Kosnov?"

"Precisely. We believe Colonel Kosnov has the letter, but we do not believe he knows who it was intended for. That, as I see it, is the reason for Series Five. He hopes the new Western agent will lead him to the guilty party – or parties."

Grodin handed Potkin another drink.

"Comrade Potkin," Bresnavitch said firmly, "I want to get there before Kosnov does. And I want you to help me."

"But – but, ah – ah I work for C-C-Colonel Kosnov."

"My dear Potkin, you work for him in an administrative capacity. This is a *political* issue. You cannot be simple enough to assume that Series Five is a routine intelligence operation. Kosnov has the letter but it is useless to him unless he discovers the intended recipient. Which group, which of the four was it meant for? Once this is determined, those men, or that man, will be politically in debt to their detector. That is what Kosnov is striving for and that is what I and my group want.

"We have managed to stay out of this Khrushchev fight and remain unaffiliated. With additional votes at our disposal we will be one of the most potent forces in Russia."

Potkin felt perspiration break out along his brow.

"You – you p-p-put me in a very difficult position."

"I once did you a service when you were in an even more difficult position, after the Hungarian trouble. I am now asking for repayment."

"Whatever you say," Potkin told him.

"Excellent. We simply want to know everything that happens in your department before Kosnov does."

"You will."

"There is another possibility," Grodin said, moving behind Potkin's chair. "The possibility that there never was a Western agent coming here in the first place."

"Ah – ah – I don't understand."

"Comrade Potkin," Grodin continued, "did it ever occur to you that the letter was intended for Colonel Kosnov in the first place? That Polakov was his man?"

Potkin shifted uneasily in his seat.

"An interesting concept, eh, comrade?" beamed Bresnavitch. "What if Series Five is simply a sham to throw everyone off the colonel's trail?"

"I don't believe it." Potkin spoke before he could restrain himself.

"Neither do I," Bresnavitch confided, "but none the less we may have to prove it. If things don't work out the way we wish them to – we might just have to prove it. After all, Colonel Kosnov is holding the letter."

The Highwayman walked quickly along the San Francisco street and entered the bar. He took a table near the postage-stamp stage. Lilly Laden was halfway through "Stormy Weather." Five pocket spotlights played down on the marcelled blond tresses, the heavy eyeshadow and false lashes, the rouged cheeks and the thick, moist lipstick. A bright red silk-brocade evening dress hung tightly from the bare shoulders.

The Highwayman sent a note back to the dressing room. Lilly Laden joined him at the table.

"You're needed in New York," he told the singer.

"When?" asked the shrill, hoarse voice.

"Now. I'll wait."

Lilly Laden went back to the dressing room, took off his wig and washed away the make-up. Ten minutes later the Warlock hurried out onto the street and fell in step beside the Highwayman.

CHAPTER EIGHT

THE PUPPET MAKER

PROFESSOR Martin Buley, the Puppet Maker, professor of anthropology, marched enthusiastically into the study.

"Gentlemen, gentlemen," he said, striding across the room and standing behind his littered desk. "It is good to see you. Please forgive the delay; I wasn't expecting you until morning. Not that I mind nocturnal surprises. No, no. The sooner we get operative, the better. Time is gold."

He turned to the bookshelf and hurriedly began unloading volumes onto the cluttered desk. The Puppet Maker was slightly over six feet tall. Rone estimated him to be in the middle or late fifties. His long shallow face was divided by a thin upturned nose and dotted on both sides by two grey owl eyes. The fine black hair was matted close to his head and parted directly in the middle. It was cut in a severe bang and hung low across his rectangular, wrinkled forehead.

Professor Buley placed himself efficiently behind the stacked desk, took out two folders and a yellow pad, sharpened a pencil, shot his cuffs, looked at Janis, and said, "Disrobe, sir."

Janis stood in his shorts as Professor Buley circled around him. He returned to the desk and made some quick notes. He was back a moment later examining Janis' scalp and hands. Once again he returned to the desk and pad.

"I understand you've done some wheat farming?"

"Me? When?" asked Janis.

Professor Buley threw open one of the two files and withdrew a sheaf of papers.

"You've spent a year and a half on a wheat farm and you speak rather broken Russian."

"I've never stepped foot on any type of farm and my Russian is excellent."

Professor Buley rocked back in his chair. "We all think

we speak foreign languages well," he said benevolently.

"Well, I do. I lived there for five years."

"Come, come, let's not exaggerate. You never set foot in Russia."

"I lived there for five years," Janis repeated.

Buley looked down at the records in front of him. "Might I ask what years?"

"From '33 to '35 and then from '37 to '40."

The professor read from a page he held at arm's length. "In 1935 you were seven years old and attending the third grade. You were lucky, in fact, ever to get out of it. In 1940 you were twelve and just graduating grammar school."

"Dammit, man, in 1940 I was with an assassination team trying to hit Beria – I never graduated from grammar school."

"Are you challenging the records?" Buley asked coldly.

"Professor," Rone interjected, "I think you're reading from my file."

"Impossible. I am reading Mr. Nephew's record."

"But I am Mr. Nephew."

The Puppet Maker shuffled the two files and nervously examined each of them. His eyes blinked and his nose twitched. "How odd," he could be heard telling himself as he discovered his error. "How very odd."

Janis had finished and was enraged. The Puppet Maker had ordered him to shave his beard. Rone stood before Professor Buley in his shorts. The Puppet Maker examined his scalp. The nose and ears came next. All the while he kept up a running conversation.

"Do you know much about archaeology, Mr. Nephew?"

"Only what I've read in *National Geographic*."

"Those people? Years back I did an expedition or two for them. Sticky lot. Would you mind opening your mouth?"

Rone opened his mouth and Professor Buley examined his teeth with a dentist's mirror and pick. "I prefer the Tillinger Fund. You have heard of the Tillinger Fund?"

Rone, his open mouth filled with Buley's fingers, tried to nod.

"As you know, the Tillinger Fund is a New York-based operation. Philanthropic, of course." The professor stood up. "Only two cavities. The great-grandfather Tillinger amassed his fortune in manganese or something like that." Buley made some additional notes and began feeling the muscles in Rone's neck and shoulders.

"Like many other men of his day, great-grandfather Tillinger set up a charitable fund. It specialised in anthropology with a spare archaeologist thrown in now and then." He was examining Rone's back. "Anyway, his great-grandsons, the brothers Tillinger, now operate it. Dedicated clan. Gentlemen all. They sponsor five expeditions a year. Why not drop in on them when you're in New York? I think you will find it interesting. Would you mind raising and lowering your arm?"

Rone obeyed.

"Smoothly and slowly," the Puppet Maker suggested, "like a seagull."

Rone was next asked to take various positions. Buley felt the muscles again. He moved on to the legs.

"I have some literature here," he told Rone.

"On what?"

"The Tillinger Fund. I must insist you read it. Acquaint yourself with the facts. Would you mind bending over?" the professor checked his feet and ankles. He had Rone squat. Then kneel. He examined the knees, elbows and toes. The professor nodded his approval and walked behind the desk. Before sitting he remembered something. "Just one more thing, if you don't mind. Then the examination will be finished. Drop your shorts a moment."

Rone obliged. The professor did not seem happy. He sat behind his desk.

"No matter what location we pick remember that you were circumcised by a Jewish doctor. When you were a child your parents took you on a trip to Kiev. You caught a bad cold. The doctor they took you to was Jewish. He treated the cold. He suggested to your parents that you be circumcised. He pointed out its hygienic value. Your parents were peasants. They didn't know the difference. They agreed. I know it's a rather clumsy story, but it always seems to work."

"Then we're going into Russia?" said Rone.

"Of course. Was there ever any doubt about that?" asked Professor Buley. "You can dress now."

While Rone dressed, Buley was busy jotting down notes and checking reference books. Rone sat down. The professor kept writing. He stopped, leaned back in his chair, pressed his hands together and put them against his lips. He thought for a while and walked to a world map.

"Do you know where Georgia is?"

"In Russia or the United States?"

"In Russia."

"Yes."

"First impressions are always the best. I think we'll have you come from Georgia. This is only sketchy at the moment; we'll work out the details later. The Georgians are physically big. You'd pass. You're muscular enough to have done farm work. We'll have to work on your accent, of course." The professor handed a pad of paper to Rone. "There are several things I want you to start doing now. You had better write them out. First, let your hair grow. Especially the sideburns and on the back of your neck. Use no oils whatever. Only water. Another thing: begin parting your hair more in the middle."

Professor Buley walked to a cabinet and took out some photographs. He gave them to Rone. "Here you see some typical Georgian farmers. These are from the north, these from the south. You will most likely end up coming from the south. Although we can't be sure until your partner is picked."

"What about combs?" asked Rone.

"I was coming to that," said Buley, showing the first signs of irritation. "A wide metal comb will do. We will provide you with Russian combs as soon as we can get them. Until then, just plain metal. Let the hair in your nose grow out and do the same with the fuzz on your ears. Now for your teeth. Stop using toothpaste. Try to brush with your finger and use salt water. It's the best thing for you anyway. If you have to use a brush, do, but as I said, I'd rather you didn't."

Rone kept writing.

"Those two fillings will have to be replaced. Where you will be coming from they usually pull teeth rather than fill them. I think we can save you that discomfort, but we will have to find out just what they drill and fill with in that locale. Am I going too fast?"

"I'm keeping up."

"Your vaccination must be covered up. I can give you a choice of two methods. Even though the time is short we could give you a skin graft. It won't be perfect when we're rushed like this. Any close examination will detect it."

"What's the other choice?" asked Rone.

"Scars. It's quicker and less painful. Burns might work in this case. Searing parts of your arms not only covers the vaccination but allows a convincing story about war wounds. Unfortunately this method mars you for future assignments. You'll undoubtedly need plastic surgery when you get back. This is all so nasty. I do wish we had the proper time but needless to say we don't. In this particular case I feel burns would be the most effective."

"Do whatever you think is best."

"Thank you. Next come fingernails and toenails. I'm not sure what instruments are used in your area. I'll look into it and get you the proper equipment." The professor took a thick notebook off the shelf behind him and began thumbing through it. He found the page he wanted, snapped open the binder and handed a sheet to Rone. "This is your diet. Start on it immediately. It will be difficult at first, since there is only eight ounces of meat per week. If you feel weak, just rest. Under no conditions take vitamins. They are too easy to trace in your system. Cut out all drinks. We will provide Russian vodka and Georgian wines in a week or two. Get used to drinking as little water as possible. Drink beer or milk for the time being.

"If you can find somewhere to shovel dirt it would be helpful. Start off with half an hour a day and then after a week move it up to an hour. You'll also have to work on your hands – the skin is too soft. You've had karate, haven't you?"

"Yes."

"Go back to the hand-building exercise with the sand pail. Fill it two-thirds sand and one-third dirt. Also twist a baseball bat or something that size in your hands until you start raising some callouses. I'll send you a solution later to harden the skin on your knees and toes. Well, I think that should hold you for the time being."

Rone smiled. "I think it should."

"This will be your first time undercover, won't it?"

"Outside of this country, yes."

"Then I should explain something to you." He looked over at Janis. "To both of you. No matter how many times you go across, this still must be understood. We will be going to great lengths to prepare your cover and to allow you to survive in foreign territory, but we cannot perform miracles. I have two objectives: first to acclimatise you to the regions you'll be living in, and secondly to minimise your chances of being detected. If you are apprehended, there is some possibility you might be mistaken for Russian; it is not very probable. Any close examination will determine that you are not one of their own. In most cases it will pinpoint exactly where you are from. Remember this, and remember one other thing – close examination takes time, and that very time they spend on you may allow your associates to escape. Don't be too quick to die.

"In the provinces you should have little trouble. In Moscow it could be a different story."

The Puppet Maker cleared his throat and looked directly at Rone. "I'm telling you this so that you don't over-estimate what I can do for you. My primary objective is to get you from Georgia to Moscow without incident."

CHAPTER NINE

THE ERECTOR SET

EARLY afternoon rain swept along the Chicago pavement. Rone stopped in front of the shop window. The gold-leaf printing arced upon the glass stated: M. Berry and Son, Inc. Below it came two horizontal words: Models – Hobbies.

A gentle girl with Botticelli grace and a melancholy look glanced up from behind the counter as Rone entered.

"I would like to see Mr. Berry."

"Are you a driver?" Her voice was soft and hesitant.

"Not that I know of," answered Rone.

"Pit crew?"

"Pedestrian," Rone said in good humour. The girl remained expressionless and distant. "I'm a friend of an old friend of Mr. Berry's. I have a personal message."

The girl hesitated. She tossed her long gold-brown hair from her face with a short self-conscious turn of the head. "You'll find him downstairs at the track. Please take the second door to your left." Her eyes avoided Rone's. Nervously she reached for a catalogue. She began thumbing through it.

The stairs led down to a hallway that connected to an adjoining building. Rone walked through and came out into a large, long room lined on three sides by a single row of empty folding chairs. In the middle of the floor, stretching almost forty feet, stood a miniature car racing track. A fourteen-inch model of a Ferrari 250 GTO '64 sped along one of the eight lanes. Right behind it came a prototype Lotus 30. The two replicas hit the turn in front of where Rone was standing, skidded around it and zoomed off down a straightway.

Rone looked up to the control booth at the far end of the room. A gaunt, red-faced man who looked more like an Irish cop than a man named Berry sat guiding the models with manual thumb controls clasped in each hand. His concentration was completely on the cars. He did not notice his visitor. Rone made his way along the miniature racecourse as the Lotus began gaining on the

Ferrari.

"Mr. Berry?" Rone called out.

"Himself," came the slightly Irish accent. He still did not look at Rone. His attention remained with the replicas.

"The Tillinger Fund is forming an expedition," Rone told him as he approached.

The pressure on the thumb controls was relaxed. The Ferrari and Lotus rolled to a stop.

The man looked up at Rone.

"We're looking for an Erector Set," Rone said.

"An Erector Set, is it?"

"I have a nephew who reads a lot. I think it's time he did something with his hands."

"And what kind of reading would a little fellow like that be about doing?"

"He prefers poetry. 'The Highwayman' is his favourite."

Berry studied Rone with a troubled gaze. "He's a wee bit young to be knowing of such things, wouldn't you think?"

"We all outgrow our scooters sooner or later. Sometimes they break," answered Rone.

"And what are the things we don't outgrow?"

"Puppet making."

"Where, for instance, would a fellow like myself learn to build a puppet?"

"In Minneapolis."

Berry began slowly to open and close his hands. He moved his fingers much as a pianist might exercise before beginning to play.

"And this fellow," began Berry, "has he been working on any puppets that you can speak of?"

"He's just completed a whore."

Berry looked down and picked up a hand control. He toyed with it a moment or so and then gave it a fast, hard squeeze. The model Ferrari shot ahead and rolled to a stop.

"And how much did you have in mind paying for this Erector Set you've been talking of?" he asked Rone.

"One hundred and twenty-five thousand, whether you go in or not. If you get what they're after, another one and a quarter – or more."

Berry grew sullen and stared into his open hands. "When would you want delivery?"

"I'll take it with me." answered Rone.

Berry reached behind him and pressed the wall intercom speaker button. "B.A.," he called into the speaker, "get everything ready. The man I told you about is here."

Berry led Rone into a spacious, modern workshop on the second floor over the store.

"I want you to look at some of the devices I've come up with since I was last over the line," he told Rone.

It took Rone almost half an hour to examine all the equipment. The workshop was excellent. Every conceivable type of sound-taping, forcible-entry and photographic device was displayed. Rone had seen most of them before, but some were new.

Rone was particularly fascinated with two new inventions. One was a tiny square of transparent plastic tape which had been treated with radioactive crystals. It could be slapped onto the back or shoulder of an unsuspecting person with little chance of detection. The crystals generated enough energy to emit a signal that could be picked up a hundred and fifty yards away.

The second device was a typewriter tap. Berry produced a thin metal grid and explained it was to be placed under the arms of the typewriter keys. The grid had a series of electrically sensitive contact nodes on it. Each node touched one individual arm of the machine. Berry demonstrated. He placed the grid under the arms of an electric IBM machine and led the wires through the electric power cord. He explained that the device could be transistorised to work on non-electric equipment. Berry led the connecting line to another IBM machine at the far end of the room. This, he explained, was the control typewriter, the one the tappers would watch. It could be planted in the next room, the basement, an adjoining building or, with the use of special equipment, a parked car. He placed the grid under the arms of the control machine. The grid on the target typewriter was an output device. The one on the control was input. Every time a key was pressed on the target machine the arm raised off the node, breaking the circuit and thereby releasing exactly the same key on the control typewriter.

Rone watched the control machine as Berry typed on the other. The message read, "B.A. invented and built this machine."

"Who is B.A.?" asked Rone.

"You'll see in a minute," answered Berry. "B.A. built everything in here. Knows every splice and cross circuit better than I do. Come along, I'll introduce you."

Berry threw open a door and Rone stepped into an adjoining room. The girl he had met at the counter was sitting with her hands folded in her lap. She was wearing black leotards.

"This is B.A., my daughter," Berry announced.

"We met downstairs," said Rone with a nod.

"As I told you before, B.A. built every one of the things you just saw."

"You're very skilful," Rone told the girl.

"B.A. will be going in my place."

Rone's head jerked towards Berry.

"My hands are gone," said the Erector Set, holding his arms out in display. "Rheumatism. I'm worthless as an oyster for what you need. But I've trained B.A. She can do everything I ever could."

"My orders are to bring you back," Rone stated.

"Then bring back a fingerless gorilla," Berry snapped. He turned to B.A. "Show him the magician trick," he ordered.

"That won't be necessary," Rone tried to protest, but B.A. was already sitting on the desk. She kicked her slippers off. Long fragile toes stuck through the cut leotards. Berry threw a piece of string on the tile floor in front of her. B.A. picked it up with her toes and proceeded to tie and untie knots in it.

"She can do it underwater as well," said Berry, stating a fact rather than boasting.

"It's still you I'll bring back," said Rone.

Berry waved his hand. B.A. wheeled a framed glass window to the centre of the room and braced it with floor screws. She buckled a leather mechanic's belt around her waist, stood on a chair, jumped up grabbed hold of an overhead crossbar and started moving herself towards the window. B.A. took one hand from the bar, reached to her belt, detached a suction cup and glass cutter and passed them down to her toes. She regripped the bar with both hands and moved along to the window. With her left foot she pressed the suction cup against the pane until it stuck. Holding the glass cutter firmly in her right toes, she expertly cut the glass along the edges of the lower part of the frame. She finished cutting and cautiously pulled the suction cup towards her. The bottom half of the window came out easily, leaving a three-foot-square opening. She freed one hand, reached down, picked up the glass, suction cup and cutter, and placed them on top of the beam. She began swinging back and forth to gain momentum.

With one last swing, she brought her body as far back as she could, shot forward, released her grip and sailed through the opening in the window. Even if she hadn't landed on her feet Rone still would have been impressed.

"Well?" asked Berry.

"No women," Rone said flatly.

"And why not, if that woman can do what no man can do?"

"My *orders* are to bring you back."

"Orders, is it? since when has this lot gone back to the givin' and takin' of orders? Join yourself up in the Army if you wish to live by orders."

"It's you who goes back."

"Now listen to me, Mr. Young and Smart Fellow, your friends owe me many a favour. I've waited a long time for the big job to come along – I knew it would. When my hands went I got B.A. ready to take my place. That share of the money's mine. I risked my skin on many a day for their pennies. Now it's dollars and I'm staking my claim with the girl. Even if you could find someone else in short order to do my job – which I know you can't – even then, no one is as good as she is. I trained her, I trained her well. She's more man than woman when it comes to working, but as a woman—" Berry hesitated and bit his lip – "as a woman, I've prepared her for what she may have to do."

Rone looked at B.A. She was standing near the portable window. He caught the profile of high firm breasts and long, lithe legs.

"How do you feel about this?" he asked her.

B.A. looked down at the floor.

"Tell the man what's on your mind," ordered Berry.

"I promised father," she began softly, "that I would do one big job in his place if it ever came up. I would like to get it over with."

"I'll make a bargain with you," Berry said arrogantly. "I'll let the girl do one last thing to convince you. If you still don't want her, I'll go along back with you."

Berry pointed to a series of floor safes lining the wall.

"Choose one," he told Rone.

Rone indicated one in the middle.

"These are all new boxes. The girl hasn't had a chance to see any of them." Berry crossed the room and returned with a small metal device with three dials on it. "This little darling, in case you're curious, is a time bomb capable of blowing the sides out of any of them beauties. How much time shall we give the lass? Half an hour? Twenty minutes? I'll tell you. Why make it easy? Fifteen minutes is what she has."

Berry adjusted the timer and placed the mechanism inside the safe Rone had chosen. He locked the door and spun the combination dial.

"Just so you don't start thinking we're pulling a windy-do, we'll have the girl work with only one hand. What's your pleasure, right or left?"

"Either one will do."

B.A. picked up a tool case and moved in front of the safe. Rone and Berry sat at the far end of the room.

"We'll not be hurt at this distance in case it goes off," he told Rone. "It's only the girl that could lose an arm or two."

Rone watched B.A. begin skilfully to manipulate the dial with only one hand. Why not? he began to tell himself. Why the hell not?

Thirty minutes later Rone and B.A. left the shop, carrying the tap typewriter.

"What's your name?" he asked her.

"B.A.," she answered in confusion.

"But what does B.A. stand for?"

"Barbara Arlene."

"Well, Barbara—" Rone began.

"Arlene," she interrupted. "I've always wanted to be called Arlene." Then she thought better of it. "No," she told him "B.A. will do."

It was only after they were on the plane to New York that Rone wondered if it was actually a bomb Berry had placed in the safe. And if it was, he wondered, had he really set the fuse?

CHAPTER TEN

THE TILLINGER FUND

RONE and B.A. walked up the steps to the Tillinger mansion, rang and entered.

"I do believe it's Doctor Nephew," said an effeminate man with long blond hair sitting behind a Louis XIV reception desk. "But what is this?" He motioned to Arlene.

"A surprise," said Rone.

"The founding fathers aren't partial to surprises. None of us is."

Rone and B.A. climbed the marble staircase to the elegant wood-pannelled study on the second floor. Ward and the Highwayman, resplendent in double-breasted pinstripes with waistcoats and key chains, looked at the pair in disbelief.

"A girl?" Highwayman said, trembling. "You brought back a girl?"

"It's Berry's daughter. He's trained her," Rone tried to explain, setting the typewriter on the floor.

"Your orders were for Berry himself," he shouted.

"He has rheumatism. He can't use his hands."

"Are you a doctor?" snapped Ward.

"A girl," the Highwayman repeated with mounting anger. "You brought a girl back here?"

"She's the best I've seen. She can do anything," Rone said defensively.

The Highwayman's face flushed bright purple. "You've *seen*? And how much have you seen in your long and *busy* career?"

"Give her a chance. See what she can do," Rone demanded.

The Highwayman gasped with rage and turned to Ward. "I told you all along he was the wrong choice. He's irresponsible, just as the reports said. This is what you get for picking him. This is Jehovah's vengeance for taking on a wet-eared pup. Didn't I warn you that none of these modern-day schoolboys was capable?"

"Capable of what?" snapped Rone. "Pushing back the clock to the dark ages of intelligence? Or taking a reel out of some third-rate cloak-and-dagger film of the forties and calling it the Holy Gospel? All I've seen around here so far looks like a rummage sale of outmoded espionage artifacts – with one exception, this girl."

"Get him out of here," the Highwayman shrieked to Ward. "Get him out."

"Wait across the hall," Ward ordered.

As Rone reached the door he turned to the Highwayman. "Look at that goddam typewriter sitting there. The girl built it herself. See if any of your obsolete henchmen can do as well."

Rone waited in the room for almost two hours before Ward came in.

"Well, Nephew, are you pleased with yourself?"

"No, but he didn't have to lay into me," answered Rone.

"Lay into you in front of a pretty young lady?"

"That wasn't it."

"Then what was? You've taken worse abuse than that in the Navy. You weren't striking back, you were giving a speech. Speeches usually take a little time to prepare."

"I saw Berry's hands and I saw what the girl can do. I felt it was worth the risk bringing her. Have you seen what she can do?"

"We've seen."

"Well?"

"She's impressive, but you've put us in a rather awkward position, Nephew. First off, you brought her here, so she knows who and where we are. Secondly, you more or less forced her on us. I have a hunch your motives weren't necessarily charitable."

"Don't fool yourself. I have no interest in her."

"I didn't say you did. I just wonder how much interest you have in us – or *against* us."

"You'd better watch it or they'll be coding you out as Mr. Freud."

Rone hardly saw Ward's arm move, but he felt the stiffened fingers drive into his stomach. Pain surged through his body. His knees weakened, he doubled over and dropped to the floor. Ward sat down in a large over-stuffed chair and waited.

It took Rone longer than he had expected to regain his strength.

"Stand up," ordered Ward. Rone got unsteadily to his feet. Ward reached into his pocket and threw him a switchblade. "There comes a time, Nephew, when every smart-assed little boy must get his comeuppance. You're seventeen years my junior, and according to that record of yours you're a pretty good street brawler. Now I haven't had any high-priced training in all those fancy Oriental styles you got such good grades in, but I'm going to take you. I may even kill you in the bargain. So when I come at you, just use that shiv well."

Rone shook his head in disgust and tossed the knife on the couch.

"You still sound like a third-rate film," were the last words Rone got out before Ward threw a left.

Rone ducked the punch and reached up for Ward's arm only to have his feet kicked out from under him. As he fell forward Ward's knee crashed into his face and the side of his hand slammed into the back of his neck. He remembered nothing else. Charles Rone had never been knocked unconscious before. When he came to, Ward was sitting in the overstuffed chair tenting his fingers.

"Let me know when you're ready again."

Rone tried to rise to one knee. It took two attempts.

"While we're waiting for the re-match," said Ward, "I think it's your turn to answer some questions."

"You've earned the right to ask," said Rone, easing himself onto the couch.

"Something's bugging you, Nephew, and it's certainly not that old man in there. Let's get it out in the open."

Rone spoke before he could edit himself. "This is easily the most disorganised, archaic, inefficient operation I've ever seen."

"Is that all that's upsetting you?"

"It's enough. Look at the people involved. The Whore. The Highwayman. The Professor, who begins examining the wrong man. And now that drag queen at the desk. They're like a bunch of comic-book characters."

"Is that why you brought in the girl? To get even with my bad casting?"

"No. I brought her because she was good and I had no other choice. I was under the impression that I could do some thinking for myself."

"No one said you couldn't."

"Well, at this mad tea-party, eccentricity seems to have priority over intellect."

"Now look here, Nephew. I didn't know what they taught you in the classroom about intelligence and espionage. I learned what I know on the street, and I can tell you one thing for certain: it has no form or size or rules. At best it turns out to be what you least expect. So you learn to expect anything. You don't put your own private rules and evaluation on people, places or events. If you want order in the universe, take up mathematics. Where we're going the world will most likely be upside down and sideways."

"I know where we're going," said Rone, "but I don't know why."

"You'll find out when the time comes, but I can assure you one thing: you'll crawl before you walk. If that girl and you wanta be in on the fun you better shag right down stairs and get ready for your first steps."

"Then you're keeping her?"

"She might suit our purposes, but we're going to make her prove it pronto."

CHAPTER ELEVEN

ELEVEN MEN

IT had not been one of Potkin's good days. It began badly before breakfast, with the persistent ringing of the doorbell. Potkin was waiting for a phone call in the office on the first floor of his New York town house. The staff was not awake, so he answered the door himself. A delivery man handed him a package. It was the new portable stereophonic record player he had bought for his daughters two days before. When they had first asked for it he had refused, not so much on ideological grounds as out of fundamental parsimony. He submitted, but rather than buy the model his daughters had suggested, he scanned the newspapers for bargains and finally found a sale in the Bronx that offered sets at fifty per cent off. He and his daughters took the trip up-town, only to find that the models were reconditioned rejects of little-known brands. The girls objected to their father's mean-ness. Potkin held firm. It was either one of these or nothing. Holding back the tears in their eyes, his daughters reluctantly agreed.

If Potkin had believed in deities he might have felt the delivery at seven in the morning was an evil omen. When the girls awoke at seven-thirty they found the unopened carton sitting inside their door. Ignoring calls to break-fast, they tore apart the cardboard, unwrapped the set, plugged the cord into the socket, placed their favourite record on the turntable and switched the machine on. Not only did all the fuses blow, but the wiring caught fire. Before anyone could reach an extinguisher, smoke began pouring from their room. Potkin could not avoid calling the fire Department. The burning wires were soon put out, but the house was left without electricity. The power failure cut off the automatic furnace and somehow caused the basement to flood.

Potkin's staff spent most of the morning watching elec-tricians and plumbers meander about the house repairing the damage. The workmen resented the close scrutiny. Furniture was accidently tipped over, and several odds and ends were broken, which better hospitality might have preserved. When the workmen left, Potkin's staff methodically checked the house for damage and most of all for bugging. This took most of the day.

While the staff secured the house, Potkin took refuge in an upstairs bedroom, working through his files. He examined the final report on potential American agents. At first he breathed a sigh of relief. After almost three months of work the whereabouts of only eleven men were unknown. As he read, however, he changed his mind. Photographs and biographies had been obtained on ten men, but for the eleventh there *were* no records – just a name.

Potkin knew that in the bureaucracy of the United States it was almost impossible for a citizen not to be recorded on paper in some easily accessible file. From birth to the grave the life of an American was one long series of city, state, federal, institutional and industrial documentation.

Potkin had always scoffed at America's obsessive condemnations of totalitarian governments' police systems. No country in the history of the modern world kept more recorded material on more of its population than the United States of America. In the land of the free more was written down than anywhere else. Telephone books alone located almost a fifth of the populace. Women were sometimes difficult to find because of marital name changes, but the average American male was easy to locate and investigate, and government employees were even easier.

For Potkin, the simplest by far were members of the armed services. They were bound to come up sooner or later on income-tax returns, social security lists, FBI fingerprint files, Armed Forces Insurance records or Veterans Administration classifications. These were the areas that Potkin's agents had infiltrated. Once you had the name of a current member of the armed forces or a veteran, the rest was usually automatic.

Potkin rocked back in his chair and bit the rubber of his pencil. This time it was different. He had the name of the eleventh man and that was all. As exceptional as it seemed, there was absolutely no additional information anywhere.

He took out a pad of paper and rapidly began writing a report to Kosnov. He would send a copy to Bresnavitch first. When he finished he buzzed for his secretary.

"Have this typed and sent out by diplomatic courier tonight," he ordered.

Rone sat at the monitor typewriter in the Tillinger mansion and read Potkin's report as it was being typed.

He watched as the last paragraph began:

```
Lt. Commander Charles Rone, USN, ONI,
discharged October 10, 1964.
Name appears on discharge order, but
nowhere else.  Travel orders, veterans'
files show negative information.  File
not to be found.  Deem situation
''unusual''.  It appears that all written
information concerning Charles Rone has
intentionally been removed.  Major
question is why discharge order was left
to be found.
Summation:  Situation concerning
Charles Rone evaluated as ''potential''.
Thorough investigation will be under-
taken.
```

CHAPTER TWELVE

PREPARATION

RONE had been scheduled to take another trip to bring back two more agents, but he had twisted his knee in the fight with Ward. The joint had swollen and he walked with a decided limp. His assignment was exchanged with the Warlock, the man with the pompadour who had first greeted him at the front desk.

For the first three days he acted as receptionist and guide for the Tillinger display of South American sarcophagi on the first floor. The public was admitted from ten A.M. to two-thirty P.M. There were not many visitors, but there were endless deliveries. A constant stream of trucks pulled up before the mansion. Crates, boxes and cartons of all sizes and descriptions were unloaded. All were stencilled with the same words: Tillinger Fund – Tasmanian Exhibition. Each one was earmarked for a specific member of the operation. Professor Buley and Dr. Set were the most often named.

From two-thirty until eight, Rone, along with Buley and the beardless Janis, who had arrived the day after Rone and B.A., distributed the cargo throughout the house. Most of the deliveries were taken right through to the house behind the Tillinger mansion. The Puppet Maker had requisitioned the basement, sub-basement and kitchen areas of this house. The two-storey-high ballroom was assigned to the Erector Set. The third floor was divided between communications and printing. The fourth and fifth floors were living accommodation and classrooms. Briefing rooms were established on the fourth floor, the dining room adjoined the ballroom.

The Tillinger mansion itself was to be used for living accommodations and offices. It had its own kitchen and dining area.

In the evenings Professor Buley and Rone worked together. The first two evenings they unpacked Russian foodstuffs. The canned goods were meticulously sorted and put onto shelves according to the regions they came

117

from. The same geographic classifications were used in the large walk-in refrigerator for the imported fresh vegetables and the frozen Russian meats.

On the third night Rone was fascinated as they unpacked specimens of Russian water. Buley gave them his undivided attention. There were some twenty-five quart bottles in all. Each had a chemical analysis attached to it. Rone followed Buley into the basement, where a complete chemical laboratory had been built and outfitted. In an adjoining room stood half a dozen five-hundred-gallon aluminium water tanks. They spent several hours cleaning them. It was well past midnight on the third night when Buley turned to Rone.

"And now we'll start manufacturing Russian water," he announced.

"Why?" asked Rone.

"Why would you think?" countered the professor.

Rone thought. "The chemical composition of Russian water must be different. Therefore if we drink it and are captured we could pass a chemical analysis test. No, that doesn't sound right."

"It's partially true. You will be drinking this water and you will be washing and bathing in it. If you are captured and the Russians take the time to analyse your chemical components, they will undoubtedly be convinced that you have been using Russian water. This would be done at an autopsy, of course.

"But there is another reason: Americans are used to much purer water than any other people in the world. Therefore our systems have become rather weak. We have a very low tolerance for impurity in liquid as well as in food. Americans abroad have always had difficulty adjusting to the drinking water of foreign countries, and rightly so. In some places it's half poison. We're highly susceptible to dysentery and other diseases contracted from impure water. This is almost always the way to spot an American in poor water areas. Perhaps this is why the majority of the world doesn't bother to drink water at all.

"What we will be doing is starting each of you on the poorest-grade water from the area you supposedly came from. Slowly we will build up your resistance. Then we will move you on to the areas you will be travelling through to reach Moscow. Some will come from the east, others from the west, north, south. Once your resistance has been established, we will switch you onto Moscow water. If you adjust to the worst, then you can easily take the best."

"Why don't you do it the other way round?" asked Rone. "Why not start with a high-grade water which in itself might be hard to drink and then slowly work down the grades?"

"That would of course make more sense – if we had the time. But we don't. Most of you will get along fine, I would guess. However, one or two are in for a few bad days. Shall we begin?"

Buley put the two large water distillers into operation. When he had about fifty gallons of pure water he poured them into ten five-gallon containers.

"Let's begin with you," directed the professor. He went through his specimen bottles and took out two. He read the charts and went back into the chemical lab. He returned with a tray of apothecary jars filled with different chemicals. Meticulously he added the formula ingredients to one can. He waited until the elements dissolved and then poured Rone a large tumbler.

"It's not quite the real thing," Buley said apologetically. "But it should do the trick."

Rone drank it down. It didn't taste different from any other water.

"Now I think you had better toddle off to bed. Don't drink anything else. We'll know by morning if you're immune."

Rone got his answer in the middle of the night.

CHAPTER THIRTEEN

MATRICULATION

AT six-thirty the next morning Rone made his way down to the dining room. He was still sick. The Highwayman, Ward, Janis, B.A., the Warlock and Professor Buley were already seated at the table. So were four additional men. The Highwayman quickly introduced them as the Casket Maker, the Ditto Machine, the Priest, Clocker Dan and the Transom Man. Rone was in no condition to remember names. When he looked down at his plate he felt even worse. One single dried fish and two roots was all that was in front of him. No knife, fork, or spoon, no juice or coffee; just a dried fish and two roots.

"And now, gentlemen," Buley said, standing, "for your first home-cooked Russian meal. In front of you you will see the sumptuous fare of that part of the USSR you supposedly come from. The water in your glass, for those of you who have water, is also of that area. Drink that later, since Russians do not use such liquids with meals. Some of you have beer, others wine or milk. Some of you have eating utensils, others do not. Those of you with forks, please place them in your left hand. The Russians eat continental-style, except in regions from which none of you come. Now do like me."

The Puppet Maker proceeded to demonstrate the table manners of the various regions. He also displayed how to eat without cutlery. He picked up a dried fish, bit off the head and swallowed it. He began chewing on it much as a child would eat a bar of toffee.

Rone picked up the fish and took one bite before abruptly pushing his chair back from the table. After breakfast they withdrew to the adjoining study for Russian coffee. The Highwayman got up and officially welcomed everyone. He explained that the group had been brought together for a specific mission.

"The project will have three phases," he told them. "Training, Interior Action, and Exterior Action. All of you will participate in the Training and Interior Action.

Only some of you will be asked to participate in the over-seas operation. This is a matter of circumstance rather than failings on any of your parts. Each of you is a specialist, but we still must determine our action plan and which of your skills will be required. For reasons of security no one will know the exact objective of the mission until the latest possible moment. Knowledge or lack of knowledge of this objective will in no way indi-cate you are, or are not, being selected to go on the expedition."

Ward took the floor next and reviewed the financial arrangements. Everyone in the room would receive the basic payment of one hundred and twenty-five thousand dollars. Those who were selected to go on the expedition would receive an additional hundred and twenty-five thousand as a danger bonus if they accomplished their objective. There was also the possibility of uncovering a cache during their mission of another million dollars or so. This would be thrown into the pot and divided by those who were selected for the expedition. There were grave risks involved. Some might not make it out.

"If we don't make it out, will we handle the danger pay and additional money in the usual way?" asked the Priest.

"That's up to all of you," Ward answered.

"I'm for the usual way," the Casket Maker let it be known.

"The usual way," Ward explained to Rone and B.A., "is that only the survivors of the expedition share in anything above the basic guarantee. They can decide among themselves whether they want to give anything to those who stayed behind or to the relatives of those who might be lost."

"It's superstition, boys and girls," Janis added. "Super-stition says this is the best way to handle it."

Ward asked for a vote. The first eight men raised their hands in approval of survivors take all. Rone and B.A. made it unanimous.

Ward next explained the domestic operation. The Tillinger mansion would be manned by a hand-picked staff that would arrive the following day. The house behind it, the one they were now in, would be the security area. It was completely restricted to the people in the room and those few specialists from the Tillinger mansion who were required from time to time. The Tillinger mansion was mainly clerical. The heartbeat of the project would be where they now were.

"How big a staff will be moving into the mansion?" asked the Casket Maker.

"Sixty-five," answered Ward.

"Do they know what we're about?" asked Clocker Dan. He was a jolly little man, no more than five feet six. A blue silk scarf was tucked into his expensive tweed jacket. A blue silk handkerchief peeked from his breast pocket. He wore dark cashmere trousers and brown suede shoes. His hair was silver and his face round and red. With a white beard, Rone thought, he would look like Santa Claus.

"The staff are all selected intelligence personnel on loan to us from various organisations. They know they are on a high-classification project, but that is all."

"Even so," pointed out the Priest, "those who work in the labs or special sections are bound to get some idea of what is happening."

"That's true," answered Ward, "but we've taken two precautions. First, the staff is exceedingly large, so no one will have to work in more than one area, and secondly, they will not be able to leave the house individually."

"That protects us during our stay here," the Priest said, "but what happens when we go over the line?"

"As I said before, they are all volunteers. They have agreed to quarantine until we have returned or are captured."

Training would not begin until the following morning. Rone spent the afternoon checking in more equipment and helping the Ditto Machine organise his ultra-modern printing and engraving shop. Crates of Russian paper of every description were unpacked and catalogued, the same paper that the Soviet government used for passports, money and a dozen official documents. Even the inks had been procured in Russia.

In the evening Janis and Rone helped B.A. unpack and catalogue five television cameras, ten television sets, and quantities of recording and film equipment. As Rone was going through the receipts he noticed an item for two lorry loads of a new transparent plastic board. The purchase price was listed at seventy-five thousand dollars.

It was past midnight before Rone got to his room on the fifth floor. He showered and was prepared for bed when he heard the knock. He opened the door. B.A. came in.

"Is anything the matter?" he asked.

She shook her head without speaking.

"Come in. Sit down."

Once again she shook her head, making the long soft hair swirl about her features.

"Then just stand there," Rone told her gently.

"I've never been away from home," she said quickly. "I've never been away from home and I've never done any of those – those other things my father talked about. You know. Those physical things, I told him I had, but I haven't." She turned and ran from the room.

CHAPTER FOURTEEN

YORGI IVANOVITCH DAVITASHVILI

BREAKFAST was at six-thirty A.M., and for Rone it consisted of one small bowl of kasha. The typewritten description beside it explained that it was the equivalent to American hot cereals. Rone had grown so hungry that even the coffee tasted good.

The first Interior Action briefing took place in the basement meeting room directly after breakfast. Ward took the floor.

"To accomplish our mission," he began, "it will be necessary to establish a headquarters in Moscow. One that can be used for six months or longer. Ideally we would like enough room to house eight men. Since every last inch of space in Moscow is under government assignment, this creates a problem. Our best chance is to find a house or apartment that belongs to a Russian who doesn't use it very often. People who fall in this category are usually high-ranking officials on foreign assignment, those stationed out of the country. We have picked a target. A man presently residing in New York. The objective of interior action is to convince him to co-operate."

The lights were switched off and a picture of a dour, round-faced man flashed on the screen.

"Let me introduce Captain Potkin, head of the Soviet Third Department's United States operation. He travels under diplomatic immunity, as a member of a United Nations delegation. This mild-mannered, devoted husband and father murdered his first man when he was just fifteen – by strangulation. His victim was in his seventies and partially blind. He had razed his first village by sixteen.

"Potkin developed his craft under Beria. During World War II he was sent into Germany and skilfully infiltrated the Reichshauptsicherheitsamt. His rise to Nazi trust began in the political prisons, where he efficiently persuaded suspects to give up secrets they had never possessed. Potkin was promoted to the rank of S.S. Haupt-sturmfürer, Sicherheitsdienst, Gross Paris. His duties included interrogation, reprisal, procurement and the infiltration of Communist intelligence. He kept quite busy. So busy, in fact, that he barely managed to set up three underground networks and assassinate twenty-eight of his fellow German officers. After the war he accompanied Russia's first delegation to the opening of the United Nations in San Francisco. We next heard of him in northern China, as an adviser to the training of Red Chinese guerrillas. As a cultural attaché to Hungary he had not forseen the Budapest uprisings of 1956, so he was brought back to the seclusion of Russia. His fall from grace lasted four years. Then he was assigned to a highly powerful counter-espionage operation – Colonel Kosnov's Third Department. The appointment was arranged through Aleksei I. Bresnavitch, whose name will come up later. Potkin's star began to rise. He was assigned a new apartment in Moscow and made second-in-command in the Division of United States Affairs. Later a new car and a summer house near Moscow were awarded him. Kosnov elevated him to head of all North American affairs. He has held that position for three years now. That more or less is a capsule view of our subject. You can read the details in your brochures.

"Captain Potkin seems to have no exploitable vices, so we must start with the obvious possibilities."

A picture of an old woman and two young girls flashed on the screen.

"These are his wife and daughters."

From the lecture Rone went to a basement classroom for his first language instruction. It was given by Clocker Dan, the little cherubic man with the tweed jacket. He was extremely patient and extremely tolerant.

"Now, let us hear your Russian. Take any one of those books on the table and read," he instructed politely.

Rone picked up a volume of Gorki and began.

"Excuse me a minute," Clocker Dan interrupted. "I forgot to turn on the tape recorder."

He snapped on the machine and Rone began again. He read for almost half an hour. Every time he looked up from the page, Clocker Dan was staring at the floor, nodding and smiling to himself.

"We do read very well. Yes, we do," he finally said, taking the book from Rone's hand. "One would think we came from Leningrad itself. Only we're from Tiflis. Now let me see. You must have learned the language at that Army school in California – the one out near Santa Cruz, perhaps?"

"Yes," said Rone. "The Army Language Centre."

"Well, don't worry about it," he said hopefully. "We'll get you back on the right track in no time. Class dismissed."

Rone left. He could hear Clocker Dan replaying his voice as he walked to the next appointment. Ten A.M. to twelve noon, personality instruction – basement room C – Professor Buley. When he entered Professor Buley was waiting with folded hands.

"Now then," he began chipperly. "What name would you like? To me you look like a Josef or a Jakob. What do you look like to you?"

"Either one will do."

"Good. Then we agree. Josef it will be. Or should it be Yusev? What about Yorgi? I feel Yorgi is even better." He examined Rone close up and then from a distance. "There's no doubt about it. You're a Yorgi. Now for the patronymic. Something patriotic, would you say? Show how much your poor departed grandparents loved Mother Russia?"

"What about Nicholayevitch?"

"Oh-ho-ho-ho. That would put you in the soup, wouldn't it? Once I knew an agent who took the name Nicholas before going across. They shot his brains out for no reason at all. I always attributed it to the name. I think Ilya would be nice. You can never go wrong with that. Or perhaps your father could be Ivan. It's always best to be simple, I think. Shall we settle for that – Yorgi Ivanovitch, son of Ivan?"

Rone nodded.

"Now for the last name I think we should have something historic – historic to Georgians, anyway. It's a little risky using Djugashvili. Might still get the police in a tizzy. Ah. How does Davitashvili strike you?"

"Smashing," said Rone, "but will I ever learn how to spell it?"

"It won't matter," Buley smiled. "You're supposed to be semi-illiterate."

Yorgi Ivanovitch Davitashvili followed the professor out into the hall, where a row of school lockers stood.

"This one is yours," said Buley, throwing open the door and taking out some rumpled, smelly clothes. These are your new uniform. They were lifted right off the back of a peasant heading for Tiflis less than three days ago."

"Will they be washed?" asked Rone.

"And ruin the effect?" Buley was shocked. "If you're to be a peasant you must eat, drink, sleep and smell like one."

"It's something like method acting, isn't it?" Rone concluded.

"You could look at it that way. Stanislavski did not come from Des Moines, Iowa."

Rone put on the clothes while breathing through his mouth.

"Yes," Buley finally declared after examining Yorgi from all sides, "yes, you have a great potential as a peasant. Now shall we settle down and find you some parents and a random relative or two?"

After class Rone changed his clothes and rushed back to the room. The Whore was lying on the bed reading a comic book.

"You smell awful," he said to Rone. "Where the devil have you been?"

"Have you had your personality session with Buley yet?" asked Rone, tearing off his clothes and heading for the shower.

"No."

"Wait."

"Hold on, old man. You're only supposed to wash in Russian water."

"Tomorrow!"

After a lunch of thick, stringy vegetable soup, black bread and a glass of tea, Rone went to the fourth floor, where an improvised dental office had been put together. He had never seen the dentist before and assumed he had arrived with the staff for the Tillinger mansion. He explained to Rone that his two fillings would have to be removed and replaced with Russian dental cements. He gave Rone Novocain and then picked up hand tools and a manual drill and began opening the cavities. Buley had explained the dental story to Rone. Yorgi had served with the Red Army in the final days of Stalingrad, and the teeth were drilled at a field dental hospital after the Russian victory. Buley insisted on using old Russian instruments, which was perhaps unnecessary, though there was a distinct difference between the effects of hand and mechanical drills. The cement would be new, but Yorgi could always explain that he had had his teeth refilled within the last two years. At an autopsy, of course, no explanation would be necessary.

Rone's schedule card indicated another two hours of personality instruction, but this time the location and teacher had changed. He was to report to the Casket Maker in the sub-basement. When he got there he found the space had been converted into a rifle range and arsenal. The Casket Maker began displaying Russian rifles and sidearms that Yorgi should have used at Stalingrad. Rone spent the first hour taking the weapons apart and reassembling them. He spent forty minutes on the firing range.

Before he left the Casket Maker gave him a thick loose-leaf notebook containing detailed information on the Red Army's defence and attack at Stalingrad. It also included pictures of uniforms, rank, insignias and machinery, as well as the names and photographs of the generals and staff officers. Rone was told to familiarise himself with all the information. The last section of the book was typed on blue onion-skin paper. It was the military history of Yorgi Ivanovitch Davitashvili. This he must memorise.

When Rone returned to his room later that night he found a neat stack of brochures on his bed with a note: "Please familiarise by morning." although there were no departmental markings on the covers, the reports looked like National Security Agency material. They were top-secret biographies and evaluations of the Kremlin's Central Committee and fifteen other high officials. There was a notation on the last biography: "of Special Interest." The brochure dealt with Aleksei I. Bresnavitch.

CHAPTER FIFTEEN

SURVEILLANCE

BREAKFAST the next morning was once again kasha. This time a peach was added to the diet. As they were eating Ward announced that except at certain lectures, only Russian would be spoken in the security area from here on in.

"The Georgians speak notoriously bad Russian," Clocker Dan announced at Rone's language lesson. "You must master their pronunciation and words. We will go back to kindergarten and work forward. Here are the school-books you would have had." He handed Rone a stack of thin, worn pamphlets. He switched on a record player. "And these are the first songs you would have learned as a child," he said as the first strains of energetic and exotic music filled the room.

When Rone arrived for his personality instruction Professor Buley led him to a room in the sub-basement adjoining the rifle range. He handed him a sledge hammer.

"If you break through the concrete you will come to dirt. Then you can spend an hour each day digging. That's what farmers do, you know."

As Rone cracked through the concrete floor Buley sat in the corner shouting more of Rone's cover story. He elaborated on the founding of Tiflis in the fifth century and began working forward. When the session finished Buley took him upstairs and gave him a notebook on the agricultural aspects of Georgia. "Memorise it by tomorrow," he told him.

In the afternoon Rone was given his first action assignment on the interior project. He and Janis were to watch every move made by Potkin's eldest daughter, Sonia. Other members of the group were assigned to his younger daughter and to his wife.

Sonia was a big-boned girl of eighteen. Her dark hair was swept back into a bun, accentuating the high forehead and square face. Even though she dressed in the latest teenage American fashions, she wore no make-up. She had thick legs and a stocky body. The loss of fifteen pounds would have left her much more feminine.

Rone and Janis had already been extensively briefed on her habits, so they knew she would be chauffeured from home to an art school on 57th Street around nine A.M. and picked up at five-thirty. Sonia had enrolled eight months before and seemed to have much enthusiasm and some talent.

At one-thirty Rone entered the art school and went to the registrar's desk.

"Are you interested in full-time or part-time instruction?" the biddy behind the desk asked him.

"Well, I'm not sure," answered Rone. "I'm not even sure I *can* paint."

"But do you *want* to?" the registrar asked with passion. "Do you really *want* to?"

"I think so."

"Oh no, young man. Thinking is not enough. Do you have the urge?"

"I have a lot of urges," Rone admitted.

"Is it a deep, burning, compelling urge, a desire that a thousand floods could not quench?"

"Now that you mention it, I guess it *is.*"

The registrar smiled maternally. "Then that's all you need to paint."

"What about talent?"

"That will develop in time."

"Don't I need any to start with?"

"What you lack we will give you. Now in my opinion the full-time course is tailor-made for your needs. Yes it is."

Rone saw Sonia come out of the cafeteria. She walked past him and turned up a flight of stairs.

". . . so if that's agreeable to you just sign this contract and leave a hundred-dollar deposit and you can start class immediately."

"You mean I'm accepted?"

"Of *course.* I knew the moment I laid eyes on you that you had great potential."

"Thank you, but I'll have to see if I can make enough free time to take all of this. Would you mind writing that schedule out for me?"

130

"Of course not." The registrar typed out the information and handed it to Rone. "If you like there is a social meeting for first-year students every Friday and Tuesday night."

"I'll try to make it, and thank you again." Rone began to leave.

"And if you want to bring someone to the meetings, please do. Every student is allowed three guests."

At four o'clock Sonia left the art school and walked slowly east on 57th Street. She stopped to look into several bookstore and antique-shop windows. At Fifth Avenue she turned north and walked into Central Park, pausing in front of the sea lion pool in the zoo. A few minutes later an attendant appeared with a pail and began throwing food to the animals. Sonia watched in great glee. Her next stop was the lion house. This seemed to fascinate her. She took out a pad and made a few fast sketches and then looked over to the tower clock. The time seemed to frighten her. She started half running along a path that traversed the park. She would run a few hundred feet and then walk until she was rested enough to run again. She continued until she was back at the art school on 57th Street. The time was five twenty-seven P.M. She stepped inside the door and waited. At five-thirty the car which had taken her to school in the morning pulled up. Sonia walked out and got in.

Rone and Janis stood across the street down the block and watched as the car pulled away.

"Are we going to follow it?" asked Rone.

"There's no need. It's only taking her home."

"Even so—"

"My dear fellow," Janis said paternally, "the Warlock set this up. He watched her first. He's the master. We must learn to listen to the master. If he had wanted her followed that closely he would have given us a car. So you just relax and watch that grocery van parked down the street."

Rone could see the driver of the van looking into his rear-view mirror. He scanned the area carefully and then started off after the car.

"Is that one of ours?" he asked Janis.

"One of ours? My dear fellow, we have too much panache to go chasing about in a common grocery van."

131

When Rone returned to his room that night there was another stack of brochures on his bed, dealing with officials in the various Russian intelligence services. The note on top of the pile stated: "Read by morning."

CHAPTER SIXTEEN

THE EXAMINATION

TACTICAL briefing number one took place in the basement meeting room after breakfast. A gaunt, lean man with a Viennese accent gave the lecture. It dealt with Russian interrogation methods. He traced the evolution of brainwashing, torture and coercion as practised in the Soviet Union for the last forty-six years. He showed motion pictures and slides of technical devices as well as quickly outlining investigation techniques.

When Rone arrived for his session with Buley he found the professor waiting with a large assortment of Russian farm tools. He instructed Rone in their proper use and then continued developing the cover story of Yorgi. Rone dug as the professor shot question after question at him in an attempt to trip him up.

The language lesson with Clocker Dan was spent singing Georgian children's songs.

In the afternoon Rone joined Janis down the block from Sonia's art school. Once again she left the building at four P.M., walked to the park zoo, sketched, then returned without talking to anyone. Just as on the day before, the car, followed at a distance by the grocery van, picked her up at five-thirty.

"That's the most ridiculous thing I've ever seen," said Janis. "That van accomplishes absolutely nothing."

"Then why are they using it?" asked Rone.

"Looks like a slight case of nerves."

"About what?"

"Maybe us."

After supper Rone was summoned to the dining room. The Highwayman, Ward and Professor Buley were waiting for him.

"Nephew Yorgi," announced Ward, "the time has come to see just how well you have learned your lessons. Each of us will be popping a few questions at you. Now, we'd like you to answer as quickly as you can, and we would also like you to be as complete as you can."

Rone nodded.

"The other night, you were given brochures on certain Soviet personages. I would like to start with Bresnavitch. What is his full name?"

"Aleksei I. Bresnavitch."

"There was a photograph of him in the brochure. Try to describe it."

"He has an angular face with a long, tight jaw. His eyes are hard-set and rather close together. His nose is aquiline. He has a receding hairline and parts his hair slightly to the right. His hair looked slightly grey in the photograph. His mouth was large. He had full lips."

"Now tell us about the report. From the beginning."

"The first page was all facts," said Rone.

"Tell us."

"Name: Bresnavitch, Aleksei I. Born: Leningrad, February 13, 1898. Father: Ilya. Mother: exact name not known, believed to be Gurla. Occupation of father: frame maker. Brothers: Boris, killed 1942. Sisters: none. Education: unknown, believed to have studied in Kiev — unconfirmed. Height: five feet ten. Weight: approximately one hundred and eighty-five pounds. Eyes: grey. Distinguishing marks: scar at base of right ear."

Rone was aware of the Highwayman's stare. "How many times did you read that page?" he asked.

"Once," answered Rone. He saw Ward nod to the Highwayman.

"Please begin with the report," said Ward.

"A. I. Bresnavitch is a master politician within the ruling clique of the Communist Party itself," Rone began. "He grew up with the revolution. His credentials are all in order. Arrest, imprisonment, exile, torture — I can give you the dates and places if you want."

"That won't be necessary," said Ward. "Just keep going."

"His political career began when he met Lenin in Germany. Later he was exiled to Siberia with Stalin. He met Trotsky at the front. Is this too brief?"

"Just keep up the way you're going," said Ward.

"Bresnavitch disliked Lenin, but supported him instead of Trotsky, who had become one of his closest friends. When Lenin died he gambled, and gambled well. This time he supported Stalin, whom he distrusted, rather

134

than Trotsky, whom he still admired. After Stalin's death he was forced into still another choice. This time he threw his weight behind Khrushchev instead of Malenkov. Bresnavitch is in no way a toady. He's a practical Bolshevik and a hardened revolutionary. He retreats when he feels he should retreat and he attacks when he feels he should attack. During Stalin's regime he openly opposed Beria. The feud became so bitter that Western Kremlinologists gave Bresnavitch little chance of survival. In the end it was Beria who fell and Bresnavitch who flourished.

"Another one of his targets was Chou En-lai. He started his attack at a time when Moscow treated Peking with confidence and respect. Once again history seems to have sided with him.

"Bresnavitch has not been without his problems. He has been openly criticised in Kremlin circles for being slightly lavish.

"One of the few positions which we know he held under Stalin was administrator of artistic restoration. A great many paintings, including a Hals, a Vermeer and a Picasso, seem to be on loan at his private residence, a rather palatial building once occupied by one of the Romanovs. He has somehow managed to keep his private collection intact even today.

"Criticism over his standard of living goes back almost fifteen years. He has constantly been accused of being pro-Western by other Russian officials. Stalin apparently warned him about it, and Khrushchev did more than that: he took away Bresnavitch's visiting privileges to western Europe. They were reinstated two years ago, but to our knowledge he hasn't used them.

"His present position in Moscow seems to be exceedingly strong. He has emerged a major influence peddler. It is doubted whether any leadership change could be effected without his support.

"Bresnavitch is particularly powerful in areas of intelligence agencies. Over the years he has more or less become the Kremlin's *ex officio* liaison man. He has smoothed over many rifts between intelligence personnel and political bigwigs. His power seems to date back to the showdown with Beria. He is, or at least was, quite close to the Third Department's Colonel Kosnov. His son-in-law, Grodin, is presently on Kosnov's staff."

The questions continued until after midnight. Finally the Highwayman asked, "You seem to retain everything you read quite well, but how do you do on what you hear?"

"I can usually remember most of it."

"To what degree?" the Highwayman said with a note of hostility.

"What degree do you want?"

"All of a spoken conversation as it was originally stated."

"That shouldn't be too hard," Rone answered with irritation.

"Well, let us see," the Highwayman said with a smirk. "Tell me what I said the first morning the entire group arrived."

"At the breakfast table or at the meeting afterwards?"

"At the meeting."

"Well, first you welcomed each of us. Then you told us that the group had been brought together for a specific mission—"

"I asked you to be specific," the Highwayman snapped. "Is that the closest you can come?"

"You stood up and turned slightly to the right," Rone began slowly. "Then you said, 'The project will have three phases: Training, Interior Action, and Exterior Action. All of you will participate in the Training and Interior Action. Only some of you will be asked to participate in the overseas operation. . . .'"

When Rone finished, Ward snapped on a tape recorder. It played a recording of the Highwayman's original talk. Rone had recited it verbatim.

CHAPTER SEVENTEEN

POLAKOV

INSTEAD of waiting for Sonia on the corner or walking along the street, Janis led Rone into an office in a building diagonally opposite the school. From the sixth-storey window they had a perfect view of the entrance.

"She'll be coming out earlier today," he told Rone.

"Why should she? She never has before."

"Seems the wires in the school cafeteria burned out last night. Left an awful stench. She'll have to go out for lunch."

At one-thirty, as Janis had predicted, Sonia came out on the street with a group of students. Rone saw that she was being asked to join them. She shook her head in refusal and went in the opposite direction. Janis produced a pair of binoculars and watched her as she walked.

"Drat it," he said, "doesn't that bitch notice anybody?"

Sonia returned to the school at two-fifteen.

Rone was left alone to follow her on her four-o'clock walk through the park. Her path and activities were identical to those of the previous days with one exception: while she was at the lion cage a rather handsome young man in sports clothes tried to talk to her. Sonia would have none of it.

Much to his surprise Rone was asked to give tactical briefing number three. It was to deal with Russian intelligence organisations, specifically with the Third Department, a subject he had read about three nights before. When Rone stood up to speak he noticed Ward switch on a tape recorder.

Rone traced the evolution of the various military, political and civilian organisations. Although he had read the brochures only once, more than a week before, he had little trouble remembering names, places and dates.

He took more time with the Third Department, pointing out that though it was nominally a counter-espionage unit it had in fact grown to be a major intelligence-gathering organisation with independent international branches. The mission of the Third Department had originally been to protect the Kremlin from external dangers but it had become the watchdog of internal matters as well. It was undoubtedly a very potent political force.

The biography of Colonel Kosnov was familiar: at sixteen a fighter in the revolution, in the thirties a Stalinist, during World War II an exceptional espionage administrator, and now chief of the Third Department.

Lieutenant Vassili N. Grodin had been the colonel's aide for over three years. He was an alert, efficient, aggressive young officer who had been educated during the post-war technological boom. He was of "New Russia." Kosnov belonged to the old. Grodin's father-in-law, Aleksei I. Bresnavitch, promoted Grodin in the intelligence services, specifically in the Third Department.

Following Rone's lecture, Ward showed slides of each of the men discussed. Then he packed up his tape recorder and left.

The following day Rone was once again asked to give the tactical briefing. This time he was to discuss the members of the Central Committee. Once again Ward was waiting with the recorder.

After the lecture Rone went on his surveillance detail. Sonia trailed into the park on schedule, talked to no one, avoided the advances of another young man, and returned to the school in time to be picked up by the car and followed by the grocery van.

That evening Rone was called to the meeting room in the basement. Ward and a tall, handsome woman in her middle forties were waiting. She wore a well-tailored tweed suit with a pale-pink cashmere sweater, a thin string of pearls and brogues. She spoke with an English accent and was introduced by her code name – Uncle Morris. A moment later Sweet Alice entered.

Ward turned down the lights and switched on the slide projector. A cemetery appeared on the screen.

"This is the graveyard outside Moscow where Polakov,

his wife, his mother and his sister are believed to be buried. We have no confirmation on the graves, since the area may be under surveillance." The slide changed. "This is one of the few photographs taken of Polakov," Sweet Alice announced. The face disappeared and was replaced by the picture of a strikingly beautiful young girl.

"This was his wife, maiden name Erika Boeck, born Hamburg, Germany, January 10, 1941. Polakov was fifty-eight. His wife was twenty-three." The lights switched on.

Uncle Morris moved to the end of the table and began talking. "Our knowledge of Polakov's history is sparse. We are doing everything we can to fill it in, but I fear we will have to work with what we have. He was born in the Moscow area in about 1907 or 1908. His father is believed to have been the second violinist with the ballet orchestra. His mother had been a painting teacher. We did not know until recently that his mother and sister were still alive. How or why he left Russia as a young man we do not know. He is believed to have attended the University of Paris in or around 1926 to 1928. It is difficult to check because we don't know what name he was using. There seems to be evidence that he studied art and languages. He also appears to have been bisexual during this time.

"Our first official knowledge of Polakov came during World War II when he fought with the Dutch resistance and acted as liaison with the French *maquis*.

"In the late forties he appeared in Vienna and was employed by French intelligence. It wasn't long before he was on his own and selling information to the highest bidder. He established a reputation for quality merchandise. Unlike other independent espionage brokers, he did not work on volume. He came to market perhaps three or four times a year, but when he did he received top price.

"His movements were well covered, but we have been able to break his activities into four specific time periods: 1956, 1959, 1962 and 1963.

"French intelligence reports that he was in Moscow in 1956 to visit his mother and sister. He was travelling under his favourite cover, as an art dealer. The French claim he was on no specific mission, but since they just gave us this information last week, we don't know what they are withholding. During this time, according to them, Polakov made contact with a Chinese he had studied with in Paris. The man's name was Chu Chang. Chang was connected with the Red Chinese Embassy, but was apparently a rather bad boy. He and Polakov cooked up some narcotics business. Chang would supply the material from China and cover the Moscow market. Polakov would act as distributor for Leningrad and the Iron Curtain countries. Chang got caught and expelled from the country. It looked as if the Russians had a strong lead straight to Polakov, but French intelligence bailed him out by sending a decoy so that his record would be clean.

"In 1959 his mother fell ill and he returned to Moscow. Up to then he had been working for the French in payment for their help in '56. He wanted his mother to leave Russia. She refused, so he sat it out there with her. Apparently he did quite a lot of reading and museum-going. He turned up at many literary and cultural affairs. It's during this period he must have made his major contact. It could have been through a homosexual relationship. Polakov seems to have remained bisexual until his marriage. He may have made the contact through his art connections. We do know that eight months later he returned to Paris and sold two Mondrians. Several months later he purchased a Picasso for fourteen thousand dollars. There is no trace of what he did with it. He remained in Paris and became active in the art world.

"In 1962 Polakov returned to Moscow. He remained there for two months, then returned to Paris. Nothing is known of his stay. There is no indication it had anything to do with intelligence except for one factor. When he returned to Paris he sold most of his art works.

"It was in 1963 that Polakov made a move. He appeared in London with information to sell. The first packet was minor, something to do with Russian-Hungarian relationships. It was purchased for five hundred dollars. It proved to be very accurate. The next packet dealt with the Russian army. Polakov showed off only part of it. He jumped his price to five thousand and got it. From then on, the information began to flow. He asked an average of five to ten thousand a folder. The information was excellent. During an eight-month period it is estimated that Polakov was paid slightly more than four hundred thousand dollars, without ever revealing who his contact was.

"It was at this time that two things happened. One, Polakov got married. We have very little information on his wife. You've seen her picture and you know her birthday. We've tried a trace and found almost nothing. She turned up in Paris eight days before he married her, then she disappeared with him. The few people who met her during this period describe her as destitute, highly neurotic, and apparently very much in love with him.

"The second thing was Polakov's arrival with a message from his contact. Polakov explained that the man was a high Soviet official involved in a power play to take over from Khrushchev. He felt he could rally pro-Western sentiment in the Kremlin into a strong enough force to oust the premier. Polakov produced detailed information on these manoeuvres. For good measure he sold us information concerning the Cuban situation – it was our first indication of what was to come.

"The Pepper Pot said the decision had to be made within twenty-four hours. He wanted either State Department or Foreign Office verification, written verification, that we would go along with a plan he would outline. The idea was that the document would be tangible proof to his contact's supporters that a deal with the West was a realistic political possibility.

"What he wanted in writing was an Anglo-American guarantee to assist the Russians in destroying China's atomic-bomb project at Lop Nor.

"The Anglo-American intelligence officers dealing with Polakov said they needed more time than twenty-four hours. Clearance would take much longer than that. Polakov said if his man was to act it had to be within twenty-four hours or not at all.

"The next evening the letter was ready. Polakov was in Moscow with it the next morning."

"They actually agreed?" Rone uttered in disbelief.

"Not only did someone agree," Sweet Alice said with a sad smile, "but they also consented to sending it in unaddressed. It was simply the body of the letter and a

CHAPTER EIGHTEEN

SONIA

RONE told Janis what he had seen in the park that afternoon.

"She talked to them?" he asked Rone in anticipation.

"For almost twenty minutes. She even ignored her lions."

"Describe them again, carefully."

"It was a Negro couple. Well dressed. The girl looked about nineteen or twenty. The man about twenty-four. He was about five eleven and—"

"Which one did she talk to the most?" Janis interrupted.

"It seemed pretty even," answered Rone.

"Be ready to go in an hour."

Janis, Rone and a dapper Negro named Fred Firm drove slowly through Harlem. It was a Friday night. The streets teemed with people. "When you see somebody who looks like either of them, let us know," Janis ordered.

They stopped at half-a-dozen bars and restaurants before Rone saw a girl who vaguely resembled the one Sonia had talked to.

"Hey, baby, that's Jamaican stuff if you ask me," said Fred, almost staring in the girl's face.

"Forget national origins, old fellow. Do you have anything like that in stock?"

"Daddy, what Fred don't have in his pocket, he's bound to find in his wallet. When do you need her?"

"Yesterday."

"Cool, man, cool."

The following Monday, Rone and Janis were back at their 57th Street vigil. Apparently the cafeteria had been repaired. No one came out. At noon Janis told Rone he would take the afternoon shift himself. Rone started back for the Tillinger mansion. He was just about to hail a cab when someone tapped him on the shoulder.

"You naughty boy."

Rone turned and faced the art school's registrar.

"You should be ashamed of yourself. It is your responsibility to share your gift with the world."

"I was thinking of coming, but I just couldn't find the time. Maybe I'll start next week."

"Oh, no you don't. You'll have to wait until next autumn. It serves you right, too."

"Why can't I start?"

"We've reached this term's quota. We have our full fifteen. Our staff can't accommodate any more. However, if you're *sure* you're coming next week, if you positively *promise*, then I might make an exception to our rules."

"When did you get the new students?"

"That's none of your business. But I got them all right."

Rone reached into his pocket and handed the registrar fifty dollars. "Here's my deposit. I'll be there Monday. Now tell me about the new students."

The registrar was slightly stunned. "Why in the world should I?"

"Well, I told several friends of mine about it. I just wanted to know if they were the ones who registered."

"Oh, heavens no! These four people just flew into the country this morning. They are foreign artists."

"Foreign?"

"They're scholarship students from the Jamaican Art Lovers League."

Rone had expected to spend Tuesday with Clocker Dan and the Puppet Maker, but early that morning his orders were changed. He, the Priest and the Warlock took a taxi to Greenwich Village. They joined Janis at a corner table in a Bleecker Street coffee house.

Janis motioned to a table across the room. There sat Sonia with a stunning Negro girl. The girl was talking with her eyes down. Sonia listened without expression. The girl bit her lip and continued talking. Sonia said a a few words every now and then.

It looked to Rone as if Sonia was trying to console her weeping friend, but didn't know how. The conversation continued this way for quite some time. Then Sonia took the offensive. She leaned over the table and tried to look into the girl's face, but the girl turned away. Sonia seemed troubled and hesitant. She looked at her watch. She paused, leaned forward again and said something that made the girl lift up her head and smile. Sonia smiled back, rose and left the coffee house.

After she was out of sight the girl paid the bill and started to walk out. When she passed Rone's table she stopped and looked at Janis.

"It's set for Thursday at five," she told him.

"Do you think it will come off all right?" asked Janis.

The girl flashed a captivating grin. "Honey, when you pay for the best you get the best."

Potkin's agents had located one hundred and eight Charles Rones in forty-two states. None proved to be the right man. Now Potkin had his first valid lead. A Czech refugee by the name of Buka had supplied the information.

Buka specialised in extorting money from American families with relatives behind the Iron Curtain. To do this he needed the co-operation of Communist officials who would provide false verification that if money was paid, relatives would be permitted to come to the United States. A great many dollars crossed the ocean, but very few relatives did. Over the years Buka had become friendly with both Iron Curtain and Western officials interested in extra income. He had expanded and diversified.

Potkin had bought information from him in the past and had always found it worth the price. Still, he did not trust Buka. When the Czech first said he had information concerning Charles Rone, Potkin was quite perturbed. How could Buka even know the Russians were interested in Rone? Then he remembered that often in the past Buka knew what he was not supposed to. Potkin felt him out cautiously. He demanded evidence, and the source of the evidence.

For five hundred dollars Buka was willing to sell Potkin a copy of Charles Rone's birth certificate. This, of course, was worthless, since Potkin would have no way of knowing if it was the man he wanted or not. Days passed. Then Buka offered to sell a copy of Charles

Rone's Navy physical fitness report. When Potkin demanded the original report, Buka upped the price to fifteen thousand. They settled for twelve. Potkin's staff determined that the report was authentic. Now he had a physical description of his man. In short order, and for more money, Buka supplied originals of Rone's Navy driving test (with the name of the test administrator cut out), his Navy IQ test (administrator's name cut out), and his request for transfer into Naval Intelligence. All the documents were valid.

Potkin was convinced that Buka had access to the Rone file. Then Buka made his offer: for two hundred and fifty thousand dollars he would turn over to Potkin the entire Rone file. Russian intelligence traditionally disliked paying money for information, and Potkin liked it less than anyone. He negotiated. The mutually agreed figure was one hundred and seventy-five thousand dollars. Potkin contacted Kosnov for permission. It was granted, with one stipulation: he must find out where Buka got the information. To do this Buka would have to be taken.

At four o'clock Potkin went to the telephone box at 71st Street and Ninth Avenue. At four-ten the phone rang. He was instructed to go to a phone box at 35th and Third, where he would be called with further instructions. Although Potkin was to come alone, he was keeping in contact with his agents by radio.

By six o'clock Potkin had followed phone boxes into the Bronx. His final call instructed him to enter Yankee Stadium through Gate 5. Buka would be waiting for him on the field. As Potkin headed for the rendezvous he radioed his men to take positions around the stadium and wait until he had finished his business with Buka. Then they would close in.

The sun was down as Potkin walked through the open gate and into the passageway. He walked out onto the field and stopped. Buka was standing beside a helicopter. Potkin made a move to go, but was hit from behind.

When he regained consciousness he found himself tied in a wheel-chair in the centre of a large room. The wall, ceilings and floors were painted white. The room blazed with fluorescent lights. Directly in front of him was a table. Behind it sat two men with white hoods over their heads.

"Comrade Potkin," said one of the two men behind the desk, "you have something we want and I believe we have something you want."

Potkin remained silent.

"To be brief, we were thinking of going to Moscow next week. And we wondered if you would let us use your apartment. We would pay you rent, of course."

Potkin said nothing. He looked at nothing. He was neither tense nor relaxed. He was simply a man waiting, an old hand at games like this. He was unafraid.

"Now for the rental of this apartment of yours. We could, of course, give you cash. Shall we say one hundred and seventy-five thousand dollars?"

The valise Potkin had brought to Buka was spilled out on the floor. Wads of ten-, twenty- and fifty-dollar bills in front of him. Potkin, unimpressed, shook his head.

"You're a very difficult man to please, Comrade Potkin. We need you, but you don't seem to need us? Let me see if we can find anything else that might interest you."

The man sat down and conferred with his companion. Then he rose again.

"We do have three items that might be more appealing. If you'll just watch the television screens over your head."

With that the lights in the room lowered and two of the screens lit up with the face of Potkin's wife.

"Don't worry, dear – please, please don't worry. They haven't harmed me at all. They told me you would be watching. I hope you are. They're treating me very well. You must do what you think best. I don't know where the girls are. They've promised that they are all right. But even they will understand if you have to make a difficult decision."

Potkin's eyes flashed for a moment, then regained their previous vacant stare. His body gave a slight heave, but he was in control of himself again. The two screens blacked out and then lit up again. This time it was Potkin's youngest daughter.

"Daddy? Daddy? Can you hear me? Daddy, I'm frightened."

The picture shut off and the lights in the room went up.

"Comrade Potkin, we want that apartment. We want it so badly that we will turn your wife and daughters inside out to get it. What is your answer?"

Potkin said nothing.

The lights dimmed and pictures appeared on all six screens. Sonia was seated in an apartment. A Negro girl stood on the other side of the room. The girl walked across and sat next to Sonia. She tried to take her hand. Sonia shied away and stood up.

"Please, not again. I've got to get home," said Sonia.

"What's the matter, honey, don't you love me no more?" asked the girl.

"I like you, but I've got to get home. You don't know how my father is."

"Well, at least let me kiss ya goodbye?" The girl gently reached out and touched Sonia's cheek. Sonia's eyes closed. The girl moved against her and began kissing her lightly. Her lips and tongue slid quickly around Sonia's face. Potkin's daughter began to respond. Sonia clutched the girl and kissed her passionately. The girl lay down beside her. They embraced. Their bodies pressed together. The girl began unbuttoning Sonia's blouse. Sonia unzipped her skirt and slid it off. She pulled up her slip and pushed down her panties.

"It is a fake!" cried Potkin. "I know how these films are made. You can duplicate anything. It isn't even my daughter in the first place."

The men came from around the desk and wheeled Potkin through the door and into the large, darkened ballroom. Television cameras with hooded operators encircled the observation apartment erected in the middle of the area. The room behind the one-way plastic was lit up like a jewel. Sonia was completely naked except for the slip gathered up at her waist. She tore at the Negro girl's clothes. She began biting the girl's lips and twisting her hand in her hair. Slowly she slid down the body, kissing the dark flesh as she moved.

"Sonia, stop! Stop!" shouted Potkin. "You don't know what they're doing to you!"

"She can't hear you," said Ward. "You can shout all day and she can't hear you, but she can still be saved if you agree. If not, we'll turn her into the most perverted

148

human being our minds can conceive. And after we've finished with her we'll start on your other daughter – and then your wife."

Potkin slumped in his chair. "Even if I gave it to you it would be no good. Kosnov will know."

"What will he know?"

"Too many things. It will never work."

"It will work perfectly," contradicted Ward. "You'll have the complete Rone file. We *want* Kosnov to have it."

"And what about my family?"

"They will be kept with our men in this country until either we get back or are caught. No harm will come to them."

Potkin was broken. "I will do whatever you say." He was wheeled back into the other room.

Ward slid back a panel, walked into the plastic room, and roughly pulled the two women apart. "That's enough for now, girls," he said.

Rone awoke when the doorknob turned. He saw B.A. step into the room and close the door quietly behind her. She stood in the darkness, not moving. Finally she stepped lightly across to the bed. She saw that Rone was looking up at her.

"He told me they did such things, but I never believed him," she said nervously.

"You do what has to be done," he answered softly.

"Don't talk. Don't say anything. Please."

She sat on the end of the bed a long time, looking out into darkness. Then she stood.

Rone heard the gentle rustle of cloth. She slid under the covers and lay on her back as far from him as possible. Time passed slowly.

"This will be my first time," she finally said, moving up against him.

CHAPTER NINETEEN

ALERT

THE pace increased. The schedules were longer, the training more intense. Rone's Georgian accent neared perfection. He mastered the songs and dances of the area. His cover story was complete. Relatives, birthdays, deaths, anniversaries were second nature to him now. More important, he had become Buley's Georgian farmer. Rone could now distinguish the variation of soils, fertilisers, and irrigation as well as their effects on the produce of the region. He could even tell if grapes had been grown in the valleys or on the mountain sides. His muscles bulged just where Buley wanted them to.

The tactical briefings had reached thirty-five in number and covered every conceivable facet of Soviet politics and intelligence. The last five of the briefings had been detailed studies on life in Moscow, pinpointing everything from underground routes to the cost of renting a boat in Gorki Park. Special attention was given to identification papers from passports down to burial certificates.

B.A. had come to Rone's room almost every night throughout this period. She would always wait until she thought he was asleep before quietly opening the door, undressing and slipping into bed beside him. She would never let him talk, nor would she, for that matter, say more than a hasty good night. She would avoid his glance during the working day, but she would be beside him at night. She had come to him a child; in the dark, at least, she was fast becoming a woman.

Three weeks from her first visit passed before she told Rone, "I think I am in love."

At eight A.M. one morning Rone was ordered to appear at the dispensary. The Priest injected his left arm with Novocain. While they waited for the numbness to set in, Professor Buley took Rone's other arm and gave him his first series of inoculation shots. When he finished they strapped Rone to the operating table and burned off his vaccination. The Priest seized his left wrist, put a forceps to the thumbnail and pulled it off. Without further explanation they bandaged him.

All regular training ceased. At noon Rone had his first session with the Ditto Machine. Photographs and fingerprints were taken. A Soviet birth certificate, work papers and travel papers were given to him. He was also issued one hundred and ten Russian roubles and sixty-five kopeks.

Late that night Rone was assigned a house-cleaning detail. He, Ward and Janis rolled the unconscious bodies of Potkin's wife and daughters up from their basement rooms and placed each of them in a softly upholstered wooden box marked: Tillinger Fund – Arkansas exhibit.

When Rone returned to his room he found a new set of clothing laid out. They were much brighter and newer than his others. Buley entered and explained that these were his Sunday clothes, the clothes he would be travelling in. Buley also gave him photographs of his Georgian mother and father and the latest photographs and maps of Tiflis. He must study the changes.

The next morning Rone returned to the dispensary for additional inoculations. He was also fitted for a plastic thumbnail. His hand was still too tender to put it in place, but he was allowed to see it. It was filled with poison. If he was captured all he would have to do was bite through the nail and suck the liquid into his mouth. Death would be almost instantaneous.

At supper that night Ward announced that the final selections of those "going across" would soon be made; until then they all were restricted to their rooms unless ordered elsewhere. Rone saw B.A. pale and look over at him.

For the next three days Rone had his meals in his room and left only for afternoon sessions with Sweet Alice. Every detail concerning Polakov and the letter was reviewed.

Even though his briefings continued and even though he had his "whoopie thumb", as the other called it, Rone was not convinced he would be chosen for the trip. He had long since realised that the Highwayman's methods were unpredictable. Seven weeks ago he had been fed up with the operation and wanted to get out. Now it was different. He wanted to go into Russia. He wanted to go very badly.

It was late in the evening when Ward came to his room.

"There is something you should know about," he told Rone. "We have decided to get Kosnov out of Moscow for a time."

"Before the men arrive?"

"At about the same time." He threw an envelope on the bed. "Here's the list of those who are going." Before Rone could reach for it he said, "Don't worry, you're third in command. In fact, you may damn well end up number two. We may lose a man on the way in."

Rone was relieved. Then he weighed Ward's words. "The Highwayman?" he asked.

"Could be." Ward handed him a folder. "Inside is a floor plan of the Potkin apartment in Moscow. Study it and make the room assignments. Also, work out a communications set-up. Each of the agents will be making reports. I don't want them to know who is receiving the information."

"What about telephones?" asked Rone.

"Not enough public phones in Moscow. I want something that will work at the apartment itself."

"Without them knowing who receives the information?"

"Yep." Ward was sitting on the edge of the bed with one leg thrown over the other. As he talked he seemed to relax. "If I don't make it, then you run the show however you want."

"I don't know enough about the case," Rone protested.

"You know almost as much as I do. If I don't make it, an agent stationed in Prague will contact you."

"Why don't you give me the additional information now?" asked Rone.

"I'm not dead yet," Ward snapped.

"Is the girl going?" Rone asked.

"Why?"

"Well, she seems a little nervous."

"Is that all?"

"And inexperienced."

"So are you."

"I just meant—"

"Look, Nephew, just because you've been shacking up with her on the side don't give you any rights. We pick who we need for what we need. You should have thought about this before you brought her here in the first place."

Rone could think of nothing to say except, "When will I be leaving?"

"That all depends on a snowstorm in Siberia."

Ward left. Rone opened the letter and read the type-written list:

```
Highwayman
Ward
Virgin
Whore
Warlock
Erector Set
```

SECTION THREE

CHAPTER TWENTY

EMBARKATION

THE following morning the entire group was called together for breakfast. When they finished eating Ward announced that the selection would be revealed in the next twenty-four hours. Sweet Alice talked next.

"It must be made clear to all of you, those selected and those remaining behind, that you are in the employ of an independent agency. You have no contact with any country. We have trained in the United States because your organisers had facilities here. It could just as well have been a dozen other countries. You are on your own. If you run into trouble when you're across do not look for help from any Western embassies. Do not go near them. That is part of the agreement."

After the meeting Rone was told to go to the basement conference room. Uncle Morris was waiting. Sweet Alice and Ward soon joined them.

"I would like to continue the Polakov story," Uncle Morris began. "While he was in Moscow delivering the letter either the White House or 10 Downing Street heard what was happening. One certainly contacted the other when they knew. Both were enraged and ordered the responsible intelligence agency to stop Polakov and get the letter back.

"It was almost two weeks before he could be contacted. He was told to get the letter back. When he objected he was threatened. A week later he returned to England and said that his contact would agree to sell back the letter for one million dollars."

"That seems implausible," said Rone. "Why would a man give up the possible control of Russia for money?"

"I would have come to that point," Uncle Morris said shortly. "Polakov explained that his contact feared

155

the West would openly refute the authority of the letter. This would completely destroy his power. Also he was meeting resistance in forming his coup. There was a chance he might have to leave Russia under any conditions. He would need money for that."

"It just doesn't sound reasonable," Rone protested.

"We were not on the case then," Uncle Morris rejoined acidly. "I can only report what was told to us. Anyway, half a million dollars was finally agreed upon. Part of the bargain was that Polakov would not have to go into Russia to get it, since he claimed his contact blamed him for the reversal.

"Polakov was held in isolation. They tried to find his wife, but she had disappeared. The arrangement called for a deposit in a Swiss bank and the return of the receipt to Polakov. Polakov was to write a note. This note would be delivered to the contact at a specified rendezvous and the letter would be turned over. Everything was done according to instruction, and the agent was sent in. He never returned. Ten days later we were advised that he had taken his own life while being apprehended by Kosnov's Third Department.

"Polakov wrote a second note and another agent was sent in. He also did not return. He was captured, interrogated and executed by Kosnov. Luckily he had no pertinent information. He was not even sure whom he was to meet or what he was to receive.

"It was then decided to send Polakov himself back in. He refused on a dozen pretexts and was apparently genuinely afraid. He was given an additional half million dollars in credits just in case his contact was holding out for the original sum. Polakov was escorted to the border. Two weeks later he was dead in one of Kosnov's prisons.

"At this time it was decided that the case should be given to a neutral agency. This move had been contemplated weeks before, and Sweet Alice and I had already been retained as observers. We do not know who our sponsors are even now. We have the co-operation of seven governments and money from them as well – but it could never be proved. We in turn sub-contracted, if you will, to the Highwayman. It is only fair to tell you that we are making arrangements with other groups in case of foul weather.'

"Two additional bits of information have come through in the last week. The half-million-dollar draft which Polakov took with him into Russia has been drawn upon. It went to the same Swiss account we originally deposited the first half million in. We also know that shortly before Polakov's death the entire amount was transferred out of that account. We are still trying to trace the circumstances.

"The last item is unconfirmed. It claims that Polakov and Kosnov held a secret meeting in Paris four days after the letter was delivered. You will have to interpret this in your own way. It has always been my private conviction that Bresnavitch was the man for whom the letter was meant."

Rone checked his papers and clothes. He thought about the Highwayman and Ward. Ward had been melancholy – the same sadness Rone had seen in the churchyard when they first talked. All through the training period he had noticed that the Highwayman had progressively less to do and say. Not that Ward tried to take over. He did not; in fact he was embarrassingly solicitous of his superior. It just seemed to Rone that Ward was running the show because the Highwayman was no longer able to. Something was happening that only Ward and the Highwayman knew about.

There was a knock at the door. "You're on," said Buley.

The floorboards of the converted World War II A-26 were lifted and Rone and Janis were helped out by a heavily moustached Turk. It was still dark, but Rone could see the outlines of mountains dead ahead. The pilot was flying at a very low altitude.

The man with the moustache handed them two baskets full of fruit and two old, battered suitcases. Janis opened them quickly. One was filled with tea, and the other with oranges and lemons. Rone put the extra clothing he was carrying in the suitcase with the fruit. The man handed them steamship and rail tickets.

"Where are the fish?" Janis demanded.

The man pointed to a paper bag sitting near the wall. Janis tore it open and took out six long narrow packages

157

and unwrapped them. There were six dried fish. Janis examined each one carefully. Then he nodded his head.

"Damn good job, don't you think?" he said, handing one of them to Rone.

Rone held it in his hand and studied it. It looked like a fish, felt like a fish and *smelled* like a fish.

Janis explained that it *was* a fish – inside of which was a compressed brick of heroin.

The plane flew low over some high hills, soared up over a small mountain range and dropped into a valley, landing on a farm field without cutting its engines. Rone and Janis jumped out, carrying their baskets and suit-cases.

"That's Tiflis behind you," said the moustache, pointing north. "And Batum ahead. The mountain range to your right is the Caucasus."

Rone and Janis ran into the orchard a few yards away as the plane opened its throttle, jiggled along the uneven earth and took off again.

"Welcome to Russia," Janis said as he turned and headed through the orange trees for Tiflis.

Ward stood in front of Da Vinci's "The Virgin of Benois" in the Hermitage Museum in Leningrad. He was wearing a dark Russian business suit and overcoat.

"Your first trip to Leningrad?" asked a guard, walking up behind him.

"I was here once when I was a child."

"Where is your home?"

"Minsk. We have a good museum there, but no Da Vinci."

"Ah, that is only part of it. We have twenty-five Rembrandts."

"Twenty-five Rembrandts?" said Ward in feigned amazement.

"Twenty-five. And we have more by Rubens than you can count, not to mention Raphael and Titian."

"And what about our young Russian painters?" asked Ward. "In Minsk all we hear about is the new Leningrad school."

"Between you and me, comrade," the guard said in a whisper, "they're not worth the time it takes to look at

158

them. Come. Let me show you our Michelangelo."

"Grodin," Kosnov called into his intercom. "Come in at once." Kosnov peered at the report on his desk intently.

Grodin entered. "Potkin may have done it," he said, handing the folder to his subordinate.

Grodin thumbed through the dossier on Charles Rone. He had already read a copy at Bresnavitch's. "This certainly could be a possibility," he said.

"*Everyone* is a possibility," snapped the colonel. "But read the last two pages."

Grodin obeyed. When he finished he looked at Kosnov and asked, "Who is the Highwayman?"

"A man in his sixties by now. He was an aide to Sturdevant – an excellent agent who died years ago. By all rights the Highwayman should have been dead before him. He was rotten with cancer fifteen years ago. I'm amazed he's still breathing, let alone walking."

"But why would they send in a man like that with a novice like this Rone?"

"Probably for the very reason that we'd never think of looking for that kind of combination. An unseasoned man and a useless one. Did you see how Potkin thinks they plan to enter the country?"

"Yes, along the Kara Sea coastline. But it doesn't make any real sense. Is Potkin sure?"

"Potkin isn't sure. He can only analyse his information. If they are training in Alaska, I wouldn't expect them to turn up at Baku."

"I still don't understand it."

"That could be what makes it plausible. Even if the Highwayman is on his last legs he could still be a useful guide. He could get the Navy man into Moscow and tell him where to go from there. Two half-good men often add up to one excellent agent."

"But why land near the Kara Sea? There are easier ways to get into the country." Grodin was still unconvinced.

"How many agents do we have in or around Vorkuta?" asked Kosnov.

"I think only one – and he isn't there half the time."

"And where else do we have men in the north?"

"The nearest place is Archangel."

"Three men covering a thousand miles of coastline."

"But even so, that's very difficult country. It's easier to find someone there than in Moscow."

"Then is it your suggestion that we ignore this report?"

"No. But—"

"But what?"

"I will take proper precautions, Comrade Colonel," Grodin said in resignation. "And what about the Highwayman? Shall I go to the files for a photograph?"

"You won't find anything. He came from an age when espionage was an art. I doubt if a photograph of him exists anywhere in the world."

It had been a slow drive out of Vorkuta. The sleet and snow had kept the driver's speed under twenty miles an hour. He was now on the coast road, and the wind from the sea hit the large Diesel truck in rapid gusts, rocking it back and forth. He decreased the speed, but even so he did not see the flare until he was almost on it. A man lay beside it on his back. He eased the truck to a stop and jumped down. The man was lying with his eyes open; he looked frozen, probably dead. The driver had been in the north a long time. He had seen many men freeze and many men die. This man looked as if he had been dead for a long time. Not hours, but days – even longer. Then who had lit the flare?

The question was answered by the gun thrust into his neck. He raised his hands and saw two men move past him and pick up the frozen body. They placed it in the front seat. Then one of them jumped in beside it. He had silver hair and looked very old. The truck pulled away, leaving the driver alone on the frozen road with the two remaining men. They took him down the embankment to the sea. They walked carefully across the ice to a small motorboat. He got inside as they shoved the boat into the water and started through the heavy ocean towards a blinking light in the dark. Half an hour later he was aboard a fishing trawler being given food and hot coffee.

Rone and Janis walked through Tiflis at dawn. Old women with crude brushes were sweeping the streets.

They waited half-and-hour for a bus to Batum. Rone checked his watch. They were right on schedule; they would go by boat across the Black Sea to Odessa, then take a train to Moscow. There was a shorter route bypassing Batum and going to Sukhum and then from Sukhum to Moscow by train. This was an emergency route and would have been used only if the arrival in Tiflis had been delayed.

The Georgians on the bus were friendly and cheerful. They laughed at Rone and Janis for carrying baskets of fruit, tea and fish, but apparently it was not uncommon. Many Muscovites made the long trip for just the same reason. Since the free market had opened in Moscow, merchants from that city were constantly travelling to the south to buy fruit and tea. Petty traders from Georgia also made the trip. Their bus companions told them they should take back champagne as well.

They boarded the five-class boat at Batum, making sure to travel in the lowest class. The Puppet Maker had wanted them to go by boat because he felt they would have extra contact with people that they would not get on a train. This, he concluded, would give them even more opportunity to perfect their Georgian accents.

It was growing colder in Leningrad. Ward was spending the day as any tourist might. From the Hermitage Museum he crossed the Neva and walked up Red Dawn Street to inspect the Peter-Paul Fortress and the Arsenal. He recrossed the river and did some shopping along the Nevsky Prospekt. In the late afternoon he stood looking at the Aleksandroskaya Column in the middle of Palace Square. A passer-by told him it was over one hundred and fifty feet high and was the tallest monolithic stone monument in the world. Ward already knew it commemorated Russia's victory over Napoleon in 1812.

It was almost time. Ward walked briskly along the Twenty-fifth of Oktober Avenue until he reached the Oktober Station. The Moscow Express was late.

CHAPTER TWENTY-ONE

MOSCOW

RONE and Janis moved into the apartment without incident. Potkin had notified the caretaker to expect his "nephews" from Georgia. They would be visiting the capital for a month, maybe more. Some friends would be joining them. There was nothing suspicious in this. Living space was at a premium in Moscow. Relatives were expected to take in other relatives. The caretaker did, however, notice something. There was a strong resemblance between Janis and Potkin. His wife vociferously disagreed. It was obvious to her that Rone, not Janis, possessed the family features.

B.A. reached the Central Market by two-thirty. She strolled aimlessly among the open-air stands. Ukrainians, Armenians, Georgians, Latvians and others from every corner of Russia displayed their goods. Although fruits, vegetables and meats had been the original attractions of the market, other items were quick to appear. If you had the necessary roubles, the newly established "petty bourgeois" would sell you anything you wanted. When an item was not on display, arrangements for its procurement could always be made. The price for staple goods was reasonable, for luxury items excessive.

B.A. stopped to buy some limes. She reached inside her purse, brought out a worn leather wallet and paid the required kopeks. She put back the wallet and pushed her way through a crowd gathered in front of an adjoining stall. French and American gramophone records were on sale for approximately fifty shillings apiece. She waited in line before an ice-cream stand which advertised twenty-five flavours. Once again she withdrew her wallet, paid out the kopeks and put it back in her purse.

The man who was following B.A. was scarcely more than twenty-two. He kept close behind. He waited while B.A. finished a bottle of soda and moved into a crowd gazing down at Japanese transistor radios. The man slid into the crowd, brushed into her, deftly lifted the wallet and weaved his way into the open. The thief moved rapidly across the market and stepped behind a van. He took out the money, stuffed it into his trousers pocket, threw away the wallet, moved back into the crowds and began looking for another victim.

It wasn't long before a Ukrainian merchant with a large roll of roubles caught his eye. The man had sold all his goods and was now buying presents before his return trip home. The pickpocket trailed at a distance. When the time was right he moved in, made his kill and retired to add more money to his growing cache.

He was having a good day. Both his pockets were filled. He struck twice more within the hour. He was about to leave for the day when he spotted a housewife buying oranges. She walked the perimeter of a group clustered around the record stand. As she strained to see over their heads, the thief moved in, reached down, opened her purse and took out the money. He shoved his way out of the mass of shoppers and returned behind the van to count his take. Fifteen roubles. He pushed them into his pocket only to find his other money was gone. He reached into his other pocket. It too was empty. He spun around. B.A. was leaning against the front fender of the van displaying a thick wad of roubles.

"Is this what you're looking for?" she asked the thief. The pickpocket stepped back and glared at her. B.A. threw him the bills. "I'm new in Moscow. I wouldn't want to fall in with the wrong people."

The thief caught the roll and held it. Then he smiled. He tossed the money back to B.A. "My name is Mikhail," said the boy. "Come, citizeness, let me buy you vodka – only you'll have to pay. Some bastard has made off with my earnings."

Ward reached the apartment at four o'clock. Rone was waiting for him. He was pleased to hear the men were already in the field. He washed, had some cold chicken, black bread and a glass of tea.

"And now, Nephew, it's time you found out just what you're doing here. Unless you'd rather go sightseeing first?"

"I had it in mind, but it can wait."

"That's mighty considerate of you. Mighty considerate indeed."

They walked along Gorki Street towards the Kremlin and Red Square. It was a brisk afternoon. The streets were exceptionally clean, cleaner than any Rone had seen in the West. Muscovites came and went with an air of dispatch, and relaxation. If it had not been for the Russian printing in the shops and the cleanliness, Rone could have mistaken the avenue for one in a dozen other cities.

"Way back when we first met up," Ward began, "you asked why we chose you. As I remember, I gave you some kind of answer or other at the time."

"You said I had the ability to let someone else die in my place and not give a good goddamn," Rone reminded him.

"Is that what I said?"

"To the word."

"Looks like you've got yourself one fancy memory."

"I remember what I want to."

"Total recall, isn't that what they call it?"

"It's not total recall," Rone answered with irritation.

"Well, it sure as hell impressed us, whatever it is. Back in New York you were given three or four times as much information to learn as the rest of us put together just so that we could see. You remembered every last word that was told you. And you remembered it the first time you read or heard it. You gotta admit, Nephew Yorgi, there ain't many men can go around doing things like that in broad daylight."

"Could you get to the point?"

"I thought I was, or does it take some kinda extra-sensory perception to realise we're locked in Moscow? Our boys will be gathering a good bit of information. Now just what are we going to do with it? We can't type it, 'cause we have no typewriters. We can't tape-record it, 'cause we have no tape recorders. And we can't scratch it out with pencil and paper, 'cause the Russians might find it. So you know what we're going to do, Nephew? We're going to tell it to you. You're going to be our walking diary."

"In other words, I'm a glorified clerk?"

"I wouldn't exactly say that. I kind of see you as a two-legged computer."

"No, things have not been good," said Madame Sophie with a sigh.

She brushed the henna curls back from her ancient brow and sipped a cup of tea. Her over-abundant torso was draped in a bright blue velvet dressing gown with gold military-type braiding. Her bulbous toes were crowded into open-end gold mules. The nails were painted blue. "I am down to one girl. That thing there," she told Janis as she pointed an elbow at a skeletal young woman in a faded red housecoat. "If I were a man," she continued, "I would pay to keep something like that out of my bed, not in it. There is no more culture. There is no more love. Tenderness is dead. What's worse, the girls have to work in factories, ten hours a day in factories. When they get back here and lie beside a man, they are as romantic as a tin of sardines. Tell me, how is Dimitri?"

"They hung him," answered Janis.

"My God," shouted Madame Sophie, "he sent me some of my finest girls – and best customers. But of course that was in the old days, the golden days. He died with honour?"

"They had to hang him twice to kill him."

"Ahh," said Madame Sophie with pride.

"They didn't have the rope on tight enough before they opened the trap. Old Dimitri was so thin he slid right out and bounced on his heels."

"Great God, did he hurt himself?"

"Not badly. He was well enough to go back and get hung properly."

"Did you, did you see him – after?"

"Oh yes."

"How did he look – all stretched out and lifeless?"

"Much better than I had expected. The hanging put a little colour in his face. His nose was slightly skinned from the rope slipping over it the first time, but all in all he looked better than I'd seen him in a long time."

"Younger?"

"Fifteen years younger."

165

"I see," Madame Sophie said in relief. "What did they hang him for?"

"Nothing specific. Just on general principles."

"The poor good soul," lamented the old woman. "Did he have any last word for me?"

"You were all he talked of. He said to me, 'If ever you are in Moscow run to my little Grushenka.'"

"Grushenka? My name is not Grushenka."

"He did a great deal of reading in prison. He usually referred to you as Grushenka of Sonia. He once even called you Yerma."

"Old Dimitri said that?"

"Indeed he did," Janis reassured her with ardour. "He said, 'If ever you get back to Moscow run to my Grushenka and give her my share.'"

"Share of what?"

"Share of the business."

"What business?"

"Old Dimitri was my silent partner. It is true he had only a small share but it made him a very wealthy man. Here, this is for you." Janis handed her two thousand roubles. "That's the first part of it. I'll give you the rest when I return from Prague again."

Madame Sophie's vast body trembled as she counted the notes.

"What business are you in?" she finally managed to ask.

"The same as yours."

"Whores?"

"Ladies of the evening," Janis corrected. "The most noble industry ever conceived. Also the most profitable."

"I didn't realise they had lifted the restrictions in Prague."

"They haven't. Things are even more difficult than in Moscow."

"Then how do you manage it? How do you get girls out of the factories? Where do you find clients who can pay so much?"

"Ah, my dear Grushenka – I can call you Grushenka, can't I?"

"Of course."

"It's a matter of market research and time and motion studies."

166

"I don't understand."

"I go where the clients are. The foreign embassies. The Americans, the British, the Japanese."

"But they are all watched."

"There is always a way."

Madame Sophie nodded in agreement. "And what are you doing in Moscow? Did you say before it was a business trip."

"It *is*. You are part of it. Then of course there are other things."

"Is there anything I can do to help?"

"Would you be interested?"

"I am never averse to profit."

Janis hesitated. "I have never had a partner."

"You had Dimitri," Madame Sophie reminded him brightly.

"So I did. So I did." Janis thought it over. "No, no, it wouldn't work." He looked into the beseeching eyes of the old woman. "Well, why not? Can you get me five beautiful young girls?"

"To work in a house?"

"Of course."

"That is very difficult. They work on their own now. They walk the street or open their legs in taxis. Comfort is a thing of the past. They do everything by themselves."

"Give them guarantees," said Janis. "We will provide clients they could never get on their own. I think it would be better if we had ten girls. In Prague we had the same problems to start with. It was solved quite easily. We used girls who took narcotics."

"That is a sin," cried Madame Sophie in horror.

"A practical sin," Janis replied harshly. "It costs less money and it makes them more dependent on you. Where can we get drugs here?"

"They are very difficult to come by. I want no part of it."

"Where can I get drugs?"

"The Kitai has some, but I will have nothing to do with him. It is said he has the best merchandise, but I will not let him within a hundred kilometres of my door."

"Can you arrange for me to meet him – without him knowing we are in business together?"

"I will arrange it."

167

"And can you get me the girls who use narcotics?"

"Yes," sighed Madame Sophie. "They are usually the prettiest, poor things."

"When will I have them?"

"A few by tomorrow night," answered Madame Sophie, suddenly as hard as steel, her eyes cold and businesslike.

CHAPTER TWENTY-TWO

THE SOFT UNDERBELLY

"POLAKOV was a muck runner," Ward told Rone as they started back towards Potkin's apartment. "He infiltrated what he liked to call the soft underbelly. He was the first to spot that Moscow was beginning to rot. It's a funny thing about social decay – it always expands in proportion to peace and prosperity. When you've got a nice healthy war or depression on your hands, everything seems okay. Take away fear and poverty, and Sodom walks right in. Maybe folks just can't handle time on their hands. Maybe we just ain't equipped to do anything better than blow one another's brains out."

Ward caught himself and got back to the point. "Anyway, Polakov was right there when Moscow's gut started weakening and that soft underbelly started popping out."

"And is that where we're going hunting?" asked Rone.

"We're jumping right in after him. People develop new and different appetites all the time. Their needs and loyalties change. Men usually betray other men out of desire, not coercion. To my way of thinking, Polakov bumped into his contact paddling through the muck, not kneeling in church. It could have been a hophead or a fag or just someone with an axe to grind, but it was someone pretty high up in the Kremlin, wasn't it? Who he was and what he was doing in the sewer would be mighty interesting to know."

"Is what you call the sewer our only point of concentration?"

"Yup. That's why I was hired in the first place and that's why I picked the men I did. They wouldn't be much use at a Sunday social."

"You picked?"

"That's right. The Highwayman was the planner and I was the casting director."

"It took Polakov almost nine years to set up his contact," Rone pointed out. "What makes you think we'll find him any faster – if at all?"

"He was only one man." Ward spoke without concern. "There's five of us and you. The Pepper Pot was what you might call a general practitioner in Sodom, but we've brought in a kitful of specialists."

"And what if we don't find our man in the soft under-belly?"

"Then we'll just have to snoop around somewhere else," answered Ward.

"That could take almost a year," Rone said.

"You got somewhere else you wanta be?"

It was sunset as they made their way back along Gorki Street, Moscow's Fifth Avenue or Piccadilly. Traffic was light on the ten-lane thoroughfare. The majority of cars were Russian Pobedas and Zims. Occasionally a chauffeur-driven Zim would pass. The streets were more active. The stores were crowded with shoppers. Rone noticed that the ice-cream parlours and bookshops seemed to be the most popular.

"You don't seem too joyful with our plan, Nephew Yorgi," Ward said.

"If it works, fine."

"But you seem to put a mighty big 'if' out in front."

"Any approach has its weak points. I'm not the one to judge. Or have you forgotten I'm the Virgin?"

"That you are, but you seem to be a good student. Just imagine we're back at one of those foolproof intelligence schools you got your battle scars at. This plan is presented. What would teacher say?" Ward asked jovially. He slapped Rone on the back and winked.

Rone took it in good spirit. "When we were sitting at our desk in short pants we had to write this sentence five hundred times whenever we were bad: 'Live longer – minimise assumptions.' But we seem to be stacking everything on two basic assumptions – one, that we will pick up our lead in one *specific* area: and two, that our flanks are protected.

"Starting with number one. We are putting all our eggs in one basket. We're starting at the bottom, when we are quite sure that our man lives at the top."

"And you think we should stay at the top?"

"Not exclusively. The procedure stands. We just add dimension to it. Let me ask you something: if Pepper

Pot's man is close to the Kremlin he's already in a select group. If we took all the top Soviet officials and their staffs and families, people who might have access to the kind of information that Polakov was receiving, how many people would it include? Fifteen hundred? Two thousand?"

"Less than that. Four hundred, maybe six."

"Then why not look there at the same time? We might just come across something."

"That kind of investigation would take ten more men," Ward pointed out.

"If we had to cover everyone, yes. But we don't have to. We only have to study Polakov's movements. Even though we don't know exactly how he operated, we *do* know *where* he operated. We know the weeks and months he was in Moscow, when he took a ten-day trip to Kiev. When he spent ten days in Leningrad. We know that between March 11 and March 21 he was in Yalta."

"Where did you get this information?" Ward asked.

"It was in Polakov's dossier. Didn't Sweet Alice give it to you?"

Ward did not remember reading this, but he nodded affirmatively anyway.

"Now," Rone began, "let's start with Moscow. We take those six hundred possible Russians and check to see which ones were not in Moscow when Polakov was. Since he was here more than a year in all, we would eliminate only forty or fifty people, maybe less. That's our lesson in subtraction. For our lesson in addition we check out which of the remaining Russians were in Kiev when Polakov was. Next, those whose visits to Leningrad and Yalta corresponded with his. When we've finished our list of six hundred prospects, we'll probably be down to forty or fifty."

"Don't pull that schoolroom crap on me," Ward warned. "If that's such a good idea why didn't someone else do it?"

"Because we're the first ones in since his death."

Ward remained silent for the next block. "It might be possible," he finally said. "Only we don't have the men to spare."

"It won't take any. One of the none-Communist embassies in Moscow is bound to have it."

"Why would they?"

"Since the mid-fifties they've been doing things just like that."

Rone saw that he had finally caught Ward off balance. The Highwayman's group had been out of circulation for more than ten years. Rone realised that Ward had also been somewhat out of touch.

"We can't make contact with any embassy," Ward said stubbornly. "The Russians watch them. All we'd need to do is go dancing into one of them and every counter-espionage agent in Moscow would be riding our bones by morning."

"Who said anything about contacting the Moscow embassies? Send someone out of the country."

"I told you – I can't spare anyone."

"Then send a message by courier. We do have a courier contact, don't we?"

"No. We're isolated."

"What about the agent in Prague?"

Ward grew angry. "What the hell assurance do I have that we could find the contact this way? We could cut the list to fifty, check each man out and still come up with nothing. What the hell chance do we have finding him that way?"

"About the same as finding him in a whorehouse."

"I knew it was a goddamn mistake to bring you in here," snapped Ward.

"You have only yourself to blame." Rone was beginning to enjoy himself. "Would you like to know what else the teacher would have to say?"

"Go ahead, talk your blasted head off. I couldn't shut you up if I wanted to."

"The second assumption you make is by far the most serious. It could destroy the whole operation. We worked for weeks setting up Potkin so that we'd have a home base in Moscow."

"And we did a pretty damn good job of it," Ward said.

"The trouble is, Potkin may change his mind. Then where would we be?"

"He won't. We're holding his family. He'll keep his mouth shut."

"That is what I mean by a dangerous assumption."

"We broke him. He'll do what he says."

"Assumption," Rone said softly.

"When a man breaks, he breaks."

"Assumption."

"He won't let his family be slaughtered."

"Assumption. What happens if he is ordered back to Moscow?"

"Look, don't play the wise-ass little punk with me."

"I'm not. I'm just pointing out that our happy Moscow home may not be as secure as we think."

"Maybe you're suggesting we should kill him?"

"Then we're *bound* to be evicted. That's a pretty nice apartment for Moscow. Once Potkin's dead the Kremlin won't waste much time reassigning it. No, the way things are now he has to stay alive."

"What do you mean, the way things are now?"

"As long as we rely on Potkin and his apartment."

"And what do you suggest we do?"

"Move."

"*Move*?" shouted Ward. "Move to *where*? You know the housing situation in Moscow."

"Isn't that just like a teacher?" Rone said sadly. "They always tell you what's wrong and hardly ever let you know what's right."

"Enough of this crap. Where could we move to?"

"Sodom – the soft underbelly."

"No."

"Are you strong enough for me to go on?" asked Rone. When Ward didn't answer he spoke anyway. "You seem to think that we can hold Potkin's wife and daughters for almost a year without anyone on Potkin's staff getting suspicious. Now how realistic is that? He can say they've gone away for a month or so and get by with it. He may string it out for half a year. Sooner or later someone is going to ask questions. Then where are we?"

"We've known that from the start. It's a chance we take. A calculated risk."

"Not if we move," said Rone.

The Warlock knew the man had followed him into the bookstore across from the university.

"Good afternoon, Comrade Instructor," a student said. The man acknowledged the greeting and continued thumbing through a book.

173

The Warlock moved down another aisle and began browsing. It was not long before the professor had casually rounded the stacks and found another volume to glance through. The Warlock put down his book and walked towards him. He smiled briefly as he passed, swept his hand back through his hair and walked from the shop.

As he crossed the street he heard footsteps hurriedly coming up behind him. The Warlock slowed his pace.

CHAPTER TWENTY-THREE

THE GRAND MUTE

"YOU never take me anywhere." Erika pouted as she paced about the bedroom in her slip. She held a cigarette in one hand and a drink in the other.

"We went to a film just two nights ago," Kosnov reminded her.

"A film? What's a film? I want to have fun. I want to get out of here and do something – go somewhere."

"In two months we'll be going to Yalta for a holiday. You can swim and go boating."

"And go to restaurants?"

"Some."

"But that's *then*. What about now? I'm bored. You bore me. I hate being locked up here with you – always alone with you."

"Would you rather go back to prison?"

"Yes I would, I would, I would. I hate you."

"Perhaps we will go to the races on Sunday."

"The races? Races, films, plays – that is no fun for me. I want to go dancing. I want to have drinks. I want to be with other people. Young people. Polakov took me to all the night clubs in Berlin before you murdered him."

"There are no places like that in Moscow," snapped Kosnov.

Erika crawled across the bed and curled herself around the colonel.

"Yes there are," she said kittenishly.

"How do you know?"

"I've heard."

"They are only for degenerates."

"But who is more depraved than I?" Erika pulled Kosnov down beside her. She wet her lips and ran her hands over his shoulders and chest.

"You know all the things I like – and the way I like them. Of all the men I've had, you're the best – the best lover of all. But you're not good to me, you don't let me have any fun. Take me to those places."

"I should send you back to prison," he said.

"I might get to like the lesbians better than you."

Kosnov let Erika pull him to her. Then she playfully pushed him away. "Won't you take me to one of those naughty places?"

"You know I can't be seen there."

"Oh, I forgot. Your position." She moved to him again. "Well, if we can't go to one of those places maybe you can get me some of those funny cigarettes, the kind that do silly things to you – the kind you gave me the night you first made love to me."

Kosnov sat up abruptly. He was a man who could cope with any situation that came his way. He was a master manipulator of people. For twenty years he had been in control of himself and of those around him. But with the girl he was lost. He hated her and loved her. The hate grew out of his inability to control her. His love grew out of the fear of losing her. He had jeopardised his career by bringing her to his home, by his steadfast refusal to give her up. He knew this. He knew he should get rid of her one way or another. He could murder her himself and no one in Moscow would know or care. He had entertained the thought quite often. At times he even felt that that was what she really wanted. He couldn't. He knew she was feeding on him, trying to drag him down, trying to destroy him for what he had done to Polakov. Even so he didn't care. He could not give her up.

"I will take you to one of the clubs," Kosnov said.

"Tonight?"

"Tonight."

Erika smothered his face and neck with kisses and tried to pull him down on the bed again. He refused to move. He sat impassively as the girl continued to tease him. "You're unhappy," she said with a slight smile.

"I'll be all right."

"I've made you angry, haven't I? You don't like me now. I know when you don't like me." She bounced further back on the bed and rested against the headboard with her knees drawn up under her chin. "Do you loathe me when I'm like this?"

"Sometimes," he answered.

"Does it go beyond loathing? Do you hate me?"

"That too at times."

"When I'm like this do I sicken you?" Erika took Kosnov's silence as an answer. "I sicken you," she sang happily. Then she slid prone on the bed, her hands between her legs, massaging herself.

"Come to me. Be my lover at this very instant. When you're sickened by me. Love is best when it sickens. At least our kind is."

"Stop that," commanded Kosnov, "and keep your hands off yourself."

Erika caressed herself more fervently. "I'm thinking of a hundred men," she told him with her eyes closed, "and none of them are you."

Kosnov rose abruptly and left the room. He went downstairs into the kitchen and poured himself a glass of beer. Then he threw the beer into the sink and stalked into the dining room. A full carafe of vodka stood on the table. He drank from it in long swallows until it was empty. He started to look for more. The telephone rang. Grodin said they still had not found the missing van from Vorkuta.

"Then send more men and planes," Kosnov shouted into the phone. "But find that van. It's been missing for five days. Pull every agent out of Moscow, but find it."

"Men and planes do no good. It's been snowing. They are having a blizzard."

"Of course there is a blizzard. Do you think they would pick a sunny afternoon to come into the country?"

"I'll do everything I can, Comrade Colonel," Grodin replied.

"Send up more men," Kosnov repeated.

"We already have sent two units. They can do nothing till the storm passes. More men won't help. We don't even know if the van has anything to do with Potkin's report. It may have simply been lost in the snow. Perhaps it had an accident."

"That van may be the transportation for the two men being landed. That is our official attitude at this time. I don't care if a hundred agents turn to ice – find me that van." Kosnov slammed down the receiver.

He stormed about downstairs searching for another bottle of vodka. He couldn't find one. The affair with Erika would have to be resolved here and now. He was turning into a madman. Kosnov stamped up to her room and threw open the door. She was gone. So were her red dress and coat. He searched through the house frantically. He could not find her. Kosnov rushed out into the street. The limousine was also gone. He ran back inside and tried to get the driver on the radio-phone. The line was engaged. Erika must have taken it off the hook. He called his office and dispatched five cars to locate his limousine. He wanted to call the police, but he couldn't. It was bad enough for his own men to know what had happened; he would have a difficult enough time suppressing them.

He paced the floor. He found another bottle of vodka and had drunk half of it before a phone call reported the car had been found. The driver had dropped her off at the Praga Restaurant on Arbatskaya Square. No, he saw nothing wrong in taking her there. He often drove her to restaurants when the colonel was busy – Kosnov himself had ordered him to do so. He wasn't sure if she had gone in; he had dropped her across the street because she had said she wanted some air.

When Kosnov arrived at the restaurant he was told Erika had not come in that evening. He returned to the street, where his driver and several of his agents were waiting. He ordered the chauffeur to stay and the others to go. It had all been a misunderstanding. Everything was in order.

He did not care if they believed him. He must find the girl. He began searching the back streets, the restaurants and meeting places of Moscow's "new youth," places which did not exist officially.

It was close to midnight when he finally found her. She was dancing with a young Cuban student in a "social discussion room" on a side street near the University. There was no orchestra, just a gramophone. The record playing was not Russian. The habitués kept rhythm with their hands and shouted "Yeah, yeah, yeah" in time to the thump and crash of the beat.

Erika saw him standing at the door, but it didn't seem to trouble her. She continued dancing more fervently than before. She ground her hips and thrust her pelvis back and forth with arduous ecstasy. Her elbows were tight to her body and her fingers snapped beside her hips. As Kosnov approached she closed her eyes, opened her mouth and waggled her tongue at her partner who was at least a foot away from her. Kosnov stopped where he was. No one seemed to notice him. The gramophone record ended and Erika walked up to him.

"Well?" she said with a bright smile.

"Come home," Kosnov said hesitantly. "It's late and it's time for you to come home."

"Whatever you say, my lover."

"This whole thing is insane," Rone protested as Ward sat him in the middle of the room and slid the hood over his head.

"You thought it up," Ward reminded him, adjusting the eyeholes.

"I gave you five approaches. This was the worst. We should have used the telephones."

"Now just be still like a good little Grand Mute so that we can rehearse." Ward took a chair opposite him, picked up a Luger, flicked off the safety catch and aimed it at him. "The code is eighteen-three," he announced and snapped his fingers five times. Rone answered with four more snaps.

"Nine snaps in series one," announced Ward. "That leaves nine for the last two series." He snapped his fingers twice. Rone added two more.

"Thirteen down. Six to go in the last series," said Ward and snapped four times. Rone snapped twice.

"Just like silk," beamed Ward, lowering the automatic.

"It's still the most maniacal thing I've ever heard of."

"Nephew Yorgi, it's just a matter of percentages. Three out of five of our men have no idea who's receiving the message. If any one of them gets picked up they can only confess to that section they know about – and they can't finger who's in on the whole story."

"What if you or I get caught?"

"Do you always have to look down when you're climbing a mountain?" asked Ward. "Now let's get back to rehearsing. You miss one snap and you just might be catching a bullet in your nose."

"Wait a minute," Rone interrupted. "There are supposed to be six of us coming to Moscow – but you just

179

said 'Three out of five of our men.'"

"Did I?"

Erika went up to her room obediently. Kosnov remained downstairs. He had no idea what to say or what to do. He stood in front of his gun case and stared in at his hunting rifles. Should he kill her? Would he be happier if he did? Again the telephone rang.

"We have just found the van," Grodin informed him. "It looks as if you were right. Two men are in it – or what is left of two men. Shall I have them removed?"

"No," said Kosnov quietly. "I want to examine them myself. Keep everything as it was found and order a plane. I'll leave at once. You'll accompany me."

"We may have trouble landing because of the snow."

"Is that all, sir?"

"Yes—" Kosnov hesitated. "No, send a car for the German girl. I'm returning her to prison."

CHAPTER TWENTY-FOUR

THE TRIP TO KARA

BY dawn their plane had reached Ustusa. The storm had ended. They flew north along the Ural Mountains past Vorkuta and on to Kara, where they landed. The town was on Baydarstskaya Bay in the Kara Sea.

"They must have come across the Arctic Ocean from the Elizabeth Islands," Grodin conjectured as their car headed back towards Vorkuta.

"And they also could have come from Greenland or Alaska or Norway or Finland or Sweden," Kosnov said without much enthusiasm.

"If they came from Scandinavia they could have travelled by land. If they came by boat they would have used the Barents Sea."

"They still would have to head for Kara."

"Why?" asked Grodin.

"Because there is a railway there. There are no railways along the Barents Sea."

"What about Murmansk?"

"Murmansk is next to Finland, and unless my geography fails me Finland stretches from Murmansk down to Leningrad. They wouldn't travel by water just to land at Murmansk and take a train, when they could cross Finland by land and catch one at Leningrad. If they came by boat their only objective could be Kara – and the railway."

"If they were planning to travel by train, why did they steal a van?" asked Grodin.

"If they *weren't* planning to take a train, why did they overlook two thousand miles of coastline that is lightly patrolled and closer to Moscow?"

"For that matter, why did they want to come in through Siberia at all? There are much easier routes."

"If you were planning to enter Russia," asked Kosnov, "would you say that coming in through Kara was impractical?"

"Very impractical."

181

"Perhaps that's why they chose it. Anyway, it makes little difference now. Are you sure Erika is comfortable?"

"Yes," answered Grodin. "Her cell is furnished and meals are brought in from the outside."

"Maybe I should get her a television set," Kosnov thought aloud.

The car moved cautiously over the newly ploughed road, doing no more than ten or fifteen miles an hour. The clouds were beginning to clear and from time to time the sun broke through. The blizzard had left almost two feet of fresh powder on top of the existing three-foot layer of old snow.

"The Highwayman was associated with Sturdevant, wasn't he?" Grodin asked.

"Where did you hear about Sturdevant?"

"I dug out the files on him after I read the dossiers on the Highwayman."

"Where did you find them? They've been closed for years."

"I went to the storage depot outside Moscow. I found information on their entire organisation. They were very effective agents, weren't they?"

"They have had their day," answered Kosnov sharply.

It was eleven A.M. Rone stood in the pitch-black back bedroom and watched Janis through the peephole as he crossed the living room, took out a key and opened the top desk drawer. He withdrew a Luger, snapped in a bullet clip he took from his pocket and started for the "confession box." Rone moved behind the blankets he and Ward had hung from the ceiling the night before and waited for Janis to enter. He heard the door open and close. There were several footsteps until Janis found the chair, sat in it and scratched around on the floor looking for the flashlight. Rone saw the beam scan the room. He adjusted his white Grand Mute hood and stepped around the curtain. The flashlight was trained on an empty chair. The Grand Mute walked over and sat down. He crossed his hands in his lap and waited. Rone knew the pistol was pointed directly at his head. The snap code was twenty-seven, the series code five.

Janis snapped his fingers three times. Rone snapped his twice. One series down, four to go. Twenty-two snaps remained. Janis snapped once. Rone answered with four. Five more snaps used up. Three series to go. Another three snaps from Janis. Rone countered with one. Three series had been completed. Fourteen snaps used, thirteen to go. Janis snapped his fingers twice. Rone answered twice. Janis snapped again. Rone counted five snaps. It was the final series. He recounted quickly in his head. Five on the first, five on the second, four – or was it three? He knew it was four on the last, but was it three or four before that? He saw the flashlight waver slightly. He recounted in his head. Five, five . . . Janis' chair creaked slightly. The beam slowly moved up and down Rone's body. He felt the perspiration under his head. Five, five, four, four, plus five. Twenty-three out of twenty-seven. Four left. Rone snapped his fingers four times. The light remained on him. He could feel Janis thinking. It snapped off. He heard the clip snap out of the automatic. That goddam Ward and his ideas, he told himself with a breath of relief.

"Last night I made contact with the Kitai," Janis began in total darkness. "A friend of Madame Sophie's set up the meeting. I went to the University Medical Centre and walked down four steps to a basement door labelled Staff Clinic. There was a waiting room. There were two peasant women sitting there. The time was approximately ten-thirty last night. The man behind the desk looked Oriental. Most likely Chinese. I should have expected that. I gave him the code as I was instructed. I told him my doctor had told me to be there at ten and that I was twenty-two minutes late. He asked me who my doctor was. I told him it was Dr. Kitai. He said he had no one by that name. Then I handed him the piece of paper and said maybe I was mispronouncing it. The orderly got up and left. He was gone maybe five minutes. When he returned he told me to go down the hall to the third door on the left.

"The Kitai looked more Mongolian than Chinese. His skin was more brown than yellow. He had a flat face and a broad, pushed-in nose. His eyes looked rather webbed at the corner. I couldn't tell how old he was. He was wearing a bluish-grey hospital jacket. He didn't talk much, but when he did you could see that two of his bottom front teeth were made of some metal. Not gold, but sort of a dull silver. Bottom right front teeth. He never stood up but he looked tall, maybe six feet. He spoke perfect Russian.

"He said he had heard I was interested in buying some new medicine. I said that was wrong, that I was interested in selling. If he was surprised he didn't seem to show it. I confessed I had made contact to him by saying I was a buyer, but that I really wanted to sell. He asked me where the medicine came from. 'By way of Turkey,' I told him. He asked when he could see some. I had the heroin in a small cigarette case. I gave it to him. He looked at it, rolled it in his fingers. He smelled his fingers. Then he tasted the stuff and asked me what I was interested in. 'A distribution arrangement,' I told him. He asked me how much medicine I had. I told him as much as he needed. He closed the case and gave it back to me and said that he was not equipped to handle a large operation. I told him I had plenty of men. He said that wasn't the point, that Moscow just wasn't conducive to widespread activities. I asked if that was because of no customers. He said that it was because of the police. I asked if it had ever been tried on a large scale. He said it had, six or seven years ago. I asked why it had failed.

"I noticed him freeze a little when I said that. He tried to size me up again and asked me why I was concerned about that. I told him if I didn't work out a deal with him I'd go elsewhere or do it on my own. I wanted to know everything I could about it. He said he still might be interested and I said I still wanted to know what broke up the first ring. He said it was a Russian officer from the Third Department, a Colonel Kosnov. He arrested a Chinese by the name of Chang who ran the operation. There was a Russian involved too, but he got away. He said nothing had worked since that time. I told him I was willing to take the risk. I asked him if he was going to come in with me or would I have to start on my own.

"'I am interested,' he said, 'but if you're in a hurry begin by yourself. I will give you a few contacts. When I find out more about you then perhaps we will talk again.'"

They reached the site of the accident in the middle of

the afternoon. The van lay on its side in a gully some sixty yards below the road. It had missed a turn in the storm, crashed into the abyss, caught fire and burned itself out before the snow covered it. Kosnov's agents lowered him into the gully. Two bodies were frozen solid inside the cab. Both were burned beyond recognition. The corpse in the driver's seat still clung to the steering wheel. The other one lay on its side against the door. Kosnov noticed that the left thumbnail of each cadaver was completely missing, while the other nine nails were only charred. They were closer to Vorkuta than Kara, so Kosnov ordered the bodies taken there for autopsies. They drove behind the ambulance until they reached the city.

Vorkuta had been the site of Stalin's most infamous prison camp. During his reign tens of thousands of prisoners had perished from the cold and hunger alone in this northern wasteland. During the Khrushchev era the camp was disbanded and the area redeveloped for settlement. Although the hospital was primitive it was still modern by Vorkuta's standards. The doctors were able to establish the age of the man behind the wheel as about sixty. The dental work on his teeth was either British or American. His hands were too badly burned to take clear fingerprints. Preliminary specimens indicated that he may have been suffering from intestinal cancer. The interior walls of his heart showed definite signs of scar tissue. From a preliminary examination he appeared to fit the description of the Highwayman.

Fingerprints were obtained from the second body. They corresponded to those in Kosnov's file on Charles Rone. So did the dental chart. The dental work was either British or American.

Kosnov decided that they should spend the rest of the night in Vorkuta and leave for Moscow early the next morning. He slept fitfully. Most of the time he lay in bed smoking and thinking about Erika. A final resolution was needed. He had two choices. Marry her or do away with her. In either case their relationship would be finalised. Marriage would be complicated. The legal problems alone were almost insurmountable, not to mention the political and social reactions. He would have to make up his mind. He could not continue as he had.

185

CHAPTER TWENTY-FIVE

THE FOURTH GRAVE

"SO you think this brings Kosnov further into the picture, do you?" asked Ward as they reviewed Janis' report, on their walk.

"It's possible. We know that Polakov and Kosnov met in Paris just after the letter was delivered. Now there is the chance that they had known each other since 1956. When the narcotics business Polakov and Chang were running in Russia was broken by Kosnov, only the Chinese was caught. Uncle Morris said that Polakov got away because the French helped him out. Maybe they did, and maybe they didn't. Maybe Kosnov let him off. Maybe they were cooking something up even then."

"Mighty interesting thought, Nephew," Ward said pensively. "It would explain how Kosnov found those two agents sent from England so easily – they were supposed to see him in the first place."

"And it could also explain why Polakov was afraid to make the last trip into Moscow. It's not too easy to avoid your contact when he has the entire counter-espionage department at his disposal."

"Well, we just better put him on the probable list until we find out a little more."

Ward led Rone along a line of stalls beside the exhibition hall. He checked his watch and purchased two soft drinks.

"Sip slowly," he said, handing a bottle to Rone.

"Why?"

"Because we got a visitor. I decided to take some of your advice."

The doors of the building opened and a mass of men and women, each wearing a white identification card, swarmed out onto the street.

Rone spotted Professor Buley pushing his way towards them with an ice-cream bar in his hand. His lapel card read:

The Puppet Maker stopped a foot or two beyond Rone and Ward, turned his back to them and began eating his ice cream.

"The Whore's in business again," Ward said softly. "He needs clients from the embassies. He needs them fast. Get Uncle Morris off her fat tweed ass in Prague. Nephew's got a brain-buster too."

Rone felt Buley back into him as he began talking. "Get a movement check on the top four or five hundred Moscow politicos. Match it against Polakov's travel record. See if anything corresponds."

Buley, still licking his ice cream, moved back towards the conventional hall.

"Button your top button," he whispered to Rone as he passed. "Russians seldom leave their top shirt button undone."

Ward and Rone finished their drinks and headed up the street.

"Well, Nephew, feel better now?"

"I think it was a good idea," Rone answered.

"You got lots of good ideas. I'm even going to use another one of 'em. Janis is moving in with Madame Sophie and the Warlock's bunking down with that instructor friend who picked him up. You and me will stay on at Potkin's for the time being."

"What about B.A.?"

"She goes in with the pickpocket."

Rone tried to hide his grimace.

"Leave that morality of yours back in New England, Nephew, it gets in the way out here. The girl goes where we need her the most. Now run on home. I got to get a Good Humour route started."

"Good Humour?"

"I'm pushing dope for Janis."

B.A. would not talk or look at him. Rone could think of nothing to say. They walked more than two miles through the cold, cloudy night before reaching the cemetery and slipping through a break in the wooden fence. The grey cement-block office building was un-attended. Rone jimmied the window and boosted B.A. through. Time passed slowly.

"Four plots are listed under the name of Polakov," she told him when she came out. "There were no first names or dates, but the ink looked fresh. The cards were probably written in the last few months."

They made their way cautiously along the funereal arboured paths until finding the sites. There were only three graves. The mounds were fresh. A simple wooden marker on each read: Polakov. Rone examined the fourth plot alongside the last grave. It looked as if digging had been started and then the dirt replaced and tamped firm.

He was still kneeling and absently rubbing the soil between his fingers when B.A. gently put her hands on his back.

"I don't care what they make me do or who I have to live with, I only love you."

Rone turned to her in time to see the solitary tear slide down her cheek. He pulled her to him.

The Warlock had moved into the instructor's apart-ment as an out-of-town colleague. All he could report was that the instructor's wife was a good cook and his children were rather precocious. Everything else was slow. The homosexual society of Moscow was cautious.

Ward's area was the most difficult. The addict does not like the pusher; he or she simply needs him. Confidences are not exchanged. Yet the addict has one over-riding weakness – when his need grows great enough he will do almost anything to satisfy the appetite. Ward would have to wait and watch.

The Warlock accompanied the instructor to a dinner party at the apartment of a secretary to one of the cultural ministries. The Warlock was not allowed to know just what ministry, since discretion, at least job discretion, was uppermost in the minds of this particular group of Russian men. It was here that Polakov was mentioned.

"They say that Kosnov has married," Dimitri said confidentially. He turned to his host. "They say that his wife was once married to the traitor Polakov."

189

"Ilyushka Polakov?" asked the host. He was a thin young man in his mid-thirties. A pair of rimless glasses perched on his fragile nose.

"Yes, did you know him?"

"Why – why yes. I'd met him. I mean I really didn't know him, but I'd seen him."

"Don't hide anything naughty from us, Rudolf. As I recall, you were questioned when he was caught."

"That is very unfair of you, Dimitri. Very, very unfair," said Rudolf nervously. "You know quite well everyone in my department was questioned – not just me. This Polakov creature had come to certain lectures at the University – that's where I met him. Everyone was questioned about him. It was a – a most hideous experience." The host rubbed his forehead tensely.

"You shouldn't tease Rudolf so," said the instructor. "We all know what he went through at the time. We can't be held accountable for everyone we might casually come in contact with."

The others agreed. They felt ashamed. They apologised to Rudolf.

"Anyway," Rudolf pointed out, "I doubt if it could be the same man. I mean the traitor, Ilya Polakov. The man they questioned me about wasn't supposed to be married."

There was something about the way Rudolf pronounced the name "Ilya" that caught the Warlock's attention. The party continued with a literary discussion on current Soviet writers.

"I tell you that Osip Mandelstam is our greatest contemporary poet," one of the guests asserted dogmatically.

"Then why don't we see any of his new work? I admit he was brilliant in the thirties. What has he done since?"

"Only written some of the greatest poetry ever to come from a Russian."

"You've read them?" asked the instructor in awe.

"Certainly I've read them. And it's silly to ask why they don't publish him. Who knows why the officials do or don't publish anything? But Mandelstam will not go unheard. Like Isaac Babel, he'll be printed on the black market if nowhere else."

As the discussion turned to the recent publication of

Franz Kafka's *Penal Colony*, the Warlock noticed that Rudolf was paying no attention. He seemed preoccupied. A look of despair covered his face. He moistened his lips and fidgeted with his glasses. Finally he excused himself.

The Warlock found his host sitting in the kitchen with tears streaming down his face.

"Is there anything I can do?" he asked.

"Only answer me this question. Why are the truly good people of this world maligned and eventually destroyed? Why? Why? Why?"

The next evening B.A. and Rone rigged a time-lapse camera and hid it in a tree opposite Kosnov's house. They recovered it the following day and hastily developed the film. Nothing was on it. The following night two cameras were planted, without results. The next night a third was added. Four photographs came out. The first was the back of a woman's head standing at the upstairs window. Her hair was blond and her back was bare. A second photograph showed a profile of the woman. Her mouth was curled back as if in anger and there seemed to be tears or water on her cheek. The third photograph was of a man's back. The final picture was of the girl again, her head thrown back in laughter. Rone recognised her. It was the woman Sweet Alice had identified as Erika Boeck Polakov.

That night B.A. and Mikhail made their way into a radio shop, ostensibly to fill an order B.A. had received at the free market. They took three radios and a television set. While Mikhail was not looking, B.A. slipped some transistors and other small equipment into her pocket.

Four nights later it rained, B.A. made her way onto Kosnov's roof from an adjoining building. She lowered a rope and slid down it head first until she was beside the bedroom window. The room was empty. She lowered the upper frame just enough to get her hands through. She reached in cautiously and lifted one end of the curtain rod from its bracket and slid the curtain rings to the other end. Then she took a duplicate rod from inside her jacket and deftly slid it through the bunched rings. She lifted the old rod out of the wall brackets and put in the new one. Then she adjusted it so that the imperceptible microphone holes were pointing into the room. She silently raised the window shut and pulled herself back up the rope.

Janis reported that business was good and little else. The new trade had given the girls confidence in Madame Sophie, and requests for employment were starting to trickle in. Janis approved only the prettiest and the most addicted prostitutes.

Ward was making little headway with the addicts. A young couple, both engineers at the same plant, were becoming his most dependent customers. They had offered any services either could perform in order to keep the heroin coming. Ward was toying with the idea of letting them be sub-pushers so that he could have more free time.

Rone now spent almost all his time at the apartment. When he wasn't listening to a report he was at the radio set waiting for contact with Kosnov's house. The colonel and his bride didn't seem to be at home for the first two days – either that or they were using the back bedroom of the house. When no word was heard on the set after five days, Rone talked to B.A. about putting another curtain rod or two in the house. While B.A. was out gathering more material, voices finally came through on the receiving set.

"But you said we could stay for two weeks. What happened? Four days and we're back," said the woman's voice.

"It couldn't be helped, my darling," said a man.

"Couldn't be helped. Couldn't be helped. That's all I hear from you. Aren't you in charge of your department? Aren't you the one who gives the orders?"

"Something has come up."

"Something always comes up. What is it this time?"

"You know I can't discuss it with you."

"Then why did you marry me? You could sleep with me without marriage whether I liked it or not. Why did you marry me if you won't tell me anything?" screamed the woman.

"You of all people should know there are certain things that can't be discussed, even with a wife."

"Why should I know that?"

"I'm sure Polakov didn't discuss his work with you."

"Are you?"

"That's what you told me."

"Well, I lied."

"Then or now?"

"Then." The woman laughed. "There's that stupid look on your face again. You're not sure now, are you? Well, he did tell me things, because he trusted me."

"What did he tell you?"

"Oh, things. If you take me dancing maybe I'll tell you."

"Erika, what did he tell you?"

"I'd like to go dancing and then I think I'd like to smoke some of those cigarettes."

"Erika!"

"Come, make love to me upside down. Look. This all belongs to you officially now. How does it look upside down? This is what I was known for in the Berlin houses."

Rone heard the door slam. The woman shrieked with laughter. Then she began to sob.

CHAPTER TWENTY-SIX

THE DINNER PARTY

"BUT I don't want to go to dinner with people I've never met before," protested Erika as the car drove along Novinski Boulevard.

"I would rather not be going myself," Kosnov admitted.

"Then why can't we go dancing instead, like you promised last week?"

"If we finish early I'll take you."

"Russians never finish eating early. They stuff their fat faces for hours. You all eat like pigs anyway."

"I want no talk like that tonight," Kosnov said menacingly. He grabbed Erika's arm and squeezed it tightly. "And I want you to remember the story. I want you to repeat it, just as I told you."

"I will, I will. Now let go. You're hurting me."

"If they like you tonight then you'll be accepted by the others. That means we can get out more often. Go more places. You'd like that, wouldn't you?"

"I'll believe it when I see it," Erika said with irritation. "Who is this Bretavitch that we have to come running when he calls?"

"Bresnavitch. Aleksei I. Bresnavitch. Say it."

"I'll remember."

"Say it," demanded Kosnov.

"Aleksei I. Bresnavitch. Satisfied?"

"Just remember it and do not drink too much."

"If I embarrass you why did you marry me?"

"Because I love you."

"I'll make you sorry for that."

"It had better not be tonight," Kosnov told her coldly. Erika believed him.

"Well, who is this Bresnavitch, anyway?"

"He is a very powerful man in Moscow."

"Is he your boss?"

"In a way."

"Then I'll sleep with him so that you can get promotion."

Kosnov slapped her across the face before he realised it. Erika took the blow cheerfully. She smiled at her husband and began rearranging her hair.

Seven people sat around the dinner table: Bresnavitch himself; his daughter and her husband, Grodin; Kosnov and Erika; and Gregori Kazar, a high-ranking Kremlin adviser, and his wife.

Bresnavitch proposed a toast to the newlyweds. Erika sat to his right, Kosnov to his left.

"You are so beautiful as they say," Bresnavitch said.

"Thank you."

"We understand you were one of Colonel Kosnov's agents in Germany," Kazar's wife said inquisitively.

"Yes."

"That must be very dangerous work for a woman," she commented.

"There is no danger when you believe in a cause."

"Well spoken," Bresnavitch interjected. "And how do you find Moscow?"

"It is a beautiful city," Erika answered.

"I would not have the courage to be a spy," said Kazar's wife. "I would not have the duplicity required. It is rumoured that you married an agent and lured him into Russia to be captured."

Erika felt a sharp chill race through her body. "I married the man Polakov on orders from Colonel Kosnov. My mission was to stay with him and learn of his activities. I led him nowhere. He came to Moscow on his own. I accompanied him as any wife would."

Kosnov watched Bresnavitch. The remark did not seem to affect him.

"Why did he come here?" asked the woman.

"I am afraid that is classified information," Erika said.

"Oh," said the woman, at a loss. "I do so much like to hear about spies. Can't you make her tell us?" She appealed to Bresnavitch.

"That is up to Colonel Kosnov," Bresnavitch told her.

"I assume we are all above suspicion, colonel," Kazar said genially. "I would like to hear your wife's answer if it is permissible?"

Kosnov thought for a moment, then he nodded to Erika.

"Polakov came to Moscow to make contact with a high Soviet official who was willing to give information to the West." Kosnov froze and glared at Erika. This was not what she had been rehearsed to say. He recovered quickly enough to notice Kazar staring at Bresnavitch. He seemed unperturbed.

"Might I ask who the contact was?" Kazar asked intensely.

"Now, now, now," Bresnavitch interrupted. "That would certainly be information Colonel Kosnov would prefer to keep to himself."

"It turned out to be a false lead," Erika offered gracefully. "His motives were completely domestic. He came to Moscow to introduce me to his mother and sister. I had married him in vain." She smiled across to Kosnov. "Darling, the next time you have your wife get married I hope it will prove more productive."

Everyone at the table laughed.

"Is that true, colonel? Is that why Polakov came to Moscow?" asked Bresnavitch.

"On that trip, yes. But he had been here before. Erika found that much out. The trip she accompanied him on was unofficial. We had not known before that time that Polakov had a mother and sister living here. We were not really sure he was Russian. Once we knew he was in Moscow I didn't want to risk losing him. I had him picked up."

"That seems like rather strange intelligence protocol," observed Kazar. "Why didn't you follow him until you found his contact?"

Bresnavitch interrupted again. "Colonel Kosnov is a very effective interrogator. His methods are quite extraordinary. Very few men fail to talk once he has captured them."

Kosnov saw Erika take a long drink of wine. For the remainder of the meal she did not look up at him. He knew that Bresnavitch was also watching.

After dinner Bresnavitch took his guests on a tour of his paintings. They returned to the living room for coffee and cordials. Grodin's and Kazar's wives seemed taken with Erika. Bresnavitch suggested that his daughter show the other two women the house so that the men could discuss a little business.

"Colonel," began Kazar, "I would not want you to misinterpret what I am about to say. Obviously you are aware of the complete re-evaluation of Comrade Khrushchev's politics. This type of activity is commonplace with a change of leadership. None of us is immune. Each must be prepared to answer for his activities over the last ten years. What I am asking here tonight is completely unofficial. It is really a clarification of certain matters and especially expenditures. You have made no secret of the Polakov matter, and for that I thank you. I am sure other camps within the government will be talking to you about it soon, if they haven't already. I don't believe it's a secret which elements I represent, and there are certain questions that we wish to put to you. If you prefer to remain silent that is your prerogative. If you accommodate us and clarify certain points we would be appreciative. If you are willing to accommodate us but prefer doing it at some other place and time, we will certainly honour your suggestions."

"I'm quite willing to discuss it," Kosnov answered calmly. He had known this was coming for months. He was prepared.

"Comrade Kosnov," said Bresnavitch, "let me first say that we are not interested in your investigation of ourselves and other Kremlin officials. We know it must take place under the circumstances. If the man Polakov was indeed in contact with a defector of high rank, we, as much as you, want him found. Each of us is at your disposal, and we accept the fact that you must proceed as you feel best."

"Thank you, Comrade Bresnavitch," answered Kosnov, slightly surprised.

"What concerns us more is the immediate security," Bresnavitch said sombrely. "You have spent great sums of money to determine which foreign agents might be sent to contact the traitor. We have learned, and not through my son-in-law, about the incident at Vorkuta. We compliment you on your ability to find them so fast, but your procedure and your conclusions have led to some confusion in our minds. Is it your opinion that the two men in the van were the enemy agents sent in to contact the traitor?"

"They most likely were," answered Kosnov.

"And you are satisfied that the two men in the van were definitely the two men you were looking for?"

"They were most likely the two men we were informed would come to this country."

Bresnavitch walked across the room and returned with a folder.

"Colonel, I have here a medical report on the two bodies found in that van. Unlike your report, ours was made by Moscow doctors."

"How could they give a knowledgeable opinion without having examined the bodies?" asked Kosnov.

"Comrade Kazar and I had the bodies flown to Moscow. You can look at this later. In effect, Colonel, our two doctors feel that there was a definite time difference between the deaths of the two men in the van. They agree with your official findings that the man known as the Highwayman died of suffocation and burns. They also feel that Charles Rone died of a concussion, but that he died three days before the other man. Your report claims that both men died in the crash and that their bodies were subsequently burned. When the fire burned out, what was left of them froze. Our doctors claim that this is true only of the Highwayman. A dermatological report indicates that Charles Rone was dead and frozen before the fire began. Skin samples indicated that flesh was frozen, began to thaw slightly and then was burned. Subsequently it froze again."

"That is possible," answered Kosnov, quite unconcerned.

"This fact interested us. We were able to get dossiers on the Highwayman and his associates, especially the man he worked for in the past. Sturdevant. We studied them quite thoroughly. Sturdevant seemed to have an interesting pattern. Every case he worked began with a diversionary move, a decoy if you like."

"And you think that is what happened here?" said Kosnov. "While we were watching the Kara Sea other men slipped in and made off with the Caucasus?"

"We would like to hear what you have to say."

"Your doctors could have been right," answered Kosnov.

"Is that all?" Bresnavitch asked, somewhat surprised.

"That's all I can agree to, and I have some doubts there."

"This is a rather dangerous attitude," said Kazar. "It looks as if you were completely fooled."

"Where is the proof?" Kosnov remained untroubled.

"In the facts as they stand," Bresnavitch snapped. "A dead man was carried into this country. A perfect decoy to draw your attention to one specific area. A manoeuvre which is repeated throughout the operation of the Sturdevant organisation."

"May I see the report?" Kosnov asked. He read through it slowly. Then he snapped it closed. "First of all, the report states that the agent Rone died anywhere from one day to three days before the Highwayman. But it does not state when the Highwayman died. The van was missing for five days in a blizzard. Rone could have been killed accidentally after they landed. His body could have frozen while the other man tried to get a van. If they entered the country by sea, Rone might have died on shipboard and they might have decided to bring his body in anyway. Even then I'm not convinced. The theory of oxidation in burned frozen skin has never been clearly established." Kosnov was bluffing on this point, but it seemed to be working. Bresnavitch and Kazar exchanged looks.

"We thought of all this in Vorkuta," Kosnov continued. "We noticed that there was a difference in the degree each body was burned. Certainly a frozen one would burn slower than a warm one. But you must take into consideration the position of the two men in the van. The vehicle fell almost two hundred feet into a snow-filled ravine. It came to rest in eight feet of snow on its side. Rone's body was thrown to the bottom. It lay on the floor. The other man was pinned behind the wheel above Rone. His door was thrown open. The fire broke out in the petrol tanks under the cab and roared through the floorboards between the two men. Rone was below it and the Highwayman was directly in it. The open door above the Highwayman acted as a chimney. The flames swept up and around him and shot through the door out of the cab. In short, there was a difference in heat. It was hotter for the Highwayman than for Rone. The bodies would therefore burn differently.

"But something else enters the picture. The fire was *put* out. It didn't burn out. That is why there were at least some remains. The van was lodged at the foot of the ravine against a solid wall of frozen snow. The flames shooting out of the cab melted the snow, and water poured down the hillside into the cab. Eventually so much fell that the fire went out. As the water began dripping into the cab it fell to the floor and collected in a pool around Rone. This is another reason why his body was not burned as badly as the other one. Rone had to be chopped out of a solid block of ice. Under these conditions it is quite conceivable that one man appears to have died much earlier than the other."

This was complete fantasy on Kosnov's part, but it was convincing.

"Even if there was a time variation, it was of little importance," the colonel continued sharply. "We knew the van was missing five days before. Every road in the area was blocked at fifty-mile intervals. The wreck was found one hundred and ten miles from Kara along a forty-mile stretch where there were no side roads. The temperature was almost constantly fifteen to twenty degrees below zero. Even if two dead bodies had been placed in the van and rolled over the embankment, how would the perpetrators of such a stunt get away? They couldn't drive very far in the blizzard, and even if they did they would have to pass one of our checkpoints. But there was no traffic in that sector. None whatsoever. It was also impossible for anyone to leave the accident on foot without freezing to death. Even Eskimos couldn't have moved about in that storm."

Bresnavitch and Kazar were showing the first signs of defeat. Colonel Kosnov did not let up.

"The other theory could be that the Highwayman intentionally sacrificed his life for a diversionary move. Diversionary for whom? He was second-in-command to Sturdevant. Sturdevant has been dead for ten years. Why would the leader of an organisation give up his life?"

"But we don't know if it was the Highwayman," Bresnavitch said.

"Potkin gave us the information. And Potkin is usually very accurate.

"Now, as to the factor of Sturdevant's so-called pattern. He had no pattern. Our records on him were compiled only after World War II. We had some information on him before, but it was destroyed. He sometimes worked alone and sometimes with a small group of men, but there was no pattern. He often used diversionary methods. Other times he did not. If we could have established his *modus operandi* he wouldn't have lasted as long as he did. I know his record very well. To my recollection he never sacrificed a single man in what we would consider a decoy move."

"Ladies, do come and join us," said Bresnavitch, rising. Grodin's and Kazar's wives and Erika entered the room. After they were settled, Bresnavitch turned to Erika.

"Your husband has been telling us of a most fascinating spy by the name of Sturdevant, but I assume you already know all about him."

"No, I don't," said Erika.

"If I am not mistaken, it was your husband who was his downfall. Let me see if I can remember. It was quite some time ago. This fellow Sturdevant was running wild through East Germany, Poland and Czechoslovakia. We were all very concerned about it at the time. Sturdevant's men were very hard to flush out. But the colonel did it."

"Do tell us about it," urged Kazar's wife.

"It was a long time ago," said Kosnov. "I'm not sure of the details."

"As I remember," Bresnavitch offered, "you knew that three of his men were in a small Polish village, wasn't that it?"

"I think so," said Kosnov.

"And the problem you faced was determining which of the twenty-three hundred people were the three you wanted. The colonel rounded up the entire population and began to interrogate and execute each of them one by one. It seems one of Sturdevant's men got a little squeamish at the sight of children being killed and made a run for it. When the colonel's men closed in he tried to kill himself, but the poison didn't work for some reason. They struck it quite rich. The man was a unit

201

leader who had information about the entire operation. From there on it was easy. How many villages did you wipe out before you found the men?"

"I can't remember." Kosnov watched Erika. She was beginning to tremble.

"Well, once the colonel had the agent he made him talk as only he can. Did you use chemicals or physical persuasion?"

"I don't remember," answered Kosnov.

"What was it you used on that Polakov fellow?" asked Bresnavitch, watching both Kosnov and Erika. "Wasn't it acid? I've been told it's like pouring molten lead down a man's throat. One can go insane from the pain. How many days was Polakov able to hold up under torture like that?"

Erika got up and left the room. Grodin's wife went after her.

Kosnov started to rise but Bresnavitch detained him. "Now, now, colonel. She'll get over it. After all, a wife has a right to know what her husband contributes to society. What did you use on Sturdevant's men that he swore to kill you?"

"I can't remember. Please excuse me." Kosnov rose and walked into the other room. Grodin's wife told him that Erika did not feel well and had gone home. Kosnov grabbed his coat and left the house without saying goodbye.

"I met this Sturdevant fellow once," Bresnavitch told the gathering. "That is, I talked to him over the telephone. He was giving us quite a lot of trouble in the early fifties. So much so that we wanted him on our side. Somehow we received word that he was to be thrown out of Western intelligence. I went to Paris and arrangements were made for a telephone conversation. I told him what we had found out and offered him a good job with us – Kosnov's job, to be exact – only we were willing to pay Sturdevant much more. He was quite polite in his refusal." Bresnavitch sipped his drink. "It was only sheer luck the colonel caught those men of his – sheer luck."

Erika ran the first three blocks from Bresnavitch's

home. She crossed a park and headed for the basement where she had danced before. She changed her mind and started off in the other direction for the restaurants Polakov had frequented. Tears streamed down her face. She moved along a side street and then into another. She knew it was somewhere in the neighbourhood.

She finally found the restaurant and went inside. Several tables of men and women were scattered through the dimly lit room. She recognised the waiter.

"You remember me, don't you? I used to come here quite often."

The waiter studied her and then nodded. "Get me something to smoke," she demanded. "You know what I mean. Or even something stronger. I'm in great pain. I must forget."

The waiter stood staring at her for a moment and then crossed the room to a table where three women and a man sat. He whispered something to the man. The man peered over at Erika. He walked slowly to her table and sat down. "Can I be of any service?"

"I need something strong to smoke."

"I see."

"And I want a man," Erika suddenly said. "I want a real man as well."

"It will be arranged," promised Janis.

SECTION FOUR

CHAPTER TWENTY-SEVEN

ERIKA

IT was early afternoon. Sun filtered into the small room Janis had arranged for them. Rone lay on his back smoking. Erika was asleep, her blonde head nestled against his shoulder, her arm thrust across his chest. She breathed easily. She had told Rone she had not slept soundly since her first husband died. Now once again she could relax. She could sleep. They had been together every afternoon since that first night Janis had brought him to her a week ago. Every afternoon their love-making had grown longer, more torrid, more tender. And each time she would fall into a deep complete sleep when they had finished.

Rone looked down at Erika's sleeping face and laughed to himself. He ran his fingers lightly along her forehead and down her cheeks. He thought back to their first meeting, to Janis bringing him into the apartment, to the expression on Erika's face as she smoked hashish with the other girls, to the look in her eyes when she first saw Rone. . . .

"How do you like him?" Janis asked her proudly.

Erika did not answer. Rone was standing in the middle of the room. At first she just stared. Then with the cigarette dangling from her lips she circled around him at a distance.

"Make him sit over there until I'm ready," she told Janis. She returned to the laughing prostitutes. After three cigarettes she ordered everyone to leave but Rone. She leaned against the wall studying him. "Whore," she ordered, "come here."

Rone stood up and crossed the room. He stopped in front of her.

"How much do you charge?" she asked.

"Twenty-five roubles," Rone said.

"Twenty-five roubles for what?"

"No one complains."

"You have a bad nose," Erika noted. "And your chin juts out too far. I don't like your ears."

"Then I'll go," Rone stated.

"I'll give you fifteen."

"My price is twenty-five – in advance."

"And what do you charge men?" Erika sneered.

"That is for others. I specialise in women."

"Old, fat, ugly ones, eh?"

"All women are beautiful if you know how to look at them."

"And am I beautiful?"

"You'll do."

"Oh, will I, now? I suppose your own girl is prettier than I am?"

"She is more polite."

"But is she more *beautiful*?"

"No."

"Ah," Erika sighed. "That's a good little whore. Here's your money." She threw the roubles on the floor in front of her. "Kiss my feet," she demanded.

"Your shoes are on."

"Then kiss my shoes."

Rone put his lips to her shoes. As he did she kicked her foot forward, catching him in the neck with the pointed toe. Rone gagged and dropped on all fours, his head hanging down between his arms. He remained in that position until he recovered. When he looked up Erika was sitting clutching her elbows.

"Now it's your turn to hurt me," she said. "We will re-enact that old, old game called woman and man – victim and tormentor – only *we* will play it honestly. Let me explain. There is no beauty but destruction. There is no feeling in love – only in pain and suffering. If you hit me I might feel something. That sole surviving nerve may feel a twinge, ever so slight, but I will know that I'm *alive* – that I can be loved. Help to destroy me – and I will love you for it. Go ahead. Hit. Hit hard." Erika looked into his eyes with supplication.

Rone's open hand landed across her face and toppled

her out of the chair. Blood trickled from her mouth. She nodded her approval. "You are beginning to learn. Hit me again."

Rone hesitated, then he slapped her again. She asked to be kicked, but Rone refused.

"But you're the whore – the slave," Erika pointed out. "You must do as I command."

"Find someone else."

"Oh, my little priest doesn't like the game of life. We will find something else to do. Stand in the middle of the room. Ah, that's a good little whore. Now take off your jacket – slowly – take it off very slowly. Now your shirt. Slowly, now. Very, very slowly."

Rone stood stripped to the waist as Erika rose and walked around him. "Now the trousers," she commanded. "And now the underwear."

Rone stood naked in the centre of the room as she inspected him. She ran her hands over his body, ordering him not to move. She stepped away, unbuttoned her blouse and dropped it to the floor. Slowly she loosened her skirt and let it fall. Next came her slip. "Don't move. Don't move at all," she commanded as she unhooked her bra and let it fall from her shoulders. She moved to within an inch of Rone and faced him as she slowly rolled her panties over her thighs and down her legs. "You mustn't move. No matter what I do, you mustn't move." Erika snapped off all but one light in the room. She moved up behind Rone and pressed her body into his back. She reached around and ran her fingers along his chest and down his thighs. She began to scratch him lightly, then harder. Suddenly she dug her long nails into his shoulder and drew blood. Rone flinched for a moment, but then remained still.

"Poor lover, poor little whore and priest and husband – look what I've done to you. Now repeat after me: *I.*"

"*I.*"

"*Am your.*"

"*Am your.*"

"*Executioner.*"

Rone hesitated, then he spoke. "*Executioner.*"

Erika stepped in front of him. She held a knife by the blade. "Kill me," she said gently.

Rone stood watching her. She jabbed the handle of the

knife into his stomach. "Kill me or I will kill you. So help me God, I will."

When Rone did not move she suddenly flipped the knife over in her hand and swung the blade at him. He caught her arm and twisted it back. It fell from her hand. Then she was upon him, clawing, scratching, kicking, beating. Tears rolled down her cheeks. Rone spun her around, lifted her up and threw her on the bed. She tried to kick at him but he brushed her legs aside and pinned her to the mattress. She was breathing heavily, tears flowing freely. Her body throbbed with sobs and laughter. Rone pressed down on her. He pushed his lips against hers. She shook her head violently away, but he caught her hair with one hand and held it in place. He gently kissed her and moved back. Erika lay motionless. Her eyes tight, her teeth clenched. He kissed her again.

"No one will hurt you any more."

She opened her eyes and stared up at him. He smiled down at her. "Oh no, no, no," she said almost inaudibly. "Dear Christ, no." Then she clutched him to her. . . .

Rone remembered reaching over and twisting the cigarette out in the ash tray. He turned back to the sleeping Erika and shook her. "Time to get up," he said and moved off the bed.

"It isn't," Erika said sleepily. Her eyes were closed. She shook her head. "It isn't. It isn't."

"It's ten minutes past one," he said flatly. "The girl who lent us this apartment will be getting home from the factory soon."

Erika held out her arms but Rone ignored them. She watched him dress without looking at her. Finally Erika got out of bed and put on her clothes.

"Will I see you again?" she asked, standing at the door.

"If you like," Rone answered.

"You know I'd like to." Erika paused. She looked up at her Yorgi. "But we must be careful."

"A husband?"

"Yes."

"He'll never find us here," Rone said indifferently.

"If he knew about us he would find us no matter where we went."

208

Yorgi laughed assuredly. "Don't worry about him. He is just another husband. None of them are any danger."

Erika reached down and took Yorgi's hand. "Please listen to me. We must be careful."

"We *will* be. Don't worry about things that don't exist."

Erika paused and looked away. "My husband is with the government," she finally said.

"Many husbands are with the government."

"Yorgi, Yorgi," she said turning back to him. "He is an intelligence officer."

"Many husbands are intelligence officers. There is still no need to worry."

"My husband is Colonel Kosnov."

Rone looked away with practised unconcern. He walked over to the table and picked up a packet of cigarettes.

"Do you still want to see me?" Erika asked nervously.

"Yes."

"When?"

"Whenever you say."

"Tomorrow? Tomorrow at two?"

"Tomorrow at two."

"Yorgi," Erika had asked on their second afternoon, "Yorgi, if I gave you money, I mean enough money, would you stop seeing other women?"

"I make a great deal," Rone said.

"I could get you almost seventy-five roubles a week."

"It's not enough."

"Yorgi, I want to speak the truth to you," she told him the following day. "So far I believe I have. Will you promise always to speak the truth to me? No matter what it is, will you always speak the truth?"

"Yes," answered Rone.

For another eight days Erika came to Yorgi every afternoon. Her dependence increased, but she never spoke of Polakov. It was on the ninth day, as she clutched her lover tight to her, that she asked, "Are you afraid of my husband?"

"No," Rone answered bluntly.

Erika moved back and looked at him. "And do you love me?"

"Yes."

"Do you love me enough to do something very dangerous? Something that would let us be together for the rest of our lives?"

"What is it?"

"Yorgi, take me out of Russia," she asked hesitantly. "I know it will be very difficult and very dangerous. You don't have to answer me now. You should think about it. If you don't want to do it I will understand. We can still go on seeing each other."

Rone rolled away and reached for a cigarette. He lit it and lay on his back, taking long, deliberate puffs. "I'll take you out," he told her.

Erika showered him with kisses. "Oh, Yorgi, Yorgi, we will lead the most wonderful life two people have ever had." Then she hugged him fiercely.

"When do you want to go?" he asked.

"As soon as we can."

"It will take time. Arrangements will be costly. People are afraid of your husband."

"I have twelve hundred roubles saved."

"That still isn't enough."

"I get a hundred roubles a week from the colonel. I think I could manage on fifteen. That would give us another eighty-five a week."

"That would still take us over a year," Rone said pensively. "I could get more customers, I suppose."

"No, no, no," shouted Erika. "I don't want anyone to be with you but me."

"We need money not only to get out, but so that I can take care of you once we're in the West."

"Once we are out I know where there is money. Enough money to last us the rest of our lives."

"Even so, leaving Russia will be very expensive."

"I don't want you to be with other women."

"I'll look around," he told her, "and see what else I can find."

B.A. lay on the rooftop next to Janis and watched Erika slip into the alley and start for the street.

"Down there – watch," she told Janis.

210

As Erika crossed the street a man stepped from a doorway and casually followed behind her.

"You're right," said Janis. "How long has it been happening?"

"For the last two days."

CHAPTER TWENTY-EIGHT

THE MAN IN THE CAR

YORGI met Erika the next three afternoons. Each time she would ask him if he had found another way to make the money they needed to leave Russia. Each time he would answer no. Yorgi finally promised her not to be with other women. He would not see Erika for two days. He would spend the time looking for new methods of earning the roubles. When they met again he had some news.

"How well do you like the colonel?" he asked.

"Before I met you I hated him. Now he doesn't matter. I can live with him. He loves me. He's pleasant. I almost like him at times."

"And Polakov? You told me you loved Polakov?"

Erika was puzzled. "Yes. Did I tell you that?"

"Have you forgiven the colonel for what he did to Polakov?"

"Yorgi, dearest Yorgi, when you have lived the way I have, you learn to forget quickly. If you didn't you would die of agony. The colonel did what he had to do. Polakov knew that. I know it now. When you have no place to give your love it often comes out as hate, but once you can love again it takes all your strength. You have nothing left to hate with. You can't be bothered."

"I see," said Rone with obvious disappointment.

"Why? Does this have something to do with getting the money?"

"It wouldn't work, not if you feel the way you do. I'll continue with the women. We'll have the money in no time."

"Yorgi, tell me what it is."

"I don't think you would do it."

"Do *what*? Darling, how can I help if I don't know what it is you want?"

"I talked to a man yesterday who was a friend of Polakov's." Rone saw Erika stiffen. "He is willing to

212

make all the arrangements for our trip and give us money."

"If?" The hardness Rone had first seen in Erika returned.

"If we give him information?"

"What *kind* of information?"

"This friend of Polakov's thinks that the colonel is conducting an investigation on certain Kremlin officials – anyway, that's what he told me. He would like to know more about it."

Erika closed her eyes and shook her head. "Oh God, not this again. Why couldn't we be two people from a faraway land where none of this happens? What is it about me? Yorgi," she said, reaching out for him, "you don't know what these people are like. You don't know what goes on. I lived through it with Polakov because he was the first man I ever really loved. But I was a child then. I didn't know the difference between true love and gratefulness. I asked to help in his work. I'm sorry I did. It is a world where no one can win. I'm afraid of it. Believe me, darling, it is better to stay away from all of it."

"It was only a suggestion. A fast way to get the money." Rone smiled. "We won't do it. In another two months I'll have everything we need doing what I'm doing."

Erika shuddered slightly and shook her head.

"Come on," said Rone gently. "It's time to get you home. Shall I meet you here tomorrow at the same time?"

"Yes," Erika said automatically. She did not move. She continued looking down.

"Come, darling," Rone urged.

"Yorgi, if I did this you wouldn't have to see any women but me?"

"Erika, it's too dangerous. You've convinced me. I can't risk you being harmed."

"You didn't answer my question. *If* I get the information, will you not see other women?"

"Of course."

"Then tell the man," Erika said without raising her eyes, "he can have it."

"But you're frightened. Why should you risk it?"

213

"To give him a sample of what we have to offer, assure him that Colonel Kosnov is indeed conducting a secret investigation. He does most of it at home so that his aide, Grodin, won't know about it. Grodin is the son-in-law of Aleksei I. Bresnavitch. Bresnavitch and other high officials don't want the investigation. They're afraid one of their own men will be implicated."

"Implicated in what?"

"Polakov had a contact in the Kremlin."

"Do you know who it was?"

Erika began slowly. "Polakov once made reference to somebody called the Bellman. I think that's who the colonel is after."

"Do you know who the Bellman is?"

"That's all the information we'll give until we see the first money." Erika stood up and began dressing. She said nothing and refused to look at her Yorgi.

"Tomorrow?" asked Rone as he opened the door.

"Tomorrow," she nodded as she left.

At ten the next morning the Warlock arrived at Potkin's apartment to give his report. Rone watched at the peephole while he entered, locked the door behind him and went to the gun cabinet. The code for that day was thirty plus three. Rone sat motionless as he entered the dark room and shone the flashlight in his face. He drew up a chair directly behind Rone and placed the Luger at his temple. He snapped his fingers five times, Rone snapped twice. The Warlock added three more snaps and Rone countered with ten. Then Warlock snapped twice more, Rone snapped eight times. The Warlock unloaded the pistol and laid it at Rone's feet with the flashlight. He moved his chair away and began talking.

"Rudolf says he is in love with me. He wants me to leave the instructor and move in with him. I told him it was not wise to break off so abruptly. I told him I would find a way to do it soon. He claims I am the first one he has been in love with since Polakov. He cried to me about it. Polakov apparently played with him, treated him badly. They had an affair, then Polakov became a tease. He would fight with Rudolf on any pretext. He would only have physical contact with him every now

214

and then. Rudolf was sure there was another man. He thinks the man was Bresnavitch.

"When Rudolf first met Polakov he was working for a department that was in charge of the restoration of art treasures and museums. Bresnavitch was in charge of the entire operation. Part of Rudolf's job was to see that masterpieces taken from Germany and other countries were catalogued and stored in safe places. Most of the German treasures had been stolen from France and Italy by the Nazis. The Russians did not want them returned. Right after the war nobody really knew what country had found what, so Bresnavitch devised a scheme whereby several vanloads of paintings were supposedly destroyed during an attack on a German convoy. Everything was reported lost.

"It seems that the loss went further than even the Russians had expected. A good many of the treasures disappeared from storage. Bresnavitch supposedly caught the culprit, got a confession that he stole them from the warehouse and sold them to an Italian. He had the man shot before anyone else could talk to him.

"Rudolf saw Bresnavitch and Polakov together on at least two occasions. Once in a restaurant and once walking down a street. Rudolf was apparently driven half mad by the Bresnavitch-Polakov affair. He thought of confronting both of them, of getting Bresnavitch out of the way – of doing anything he could to get Polakov back. In the end he did nothing and said nothing to anyone. This was in 1959, shortly after Polakov disappeared.

"Rudolf did not see him again for three years, but he couldn't forget him. Eight months ago he was passing a small restaurant he had been to with Polakov. Polakov was sitting at a far table by himself. Rudolf approached him. Polakov was furious.

"'Get out of here, you fool, or you'll get yourself killed,' he whispered to Rudolf.

"Rudolf went across the street and hid. He tried to watch the restaurant. A car drove by slowly, pulled down a side street and parked almost directly opposite where he was standing. A few minutes later Polakov came out of the restaurant and started for the car. Rudolf ran off in the other direction, but not before taking a quick look in the car. He couldn't see the man very clearly – not well enough to describe anyway – but he was sure of one thing: it wasn't Bresnavitch.

"Four months later he received a note from Polakov saying it was urgent that they talk. He said Polakov was nervous and frightened. He had never seen him like this. He told Rudolf he was in trouble and asked if he could stay with him if things got worse. Rudolf asked why he didn't go to Bresnavitch? Polakov said it wasn't possible. Rudolf pressed the point. Polakov finally admitted that he had had an affair with Bresnavitch, but swore it was finished. The split up had caused bad blood. Polakov confessed to fearing Bresnavitch's hostility. Rudolf agreed that Polakov could stay with him. That was the last Rudolf was to see of him – alive.

"He learned of Polakov's death when the Third Department picked him up. He was interrogated by Grodin. They had searched his apartment. Rudolf was afraid they might have found the five or six books he had loaned to Polakov. Each had his name in them. Grodin never brought the subject up. The questions were quite routine. He was asked when and where and how he had met Polakov, what he knew of his background and activities. He told them as little as possible and never mentioned the Bresnavitch or car incident. He was released. A week later he was asked to return for more questioning. It was much as before and then they released him. He hasn't been bothered since."

Rone handed the Warlock the envelope with one typed question on it. The Warlock picked up the flashlight and shone it on the page. "No, I've never heard of the Bellman," he told the Grand Mute, "but I'll keep my ears open."

Later Rone and Ward went over the Warlock's report. The history of the Pepper Pot was beginning to take shape.

"Bresnavitch could easily have been Polakov's source for the paintings," Ward pointed out.

"If what Rudolf says is true he most likely was," said Rone.

"And he could damn well be the Bellman also," Ward thought aloud. "Bresnavitch was in complete charge of hiding those art treasures from the West. He thought up the scheme of making us believe they were destroyed, then he arranged for the secret storage of them. Who would have been in better position to turn around and steal them from Russia?"

"No one," Rone agreed, "but why would he do it? For the money?"

"I don't know – but I'll just bet he was the one. He was the original thief, and Polakov opened up his Paris art business to cover for the unloading of the paintings. Once they were in that far together, moving on to sell information was just the next step."

"But once again," said Rone, "Polakov got high prices for his material. Did Bresnavitch want money for that too?"

Ward drummed his fingers on the table. "Take it from this point. Bresnavitch decided he wanted to make a move in the Kremlin, he wanted the letter to show his associates he had delivered to the West. Either he or Polakov must have realised that getting someone to write the letter in the first place would be one hell of a job. It would take time and trust. What better way than to start feeding in information – information for a price, damn high-level secrets? Polakov was an old espionage hand – he would have known that paying for information wouldn't have bothered the West; in fact, the more he asked the greater the Western trust in him. No, maybe the whole idea of charging for the information was simply a come-on. Maybe they knew from the beginning they wanted the letter. Once the West began relying on the Russian data, getting the letter wasn't too hard."

"That still doesn't explain why Polakov and Bresnavitch sold the missing paintings," Rone said.

"That might simply have been Polakov's way of cultivating Bresnavitch, of getting up his confidence – I'm just not sure of that point at all."

"And what about the man Rudolf saw in the car?" Rone reminded him. "It wasn't Bresnavitch. Then who was it? Would Bresnavitch send an emissary?"

Ward shook his head. "No, I don't think so. He'd deal directly with Polakov – he wouldn't let anyone else know."

"Another thing," said Rone. "Do you think Bresnavitch would tip off Kosnov that agents are coming into

Russia to meet him? Do you think, if he was the Bellman, that he would risk having Kosnov catch those men and make them talk?"

"No, Nephew, he sure as hell wouldn't. He might kill them himself, but he wouldn't hand them over to the good colonel."

"I don't think the man in the car was Kosnov either," mused Rone. "Kosnov is too well known to meet that openly."

"Agreed. He has half of Moscow to use, and if you'll remember, when he and Polakov did get together they went all the way to Paris to do it."

"Could Bresnavitch and Kosnov be working together?" asked Rone.

"That's one helluva thought."

"It might explain their so-called feud. Antagonisms make a perfect cover."

"That they do." Ward shook his head. "I just can't see the two of them linking up. It's that man in the car who's getting more and more interesting."

"Is there any word on who's been tailing Erika?"

"Not yet. The Warlock and B.A. have trailed him as far as the University area, but then he shakes them off. Come to think of it, that fellow might be able to clear up a thing or two."

Rone sat at the receiving set. Just before midnight he heard voices come from Kosnov's bedroom.

"I passed Madame Grodin on the street today," Erika said. "She was very cold to me."

"Ignore her," said Kosnov.

"I can't. It seems to be the same with all the women. Is it me?"

"No, *golubushka,* I'm afraid it's me. The investigation has everyone on their guard."

"But why should Madame Grodin be the coldest? The same is true of her husband. I even felt it with Bresnavitch. It's different with them. Does Bresnavitch feel you are concentrating on him?"

Rone was aware of the pause before Kosnov began to explain. "Bresnavitch and I were once friends and then became enemies. It has never been the same since. We have been polite to each other, even co-operative, but it has never been the same.

"What happened?"

"I would rather not talk about it."

"You never talk about anything that troubles you. How can I be a wife if you don't let me know things?"

There was another pause. "Many years ago Bresnavitch and I had a falling out. He tried to replace me with a Western agent."

"A Western agent?"

"A man named Sturdevant. Bresnavitch offered him my job."

"How do you know?"

"Sturdevant told me. We had become friendly during the war. Even after we and the West became alienated, Sturdevant and I still co-operated. It was said I was the only man he even halfway trusted. I often allowed his groups to operate in my area, and he did the same for me. I am afraid I betrayed him. Bresnavitch was after my resignation. I had to do something spectacular to hold my position. So I broke up one of Sturdevant's rings, one that I had guaranteed to protect. The raid on the ring disrupted Bresnavitch's plans. He is not an easy loser. So you see, *golubushka,* the trouble is not with you. It goes back many years."

"What became of Sturdevant?"

"He swore to kill me, but he died before he could carry out the threat."

Potkin had seldom been nervous. Now he was. Potkin had seldom trembled. Now he caught his hand shaking from time to time. There was no one to help him look for his wife and daughters. No one could know. He must wait. He must hope. Potkin was a man alien to hoping. Since Series Five had been completed there was only routine work; he had too much time to think. He took long walks.

He strolled slowly along Fifth Avenue. The sun was setting when he reached the house and walked into his office. Lieutenant Grodin was waiting for him.

"We need you," he told Potkin.

"Wh-why?"

"We have decided to assassinate Kosnov."

Potkin stared at him.

"You will do it," Grodin said firmly.

"I am busy. I have many important cases. I can't leave."

"Comrade Captain," said Grodin, "the decision is not yours to make. Aleksei Bresnavitch is not accustomed to refusal. He has his ways."

"His ways?"

"Don't be naive, Captain. This is a serious matter. If you don't co-operate it could affect your career – your family."

"My family?"

"That is what I said. Aleksei Bresnavitch has his ways."

Potkin had never cried that he could remember. Now tears swelled in his eyes. He was an apathetic man. Now he threw back his head in hysterical laughter.

CHAPTER TWENTY-NINE

THE MAN IN THE FEDORA

ERIKA left Yorgi in the apartment, went down the back stairs, through the basement passageway and out along the alley. As she moved out onto the street a man in a wide-brimmed fedora hat stepped from the doorway and followed at a distance. He stopped and faced in the other direction while Erika looked into a shop window. He continued after her when she began walking.

Erika followed the route that Yorgi insisted she use today. Instead of walking along Pyatnitskaya Street as she had done in the past, she cut through an alley, crossed the boulevard and ducked into another alley. The man with the wide-brimmed hat quickened his pace. He turned into the alley. No one was there. He ran farther along. An arm reached out and grabbed him from behind. The man dropped to his knees, lurched forward with tremendous strength and hurled the Warlock over his shoulder. Then he turned and began running back up the alley. A knife shot through the air and drove into his back. The man took two more steps, gasped for breath and fell forward dead.

Ward walked over, pulled out the knife and turned the body over with his foot. "Well, what the hell do you know," he said to the approaching Warlock. "It's a goddam Chinaman."

B.A. and Rone found little time to spend together. When they did there was no place where they could be alone. At the most they would walk hand in hand along the riverbank through Gorki Park.

"We have both become prostitutes," she told him one day. "I don't feel any different, do you?"

The following days were mostly unproductive. The Warlock reported that Rudolf had gone into a state of depression and refused even to mention Polakov's name. Business was thriving for Janis and Madame Sophie, but none of the girls seemed to have known Polakov. B.A. and Mikhail were also doing well on the black market in stolen electrical equipment. Once again, there were no leads to Polakov's contact.

The only thing that was progressing well was Yorgi's affair with Erika. Rone felt she was falling deeper in love with him. He was surprised and somewhat embarrassed when she told him she realised they might never leave Moscow together. She didn't care. If she did it might mean her life anyway. The last few weeks with her lover were the happiest time she had ever spent. She was grateful to him for this. Just to be close to him was enough. If it ended tomorrow she would understand. Erika also had a surprise for him. It came at the beginning of the next week, on a Tuesday. He had reached the apartment before her. He made himself a glass of tea. Erika was late. She did not arrive for half an hour.

"Darling Yorgi, darling Yorgi, forgive me, but I just couldn't get away," she explained breathlessly.

"That's all right," answered Rone. "Here, have some tea."

"No, I can't stay. I have to meet the colonel. Yorgi, close your eyes." Erika stood with her arms behind her back.

"Why?"

"Don't ask. Just close them. Now hold out your hand." Erika placed a small, brightly wrapped package in his palm. "I have to go now, darling. I'll see you there tomorrow."

"Where?" asked Rone.

"Unwrap your present and find out." Erika threw him a kiss and left.

Rone opened the package. Inside he found a key and a folded note. He began reading:

Dearest Yorgi, this is a key to our new apartment. It's ours for at least a month, and maybe longer if we want. Don't ask me how I got it. It is ours and no one knows about it. It is perfectly safe. The address and apartment number are below. I love you, I love you, I love you.

Rone shook his head in frustration. The room he was now in had maximum security; Janis had seen to that. It was in a complex of five dilapidated buildings in a crowded section of Moscow. It could be entered from adjoining structures or through a common basement. Even more important, the streets below were busy with shops, vendors, small restaurants, neighbourhood inhabitants and shoppers from other sections of Moscow looking for items not necessarily available in more respectable sections of the city. Rone and Janis had feared Kosnov. They picked an area where it would be hard to be followed. They had found a room that was virtually undetectable. There was no way to link Erika and Rone. They entered the building at different times and from different approaches. Their meeting place was perfect.

Rone slipped down the back stairway, walked along a narrow alley, and stepped through the rear entrance of a neighbouring restaurant. He ordered a bowl of soup and a glass of wine. When he left he criss-crossed the crowded side streets and made his way to the underground station. He took the train for five stops, got off, rode back three. He back-tracked four more stations and got off within five blocks of where he had started. He crossed several vacant sites, made sure he was not being followed, then caught the underground once again.

The address was a new multi-storied building in one of Moscow's better neighbourhoods. Rone walked past the building several times. As he had feared, it was too isolated. There were very few people on the street. They could be spotted too easily. He walked down the side streets and behind the building. No, it wouldn't do at all. He anticipated Erika's tears. He didn't like to make her unhappy, but this time it couldn't be helped.

It was not quite noon. His first appointment was with the Warlock at two o'clock. Rone decided to walk for a while. He passed the Palace of Labour, turned right and strolled along the river. It was a quiet, peaceful afternoon. Moscow is a silent city. Cars are not allowed to honk their horns, people are generally quiet in the street. Somehow the din of other cities had never found its way into Russia's capital. Rone did not particularly care for this. In a way it depressed him. It was a city that behaved more like a hamlet. Physically it was impressive, but for some inexplicable reason even the architecture seemed muted.

He returned to Potkin's apartment shortly after one. A note was pinned to the door: "Yorgi, am waiting on the street, *à droit*. U.M."

Rone went downstairs and turned right. He had walked seven blocks before Uncle Morris fell in beside him. She was wearing the latest in Moscow styles: a heavy wool suit with square, padded shoulders and block-heel shoes.

"We have come up with something you should know about," she told him as they walked. "The Swiss bank account has been traced to Polakov. Twelve deposits were made which correspond in time to the twelve payments he received for each of the parcels of information. In fact, each deposit was made within five days after he received payment from the West. This was the same account where he subsequently deposited the first half million dollars. Two days after he went into Russia for the last time, the entire balance was transferred to another account. We don't know who that one belongs to.

"Here is what is most interesting. All of the money in the last account was then transferred to Tangier. Also deposited in that bank was the second half million dollars. Our people checked back and found that previous to this large transfer, eight smaller deposits had been made. Four were on dates corresponding to the last four small deposits he made in the Swiss bank, but the additional four deposits were made at intervals *after* he ceased supplying us with information."

"You didn't make any more payments after the letter?" asked Rone.

"None. Once we had agreed to deliver the letter there was no more information for sale, at least to us. He might have continued selling to someone else – at least that's what some of us think."

"Maybe those four additional payments came from the Swiss bank."

"They didn't," Uncle Morris informed him matter-of-factly. "As I said before, we were able to trace the original Swiss deposits. His account was cleaned out in one transfer. A subsequent transfer for the same amount showed up in the Tangier bank. And then, of course, there is that confusing issue of who made that last transfer, since Polakov was already in Moscow at the time."

"Couldn't he have posted the transfer?"

"Our information says it wasn't done by post. No, someone had to make it and someone had to be in Tangier, and I'm afraid that list of Russians and their whereabouts you wanted is of little help here. Not one of them was within five hundred miles of Africa at the time."

"Was there a name on the Tangier account?"

"Yes, but it makes no sense to us. It was Bel Aman. What do you know about it?"

"Nothing," answered Rone.

"Sorry to spoil your hopes, but it looks like that bonus money your little club was counting on is tied up in a dead man's account."

"Is there anything else?" asked Rone.

"Not from our end. What's progressing with your merry little group?"

"You'll know when we come out."

"And how's the bordello business?"

"Still looking for new and experienced girls."

"I prefer younger clients. Well, ta ta." Uncle Morris turned away.

Rone watched her disappear down the street. It was ten past two. The Warlock was already sitting in the confession booth. In five more minutes the interview would automatically be cancelled. The Warlock would leave. Rone knew he couldn't make it back in time. He turned and headed slowly towards the apartment.

When Rone was four streets from the apartment he stopped and lit a cigarette before crossing to a park, where he would wait until the Warlock was out of the vicinity. He started to cross the street, but jumped back as a black Zim roared past. In the back seat sat Grodin. Beside him was Potkin.

CHAPTER THIRTY

THE VISITATION

POTKIN's car was followed by two others. The street curved at the next corner. As Rone rounded it he could see straight down to Potkin's building. Five black Zims were parked in front. Several men stood near the door. Another man came out shaking his head. For a moment Rone felt relieved. The Warlock had escaped. Then two more men emerged carrying a body. He could see the stumpy form of Potkin approach and look down at it. He said something to Grodin. Men were dispatched in various directions. The body was put into one of the cars. All the cars drove away. The apartment was now a trap. Rone would have to warn the others.

B.A. was not due until five, Ward not until seven. He took the underground to the street Mikhaïl lived in. His mother said B.A. and Mikhaïl were not expected back until after eight. She didn't know where they were. He told her, if she possibly could, to get a message to B.A. saying not to buy meat for dinner. Then he went to contact Janis. He had no way of knowing where Ward was.

It was almost three-thirty when he reached Madame Sophie's neighbourhood. Janis usually spent his afternoons in one of two small restaurants around the corner. Rone entered the first and sat down. When the waiter approached he asked if he had seen Janis.

"They took him a half hour ago," the waiter whispered as he cleaned off the table.

"The police?"

"Police or secret police. They may still be around. Go out through the back."

"And Madame Sophie?" Rone asked as he rose.

"They only took him. Go. You'll get us all in trouble."

B.A. had six possible routes to the apartment. From the western end of the street she could approach from the west, north or south. From the eastern end, east, north or south. Rone sat in the small park three blocks east of the house. He would have to gamble. She was due in less than ten minutes. Rone saw no movement on the streets. Only two vans passed along the street. One of them stopped in the next block. As the driver got out, a man stepped from a doorway and said something to him. The driver nodded, got back into his van and drove away. The man walked down the street away from Rone and stepped into another doorway. There were five minutes left when a car pulled up opposite him. A young man and a woman sat in the front seat. The man got out, went around the car, and opened the door for the woman. He helped her to her feet and then escorted her to an apartment entrance. They stood in front of the building talking. No one came to tell them to move on. The surveillance did not extend this far. There were less than three minutes to go. B.A. must be coming from the other direction. Rone walked quickly to where the car was parked. He called to the man: "Your oil's leaking."

The woman entered the house as the man returned to the car. He looked underneath. "I don't see anything," he said to Rone.

"It's getting too dark. Do you have a torch?"

"No," the man replied, somewhat perplexed.

"Then back up the car and put on your lights and you'll be able to see."

The man got into the car, started the engine, turned on the lights and backed the car a few feet away. Before he could get out Rone was at his door. "You're dropping oil, all right. It's probably coming from under your dashboard."

"There's no oil line there," the man said defiantly.

"Don't tell *me*, comrade," answered Rone. "I'm a mechanic. I know this model you're driving. They put it together backwards. They've got everything in the wrong place. Move over and I'll show you." Rone opened the door as the driver obediently slid away. Rone stuck his head under the steering wheel. "There it is. Just like I told you."

"Where?"

"Just look down here." The man bent his head under the dashboard and searched. Rone's hand crashed into the back of the man's neck. He pushed the limp body away, grabbed the wheel and started driving for Potkin's building. As he drove he saw several men standing either inside doorways or between the buildings. They looked up at the passing car without interest. There was no sign of B.A. at the first crossing street. He continued towards the apartment. The owner of the car stirred slightly. Rone cracked him across the back of the neck. The body slumped. Two more streets and still no trace of her.

He was opposite Potkin's apartment when B.A. turned the corner two blocks ahead. She was coming towards him on the opposite side of the street. He rolled down his window and reached back to open the rear door. They were half a block apart when he jammed down the accelerator, swerved the car to the opposite side-walk, bounced over the kerb and slammed on the brakes. The car screeched to a stop.

"Get in," he shouted, throwing open the rear door.

B.A. stood frozen. "What?"

"It's a trap. Get the hell in here."

B.A. moved for the car just as a man rushed from a building and caught her by the arm. Rone jumped out. B.A. had been thrown to the ground before Rone reached her. He chopped away her assailant with two fast cuts, jerked her to her feet, and dragged her to within a foot of the car before two men lunged onto them. Rone caught the first one in the groin. When he turned to B.A. she was being pulled back towards the building. Three more men were within steps of her.

"Save yourself," she shouted twisting one hand free. "Please. I love you." She was pushing her thumb into her mouth. The last thing Rone saw before jumping behind the wheel was a man reaching for B.A.'s jaw as it snapped shut.

Rone had expected gunshots. No one fired. He had expected cars or barricades to block his way. None appeared. He had accelerated and roared from the kerb with only two men running towards the car waving him to stop. They jumped clear as he passed. He skidded around the corner and raced onto the boulevard. The last thing he saw in the rear-view mirror was a group of men bending over B.A.

No one was behind him. He took no chances. He turned down several side streets and reversed his direction twice before reducing his speed. He drove another five minutes before pulling into an alley, parking and getting out. He walked between two buildings, turned onto the boulevard, and caught a bus.

For the first time he thought of Ward. Ward would be coming to the apartment at five. He would be walking into the trap just as B.A. had. He realised there was nothing he could do about it.

Rone had less than fifty roubles with him. There were thousands in the apartment. Fifty roubles would not carry him far. It would barely get him out of Moscow, if he had any idea how to accomplish that in the first place.

He sat in the Komsomol Theatre on Chekhov Street trying to clear his mind. He was oblivious to the players and the audience. The key was clenched in his fist, the key Erika had given him earlier that day. The solitary question in Rone's mind was how much the colonel knew about his wife's affair with Yorgi. If he had been followed, and now there was no reason to believe otherwise, did the colonel know he had been meeting with his wife? They had never been seen together. They had always entered and left their rendezvous from different directions at different times. Erika usually came through the restaurant, Yorgi through the basement of the adjoining building. Rone closed his eyes and concentrated. He tried to rehear the nocturnal voices. He listened for inflections, innuendos. The words were those of a trusting husband, but what was underneath them? Had he been play-acting with his wife or had the affair escaped his notice? Maybe the colonel knew all along but refused to acknowledge it. Rone listened to the voices from his memory. He replayed certain segments as if he were operating a gramophone. He could recall no trace of scepticism in Kosnov's voice.

He had to assume that all the means of exit from Moscow would now be well covered. He couldn't risk going near any place or anyone he had known before. Hotels were out of the question. Moscow is not the kind of city where you can sleep in the park or on an underground station platform unnoticed.

He pressed the key. The idea of having a new apartment suddenly available was a little more than Rone could accept. Perhaps Kosnov hadn't wanted to catch him in the afternoon raid. Had he intentionally waited until Rone was approaching the building? Rone would see what was happening and run. Where would he run to? To the new apartment of course.

It was adding up too well. Erika could not come that afternoon. The colonel wanted her to be with him. Why this afternoon particularly? If he was conducting the raid, how could he possibly be with her? No, he wanted her out of the way; she could be under guard at this very moment. When he tried to save B.A. he had escaped too easily. He was a perfect target, but no one had fired a shot at him. Three men were within short range of him. No one fired. No one produced a gun. The men in front of the car had simply waved their hands to stop, but neither one was holding a gun. He had raced the car away expecting to be chased. He wasn't.

The play was over and the audience applauding as Rone slipped the key into his pocket. If the colonel was waiting for him to make an appearance, Yorgi would not disappoint him.

SECTION FIVE

CHAPTER THIRTY-ONE

THE APARTMENT

HE walked casually. In his pocket he carried a knife he had stolen in the last restaurant he had visited that night. If Kosnov was waiting for him, he still might be able to catch him off guard. This would even the score for B.A. He had no idea how he would get into the apartment unnoticed, but for a few minutes he would at least have the satisfaction of being the hunter.

Rone also considered the possibility it wasn't a trap. Erika might have arranged it without Kosno's knowledge. Perhaps this more than anything was what lured him there. It might be a haven after all.

Rone strolled past the building, turned up a side street, cut back and passed again from the other direction. He saw no one.

He walked around to the back entrance and tried the door. It was locked. That left only the front. He entered the small hallway and climbed the stairs to the third floor. He held the key in one hand and the knife in the other. He slipped the key quietly into the lock and cautiously opened it. The apartment was empty.

The flat consisted of a living room, a bedroom, a bathroom and a kitchen. The kitchen was modern with an electric refrigerator stocked with food, a four-burner gas stove, a double aluminium sink and modern wooden cabinets filled with dishes and canned goods. In the living room was a television set, a radio and a record player as well as two modern couches, three chairs and a small dining table. An Armenian rug was spread over the centre of the floor. The bedroom contained two bureaus, a double bed with a wooden headboard and a second radio. It was, in Russian terms, a luxury flat.

Rone took a bath and made himself a sandwich of

black bread, cheese and a processed meat that tasted like pork. He looked through the bedroom drawers. They contained a woman's clothes. An old woman.

He was exhausted; he lay down on the bed. He tried to stay awake, but he couldn't.

"Yorgi, darling, it's time to get up," Erika said with her lips against Rone's. He opened his eyes. It was daylight. "How do you like your surprise?" she asked, handing him a glass of coffee.

"Who does it belong to?"

"Us. At least for a month. Come, tell me, do you like it?"

Rone nodded and sipped his coffee.

Erika began to undress. "When did you get here?"

"Last night."

"Last night? Yorgi, is something wrong? Why didn't you stay at your place?"

"I was thrown out."

"Why?"

"My work papers weren't in order. The room goes to a factory worker. Some regulation or other."

"Then you can live here." She threw her arms around him. "You can live here where I know where you are. I'll come every free moment and make love with you."

"This is a dangerous flat. People can notice us too easily."

"I'll lock us both in. We'll stay here for four whole weeks making love. Would you like that?"

"Yes."

"It's settled," she said, nuzzling him. "The day after tomorrow I'll come to live here too."

"What are you talking about?"

"The colonel's going away for a month." Erika giggled. "And he's letting me stay in Moscow alone. Only I'm not alone, am I?"

"Where is he going?"

"To visit his mother in Yalta."

"Are you sure?"

"Of course." Erika was biting his ears. "We put her on the train yesterday," she whispered.

"We? You and the colonel?"

"Hmmmm. You have exciting ears. I like biting them. I love biting and kissing your ears."

"Erika. Was the colonel with you when you put his mother on the train?"

"Yorgi, please, no questions now. Must we always start with questions?"

"Answer me!" he said, pushing her away. "Was the colonel with you when you put his mother on the train?"

Erika rolled on her stomach and pulled a pillow over her head. "I won't answer anything until you make love to me. I'll stay under here and suffocate if I have to – but no questions first."

"Please, Erika, it's important. Just tell me – then we can do whatever you like."

She turned on her back in disgust, folded her hands over her breasts, and looked at the ceiling. "I met you, I gave you the key. I left you. I met the colonel at his office. We picked up his mother. We went shopping with his mother. We had a meal with his mother. We put his mother on the train. Together. He and I. One, two. One, two, three, yo, ho, ho, ho – the old girl was on the train. All right?"

Rone thought for a minute. "That means you were with the colonel from the time you left me until when?"

"I left you at noon and I was with the colonel until we went to bed at eleven. Any more questions?"

"Come here," said Rone, reaching for her. But deep within him he heard B.A.'s final shout.

Erika was bathing. Rone lay on the bed smoking. She had not been out of the colonel's sight the entire afternoon. He had not been back to the office or even called in from noon on. But the raid took place at two o'clock. Why wasn't he concerned? Potkin must have told him the whole story. Rone knew from Erika's previous conversations that he was obsessed about the Highwayman and the missing van. He had flown to Kara himself. Yet when he had the entire operation in his grasp he spent the day seeing his mother off. All day he had no way of knowing if the raid was successful or not. He didn't seem to care. Not only that, but he was leaving for Yalta in two days. Did that mean the others were all dead? If they were, he couldn't interrogate them; neither could anyone else. But what about Rone himself? Kosnov would certainly know that Rone was still free. Why would the colonel leave before he was captured? Rone went to the bathroom and stood beside the open door. Erika was drying her hair.

"Erika. Whose apartment is this?"

"Ours."

"You know what I mean."

"It's ours for one entire month. That's all that matters," she answered happily.

"It belongs to the colonel's mother, doesn't it?"

"Not if she isn't here it doesn't."

"How did you get the key?"

"She gave it to me."

"Why?"

"So that I could look in while she was away. That's why I was late yesterday. I stopped here to help her pack and get the key. I stopped before I met you and had a duplicate made for your present." Erika threw her towel around Rone and pulled him to her. "Yorgi, let's take a bath together."

"You just had one."

"I would like another – under the right conditions."

Rone nodded and Erika started filling the bath.

"Why is the colonel letting you stay in Moscow?"

"Because he knows I want to be alone with you."

"Be serious."

"I told him I was allergic to sun and swimming. If I went to Yalta with him I would be unhappy because everyone else would be on the beach and I would have to stay inside."

"And he believed that?"

"Darling Yorgi," Erika said, pulling him into the water with her, "the colonel *wants* to believe it. He's very much in love with me, and since I've met you, I've treated him much better. He wants to believe I care for him. He wants to believe our marriage is a good one. When a man wants to believe in something, and you encourage that belief, he'll go to great, great pains to protect his illusion."

After they dried each other Erika prepared a meal.

"Has the colonel mentioned Potkin to you?" asked Rone.

"Who is Potkin?"

"One of his agents. I believe he works in New York."

"Where did you find out about that?"

"From Polakov's friend. He wants to know when Potkin is expected in Moscow."

"I'll try to find out," she said, turning back to the stove.

CHAPTER THIRTY-TWO

THE FALLING OUT

RONE spent the evening watching television and listening to records. He went to bed early and slept until Erika returned the following afternoon. After they made love he asked her about Potkin.

"Polakov's friend was right," she announced. "Potkin is one of the colonel's agents. And he is in New York."

"Now?"

"Yes."

"How did you get the colonel to tell you?" asked Rone.

"I told him a woman in the beauty shop had asked me about him. I told the colonel she was a neighbour of Potkin's who had lent him some dishes and wanted to know when he would be back."

"What did the colonel say?"

"He laughed and told me that the woman was out of luck. Potkin wasn't expected until the end of the summer."

"When does the colonel plan to go to Yalta?" he asked.

"Tomorrow. Then we have a whole month to take baths together."

"I don't think he should go."

"Of course not, my darling Yorgi. We should invite him to dinner instead."

"I'm serious."

"And so am I, darling. Don't worry yourself. He won't be hiding somewhere to try and catch us."

Rone pushed Erika away and held her at arm's length. "He may be in trouble."

She stiffened. "What kind of trouble?"

"Polakov's friend says that Potkin was in Moscow two days ago. Arrests were made. A spy ring was broken up. An organisation that the colonel was very interested in. Only I have a suspicion he doesn't know a thing about it.

Potkin and Grodin were there – at the arrest – I don't think they told the colonel."

Erika remained rigid. "Why do you suddenly care what happens to the colonel?"

"Because it could affect you. If he is arrested, what becomes of you?"

"I had hoped you were going to take care of me."

"You know I will. This other thing could complicate matters, though."

Erika turned her head. There was no longer a smile on her face. She got out of bed and walked across to the table. She lit a cigarette and stood smoking with quick nervous puffs. "Do we have enough money to leave Russia?" she asked.

"Almost."

"What does 'almost' mean? If we don't have enough, how short are we?"

"About five hundred roubles," Rone answered. "But if he's arrested they might take you as well."

Erika turned back to Rone. She stood silently smoking. "Something has changed, hasn't it, Yorgi? You sound different. It's like someone else is talking. A person I've never met."

"Nothing has changed." Rone got off the bed and moved across to her. "Before, there was no danger. Now there is. I'm concerned for you."

Erika avoided him. "Yorgi," she said nervously, "answer a question. Did your losing your room have anything to do with those men who were arrested?"

"Of course not."

"Answer another question."

"Certainly."

Erika looked straight into his eyes. Her lips were tight. "I want to leave Moscow right away. I will somehow get us the last five hundred roubles. You can have them later today, but I want to leave Russia the day after tomorrow."

"We can't."

"Why not?"

"Arrangements take longer than that."

"How much longer?"

"A week. Maybe two."

"You told me before that once we had the money it was only a matter of one or two days."

"Things have changed. It will take longer now."

"Nothing has changed." Erika's gaze was hard. "You have known this from the beginning, haven't you?"

"Of course not. Things have changed, that's all. My man has to be cautious."

Erika did not move. Her eyes were trained on Yorgi's. "You're one of them, aren't you?"

"Of whom?"

"One of the men they are after. One of the men they didn't catch yesterday."

"What are you talking about?"

Erika lowered her head and clutched her arms. Her lips parted but at first no words came out. When they did they were hardly audible. "I really think I knew all along. I'm sure I did." She laughed gently. "What was it I said about the colonel, that he'd go to great pains to protect his illusion? Perhaps he wasn't the only one." She went to the bureau and began dressing.

"I meant what I said. I'll take you out of the country, but we have to wait."

Erika continued dressing.

"Believe me, we will leave the country – it could be only a matter of weeks. If we're lucky, *days*."

"You don't understand me." She stood facing him, fully clothed. "I still love you, Yorgi – or whatever your name is – but that doesn't stop me from despising you. In time that love might weaken. I'll pray it does."

"It couldn't be helped," Rone said.

"Oh yes, it could. Very, very easily. You knew I loved you. You knew that, even more, I trusted you. For the first time in my adult life I truly trusted. I accepted you as I first met you – in not the most noble of occupations, because I didn't care what you did or who you were – you knew that. I asked only one thing, that my love, my trust not be destroyed. There was only one way you could have done that – and you found it. I thought that you were speaking the truth to me. It's that simple. I was sure I had found the one person who would speak the truth to me. I'm tired, Yorgi, so tired of living in a world full of lies. I want only honesty and love. Was that so much to ask?"

238

Rone went to Erika and took her by the arms. She looked into his face impassively.

"I'm sorry – it won't happen again."

Erika shook her head. "It's too late. Something has died, you see. You could say you loved me a thousand times and I couldn't believe you. They're only words, now – now that I know who you are, or at least *what* you are. I'm sure you're very good at what you do; you'd have to be to fool me. I've had a lot of experience with your fellow workers – Polakov, Kosnov, and others too. To be good in your field you have to lie. The truth must have no meaning at all – otherwise you are dead."

"If it had been up to me I would have told you from the beginning. There were others. I had superiors."

"And you'll have them in the future. There'll always be someone higher up or something lower down that makes you change your story. It has to be. That's the world you live in. I believe that you'd *like* to mean what you're saying, but it's too late for both of us. For me because – maybe because I've seen too much of it. I don't want it any more, not now. And for you because you are too good at the other. You have a bright future, Yorgi. In the end you'll make the Polakovs or Kosnovs or any others I've met take notice. You have all the trappings of a great, great spy. Take it from someone who has known the best."

"I'll get you out of here. I'll take you to America."

Erika broke into a broad smile and shook her head. "An American? You're an American?" She laughed. "It certainly isn't my day, is it?"

"I'll arrange for you to come to America," Rone repeated.

"Poor Yorgi, stop when you're ahead. The image is crumbling fast. Leave me some memories at least. Did it ever occur to you that to some people the United States is not Utopia? You see, I don't *like* America – I've seen the Americans in action. I learned first-hand."

"Would you rather stay in Russia?"

"I'm not much for the war and its memories. It happened and that was that. But I'm going to tell you a little story – just a page or two out of my long and eventful life. Not for sympathy or judgment, but just as a little comparison between Russia and America.

"When the war ended I was four years old. The Americans occupied the village I was living in. On the first day of the occupation a group of American soldiers came to our house and took my mother, my two older sisters and myself into the basement. I watched as they raped them for six days. Oh don't look so horrified, Yorgi, it's happened since time began. The Germans have done it, so have the French and English and every other nationality – America had to grow up sometime.

"Anyway, it was finally decided that the town was really in the Soviet zone, so the Americans moved out and the Russians moved in. Once again the soldiers came to the house and raped my sisters and my mother. They kept them there about as long as the Americans did. But there was a difference – and whether you know it or not, there can be a difference in rape. The Russians were kinder to us. After they finished all they had to offer was their soup. Not that they wouldn't give us other things if they had had them, but they didn't. Soup was the only thing they possessed that was of any value to us. So the Russian soldiers, the rapists, went for their meal of soup and instead of eating it themselves they brought it to us. When the Americans finished they threw candy and tins of food on the floor and walked off. So you see, my American Yorgi, don't ask me to make comparisons between the Russians and Americans."

Rone was not pleased with the story. "I'm sorry it happened."

"I could have lived without it myself." Erika started into the other room. "Don't worry, I won't betray you. You can stay here if you want and I'll get you whatever I can. I just don't want to see you any more."

"I'm afraid you'll have to."

"Ah, that sounds more like the man I don't know."

"Your bedroom is tapped."

Erika flushed.

"We were using Potkin's apartment. The receiving equipment is there. Whoever is involved probably listened in and found out the bug was on you and Kosnov."

"That's their problem." Erika started for the door. Rone grabbed her and spun her towards him. She tried

240

to get away. He shoved her into a chair.

"You can think or feel whatever you like. I'm sorry I hurt you – I'm even more sorry I disillusioned you. But you might as well get certain things clear. Polakov and probably all of my men are dead – all for the same reason. And it looks like you, the colonel and I might join them. Maybe you don't care what happens to me or yourself or Kosnov, but you owe a little something to Polakov. All of these lives have been lost because of someone else: the real enemy. He's played both ends against the middle. Kosnov didn't kill Polakov – he was betrayed by someone you called the Bellman. He sold out Polakov and he probably had a hand in what happened to my group. The chances are he'll be after the three of us now. Well, I want to get to him first – as a sort of a memorial to the men I lost. I don't think you have anything to lose by paying a little tribute to Polakov as well – from what I've heard he went out on a limb a couple of times for you."

"Yorgi, you're a fool. What is worse, you're a romantic fool. No one betrays anyone in the bizarre little game of yours. Your time runs out, and that's all there is to it. Polakov wasn't betrayed. He was taking risks, risks he shouldn't have taken, to get me money. He wanted to quit, to spend his remaining years with me. He thought up a way to make all the money either of us would need. It's what he wanted to do. He failed, he's dead."

"Get the colonel to stay," Rone insisted.

"Why? So that he can be killed too? At least he loves me."

"If he goes on that trip he'll be walking back to death. So will you. Whoever the Bellman is, he probably thinks you know his identity. With Kosnov gone, what becomes of you?"

"I finally die."

"Then go," Rone said defiantly. "Get the hell out of here and do whatever you want."

Erika stepped to the door. She opened it and turned back to look at him. "What is it you want?"

"Tell him about the Bellman. Tell him in the bedroom where the microphone is hidden," said Rone. "Say that a man approached you who once knew Polakov. Say that this man told you that Polakov had two contacts

CHAPTER THIRTY-THREE

NIKOLAYEV SQUARE

IN retrospect, the very nature of the raid obviated the colonel's participation. Kosnov's department was as large and modern an apparatus as any in the world. Men and equipment were no particular problem for him. The Third Department was capable of striking in ten, twenty, fifty different areas of Russia, let alone Moscow, simultaneously. The raid Rone witnessed was on a very small scale. He had seen only four cars and perhaps ten men. The area had not been cordoned off. There were no road blocks, no shots. Gunfire would draw attention. Whose attention? Kosnov's?

No, someone else was behind the raid, but Rone would have to make sure.

Erika arrived on Sunday. She had taken a circuitous route, changing underground trains three times and taking two buses. She was sure she hadn't been followed. She sat down without taking her coat off.

"The colonel and I have changed our bedroom," she announced.

"That's up to you." Rone stood at the window and looked down at the street. "What's the name of that little park down there?"

"Nikolayev Square."

"Tonight, when you are certain the colonel is in another part of the house, I want you to go into your old bedroom and pretend you are talking to him. I want the people who are listening at the receiver to think he is there. They must think you are talking to him. Say that the man telephoned while he was out. He has received the money and is happy. The man will leave a message for the colonel. It will be the first in a series. He will identify himself – or at least his code name. He will leave it in an envelope in the base of the statue in Nikolayev Square. You or the colonel should go there tomorrow after ten and get it. Say that the man said the code name will explain many things to the colonel. Do you have gloves?"

"Not with me," answered Erika.

"There are some in the bedroom bureau," Rone told her. "Put them on and take this envelope," he said, handing it to her. "Put it somewhere under the statue when you leave. Then tomorrow at ten-thirty come back to the statue, search for the letter, find it and go right back home. When you get there, burn it."

"What's inside?" asked Erika.

"Just one word: Wimpleton."

"What does it mean?"

"Nothing," answered Rone. "Nothing at all."

"Is that all?"

"That's all."

"Then I'll go."

"Do that," he told her.

Erika stared at him. The warmth of the past flickered slightly.

"When do you want me to return?" she asked.

"You don't have to."

"And you?"

"I'll be all right. The apartment will be vacant by the time your mother-in-law returns."

Erika looked down at the letter in her hand. She reached into her purse, took out a scrap of paper and scribbled something on it. She handed it to Rone with some money. "Take this. I don't know how far the money will get you, but that address might help. It was Polakov's escape route. He made me memorise it. I don't know where it leads or who is concerned. All I know is that he told me to use it if everything else failed."

"But everything has failed. Why give it to me?"

"I still have the colonel. You have nothing." She turned and walked from the room.

As she was leaving, Rone said to her, "Try to have the conversation between ten and eleven tonight."

He stood at the window and watched Erika walk into the park. She went to the statue and sat on the base, as if to adjust her shoe. Rone saw her slip the envelope into a crevice. She looked up in his direction and left. He took up his vigil at the window just before ten o'clock that evening. There were no lights in the park. The sky was clear. A three-quarter moon shone. Rone checked his watch just before eleven. They should know by now. When he looked at the time again it was two A.M. No one had come.

"Maybe they're thinking it over," Rone told himself. At four o'clock he grew edgy. It was only an hour and a half until dawn. He doubted if they would appear in daylight. If they didn't, it was Kosnov after all. At a quarter to five Rone spotted a figure standing at the far side of the square. He seemed to appear out of nowhere. The man ambled casually towards the statue. For a short time the stone figure blocked Rone's view. The man came into sight again. He was examining the structure. There was something familiar about him, either his walk or his bearing. Rone couldn't place it. Even from a distance he appeared too tall for Potkin. It might be Grodin. It wasn't Kosnov. The man slowly circled the statue. He stopped from time to time and leaned closer, then moved on. He finally made his way around to Rone's side. Rone saw that he had a small pocket flashlight. The tiny beam skipped over the weathered stone and zigzagged its way down to the base. It illuminated the crevice and stopped. The light was switched off and the figure kneeled down. It rose again and walked back to the far end of the park. Rone saw the silhouette of a car, its lights off, draw up slowly beside the figure. The man got into the back seat. There was a flash of dark-red light from the rear-door window. Rone knew they must be photographing the letter with an infrared bulb. The car remained there for almost five minutes. Fingerprints, Rone speculated. Finally, the unknown man left the car and walked back to the statue. He replaced the letter, returned to the vehicle and drove off.

Rone slept until ten in the morning. He got out of bed, made himself some coffee and went to the window. At ten-thirty Erika arrived at the statue, circled around it, supposedly looking for the letter, and finally discovered it. Rone was pleased with her acting. He watched her trim figure leave the park, then went back to bed.

CHAPTER THIRTY-FOUR

THE EMBRYOLOGISTS

RONE was awakened by a banging on the door. He looked at his watch. It was three in the afternoon. He walked cautiously across the front room. He moved closer to the door.

"Yorgi," boomed Ward's voice. "Open the goddamn door."

"I had one hell of a time finding you," he told Rone once he was inside.

"How did you?"

Ward grinned. "I just followed Nephew Yorgi's piece of ass, that's all. She led me one hell of a chase, too, what with her getting off and on underground trains and buses, but I finally made it."

"How did you know they hadn't caught me?"

"I was on the street the night you tried to save B.A. I wanted to get some more heroin out of the apartment before you had your confession. I noticed some guys hanging around, so I swung around the long way. That's when I saw you hijack the car. Pretty neat trick, Nephew, pretty neat indeed."

"They picked up Janis," Rone told him.

"How the hell did they find out?" Ward asked without much concern.

"Your friend Potkin," Rone announced coldly. "I saw him drive by with Grodin. If you'd done what I suggested all of this might have been avoided."

"Guess you're right, but the two of us are awfully rich right now. Those three bodies were worth almost four hundred thousand."

"How the hell can you talk about money?"

"That's what we were in it for," Ward said innocently.

"As I remember we got half on account and half on delivery."

"Don't worry, we'll deliver," Ward said.

"For Christ's sake, be practical. We have this place for another five days and then we're out on the street.

246

How can we work, let alone stay alive, if we don't have a place?"

"But we *do* have one," said Ward, grinning, "and a damned good one. Come on, I'll show you."

"How did you arrange that?"

"Through the French. But it was your idea, Nephew Yorgi. You've been right more often than me, so I decided to take your advice. We were going to move the day the roof fell in. Guess my timing was just a little bit off. Say, this isn't a bad layout either." Ward began looking about the apartment. "Whose is it?"

"Kosnov's mother's," said Rone. "Erika arranged it."

"You better leave Erika a note so that she doesn't get all worked up. Then let's cut out of here."

"That isn't necessary. I can get hold of her."

"Don't get the little lady upset. We may need her."

Rone scribbled out a fast letter to Erika as Ward watched. They left the apartment and went by underground into the University district. Ward led him into a modern industrial building and up a flight of stairs. He took out a key and opened the door to a modern chemistry laboratory.

"Know anything about science?" asked Ward.

"Not too much."

"Better learn pretty quick, 'cause that's what we are now." Ward handed Rone new identity papers. "How's your French?"

"Terrible."

"Well, we'll have to get by on mine. As you can see from the passports and identification cards, we're exchange embryologists."

"How did you manage this?" asked Rone.

"Uncle Morris set it up. I would have told you sooner, but you were so damn cocky I didn't want to give you the satisfaction. As long as I'm in a complimentary frame of mind, let me throw another one your way. That was a pretty nifty little gimmick of yours."

"What was?"

"Having Erika give that cock-and-bull story about Polakov's second contact."

"How did you know about that?"

"Take a look." Ward led Rone into a small bedroom off the laboratory. He pulled open a dresser drawer and took out a small receiving set. It was one of B.A.'s emergency radios which had been in Potkin's apartment. "B.A. brought it over here the morning of that bad day. She worked it so we could pick up Kosnov's from here. I heard the whole thing last night. Figured you had to be behind anything as wild as that."

"I thought it might take some pressure off," Rone admitted.

"Off who?"

"Kosnov."

"Explain yourself, Nephew Yorgi."

"It wasn't Kosnov who raided the apartment. It was Grodin and Bresnavitch and Potkin."

"And why would they want to do this without the colonel knowing?"

"To discredit him. Ostensibly, Bresnavitch doesn't want the investigation. Neither do the other Kremlin bigwigs. What better way to boot Kosnov out of his job? What better way to put in Grodin, and whitewash over the whole thing?"

"I don't know now, Nephew, I don't know. It seems like the long way through the woods. Why don't they just kill Kosnov and be done with it?"

"They probably will when they can find the way."

"You're beating me at my own game. I thought I was the only one who talked riddles."

"It isn't easy to kill Kosnov. First of all he's well guarded."

"Since when?" asked Ward.

"Since that night he had dinner at Bresnavitch's. He suspects something. He has two men with him all the time. His own men."

"How did he manage that?"

"Flew them in from somewhere. He also has two emergency teams on constant standby. Erika overheard him talking in the dining room, giving orders to the group. She thinks Grodin doesn't know anything about this – or maybe he does. I have no way of telling. To kill him you would have to catch him without his two men and somehow cut off communications with those goon squads. That will be a nice trick to begin with. Second, you can't bump off the head of one of Russia's largest intelligence organisations without there being a little ruckus. What excuse can they use?"

"You can always find an excuse," Ward said glumly. "It's finding a *method* that might be tricky. Are you sure about this new security set-up?"

"Everything Erika has told me up to now has been accurate. I believe her."

"Well, it looks like we got a little revolution going within the revolution, but that still doesn't convince me Grodin raided our apartment."

"I saw him."

"This Grodin fellow is treacherous. Wouldn't trust him around the henhouse. Well, what do you say we get going?"

"To where?" asked Rone.

"Out to celebrate. I think this information of yours deserves some real spending. What say we take in the opera?"

"Are you mad?" Rone replied in disbelief. "Grodin and Potkin probably know our faces. A dozen of their men must as well. They're looking for us right now."

"I suppose you think we should pack up our bags and skedaddle back West?"

"We should damn well consider it."

"And let all that money slip through our hands?"

"We'll get enough."

"I want the full cheque."

"It won't do us any good if we can't spend it."

"We'll live to spend it," Ward said stubbornly.

"Then I suppose you've worked out how the two of us are going to do what five could not. On top of that, no one was looking for the six."

"Singing saints," Ward grinned. "I never knew you was such a worry wart, Nephew Yorgi."

Rone was irritated. "Then you tell me how we find Polakov's man and the letter."

"I may do just that."

"You know who he is?"

"I'm not sure of *that*, but there's a pretty good chance we're going to have that letter in our hot little fists before very long – maybe within two weeks, maybe *sooner*."

"How?" Rone was bewildered.

"Just 'cause you was lucky, shacking up the last two weeks, doesn't mean the whole world closed down. Some of us early birds was out pecking behind the barn."

"But how?"

Ward shook his head and winked. "Uh, uh, Nephew. Little by little. The suspense is good for your soul. When I'm sure, I'll tell you. Now you just gather your bones into the bath and splash about a bit. I'll race out and see if I can scare up some opera tickets."

"I'd rather know now," Rone persisted.

"Yorgi boy, you gotta learn to take some things on faith."

"As I remember I *took* a lot of things on faith. Three men are probably dead because of it."

"Occupational hazards."

"Hazards my ass," snapped Rone.

"If you think you're going to ruffle my feathers with all this carrying on then think again, Nephew. I told you I've made contact to get the letter and I have. Now if that won't do you and yours and you want to trundle on back West, you've got my blessings, except that I could use an extra hand. If you stay, you gotta act civilised. You gotta spread your wings a little. We've got five or six days to wait until we hear about that little piece of paper, and I don't intend to spend it cooped up in here. That kind of thing could drive a man neurotic. I didn't travel ten thousand miles only to look at your face. So just go into that bathroom there and get yourself washed, shined and polished. You wouldn't want to miss all that pretty singing, would you?"

During the interval they mingled freely. Rone was uneasy. Ward seemed to be having the time of his life, but during the second act Rone noticed a change. Ward was sitting slumped in his seat looking down into his palms. His cheeks were sucked in and from time to time he bit his lower lip. He gave only token applause at the curtain calls.

"When will you be seeing the girl again?" he asked Rone as they walked home.

"I don't know."

"Can you make it soon?"

"I don't know," Rone repeated.

"I'd like it to be tomorrow. We may need her."

"Erika and I have split up."

Ward frowned. "How bad?"

"It's over."

"No way to patch things up?"

"No."

"I see. Well, maybe it's for the best. By the way, were there any other reports on that last day?"

Rone had not yet told him about Uncle Morris' visit. "No," he answered, "there was no more information."

They both remained silent until they were in front of the laboratory.

"I got a little calculating to do," said Ward. "Feel like walking some more?"

"Not really," answered Rone.

"See you in the morning then."

CHAPTER THIRTY-FIVE

THE SACRIFICE

"TODAY may be the the day," Ward announced to Rone four mornings later.

"For the letter?"

"Could be. Meet me at the Ararat Restaurant at 4 Neglinnaya Street at five-thirty sharp."

Ward waited until Rone left. He went to the drawer, took out a pair of rough leather gloves and pushed a gun into his belt.

Erika watched the fashion show at the GUM store until eleven-twenty. She was at the shoe counter exactly at the half hour.

"I'm Yorgi's friend," Ward said, inspecting a pair of slippers next to her.

"What has happened to him?" she asked calmly.

"He was picked up this morning."

"By whom?"

"We think it was your husband."

"Oh no, dear God, no."

"We might still be able to do something," he said without looking at her. "Wait ten minutes, then walk right along Gorki Street for three intersections. Take another right. In the middle of the block is an alley. Go in and wait at the end."

Erika found the alley without trouble. She walked up the brick paving stones and waited in the doorway at the end. She leaned back against it as footsteps approached. The sound was fast and choppy. They ran quickly, then stopped, started again and once again stopped. There was a pause, then they started directly for her.

Erika looked up into the face of a dour Chinese.

"Where did he—" was all he uttered before falling forward with Ward's knife in his back.

"This way," Ward commanded, pushing Erika through the door. Ward pulled her quickly through the hallway and out onto the street. He opened a car door, shoved her in and slid in beside her.

"Can we go to your mother-in-law's apartment?" he asked as they started off up the street.

"Can't we talk here?"

"Look, little lady, if the colonel finds out about you and Yorgi, I think Moscow might be rather uncomfortable for you. We've got a lot of figuring to do. A car isn't the place. Now what about that apartment?"

"All right," said Erika uneasily.

Erika sat stiffly in the living room. Ward handed her a small bundle of clothing.

"These were Yorgi's," he told her. "I thought you might want them."

"How was he caught?" she asked without emotion.

"We don't know. He was just picked up off the street."

"And how much does the colonel know?"

"He knows that you and Yorgi used this apartment."

Erika stood up and paced the room, hugging her arms close to her. She lit a cigarette and looked out of the window. Her back was to Ward as he slipped on the gloves. When she turned back towards him a fist drove into her face.

Ward carried her into the bedroom and tossed her on the bed. He ripped off her dress and underclothes. When Erika regained consciousness she saw him standing naked beside her. She tried to fight. She dug her nails into his back and drew blood. Ward knocked her unconscious again and raped her. After he had finished he raised the motionless body into a sitting position. He began beating her around the face and shoulders. He punched her arms and body and legs. Blood covered her face and torso. Then he strangled her.

Ward took off the gloves and tossed them on the floor. He bathed, dried himself, placed a linen towel on his back to stop the bleeding and dressed. He undid the bundle of clothing, neatly folded each piece and placed it in the dresser drawer. He slipped a card into her purse. On it was written "Yorgi" and an address.

He left the apartment and drove to the Leningradskaya Hotel. He gave the car to an attendant and began walking along Kalanchovskaya Street. He stopped to admire a baby in a pram. He pinched it on the cheeks, doffed his hat to the nurse and continued, sprightly, on his way. He began to whistle softly to himself.

253

CHAPTER THIRTY-SIX

SHADOWS FROM GETHSEMANE

"HEY there, Nephew Yorgi," Ward shouted from a rear table as Rone entered the Ararat Restaurant. "Order and eat up. This looks like our lucky night." Ward beamed a viperous smile.

"The letter?" asked Rone.

"The letter, little nephew, the letter," Ward confirmed. "There's every chance we'll have it before morning – and guess what else?"

"What?"

"I got us tickets for the ballet tonight."

The Bolshoi Ballet's performance of *Swan Lake* was captivating. There were times when Rone almost relaxed, almost forgot his predicament. The *première danseuse* moved with perfection; her grace was unparalleled. From time to time Rone glanced at Ward. His companion was completely transfixed by the performance. Every now and then he would nudge Rone with his elbow and motion to the stage with approval. "If you live to be a hundred," he whispered, "you may never see anything like this again."

During the interval they pushed through the crowded foyer. "Wait here," said Ward. "I have to make a call."

When he returned he slapped Rone on the back. "Get cutting, Nephew," he said. "We're about to become rich."

They walked rapidly through the overcast night.

"Will we get the man as well as the letter?" asked Rone.

"I doubt it, Had to move heaven and Texas just to wrangle the paper itself." He stopped abruptly and grabbed Rone by the arm. "It's a funny thing," he began softly, "but suddenly I miss the others. I wish to Christ they were alive right now."

"You'd have to split the money," Rone reminded him coldly.

"The money be damned. They were a good lot. They should be in on this."

"Sentiment doesn't become you."

"Well I am sorry and I ain't ashamed to admit it. Especially 'bout that little girl of yours."

"Can't you keep that mouth of yours shut?"

"Sure thing."

They were at a corner two blocks from the laboratory when Ward stopped. "You go on ahead and start packing us up. Just take enough to fill one grip. Leave everything else there."

"And where are you going?"

"To pick up the goods."

"The letter?"

"Yep. I'd ask you along, but my friend is a little jittery. I'll be back in fifteen minutes – then we split from Moscow." He slapped Rone on the back and started off down the side street.

Rone watched him diminish into the shadows. Ward walked with a rolling gait. As the figure grew smaller Rone recognised it. It was the same hunched form he had seen run across the square and up the church steps into Gethsemane; the same grey figure that had searched for the letter at the base of the statue in Nikolayev Square. Ward was the man with the flashlight.

CHAPTER THIRTY-SEVEN

CONFRONTATIONS

RONE hurried through the darkened laboratory, rushed into the bedroom at the back, flicked on the light and went to the auxiliary receiving set. He snapped on the power and turned up the volume. Static crackled. He checked the tubes and wiring. They were operational. He traced the aerial up the wall to the small cut in the ceiling. It was loose. Rone gave a slight pull. The wire fell into his hands. The ends had not been frayed. The line had never been attached. The set could not have picked up the conversations in Kosnov's bedroom or anywhere else. There was only one place they could have been overheard.

Rone knew that Ward had been in Potkin's apartment after the raid. It was he who had listened to Erika's make-believe conversation with the colonel informing him of still another Polakov contact. It was Ward who had gone to the statue to find the message, and it was Ward who had read the word "Wimpleton." He had never bothered to follow Erika to the apartment, because he knew where Rone was all the time. The only reason he came was to check on the handwriting. Ward had insisted that Rone leave a note for Erika under the pretext they might need her in the future. Once he had seen both notes had been written by Rone he blithely announced that he knew Rone was behind the stunt because he overheard it on the auxiliary receiver. He took Rone back to the laboratory to prove it.

Rone opened the closet and reached up on the top shelf. The Luger was gone. He went to the desk and reached into the cubbyhole. There was no money. Ward would be back in ten minutes. Rone quickly threw a change of clothes into the grip, snapped off the light and started out through the laboratory. He reached the street door and turned the knob. It was locked. He jiggled it and searched through his pocket for a key.

"You seem in a hurry," said a voice in the darkness.

Rone wheeled around as the lights snapped on. A man was on each of his arms. They wrenched them behind him and snapped his wrists into handcuffs. They returned to the centre of the room. They fitted the description Erika had given him of Kosnov's bodyguards. The tall blond one boosted himself onto the lab table and sat there with his legs swinging. The second, the bald Eurasian with the jet-black moustache and goatee, wore a square blue skullcap with elaborate white and red embroidery. He leaned cross-armed against the wall.

Colonel Kosnov stood stiffly in the middle of the room. Beside him sat a gaunt, nervous man.

"That's him," he told Kosnov, raising a limp-wristed arm in Rone's direction. "He was on the street today with your wife. He forced her into a car."

"You are sure?" Kosnov asked.

"That is him."

Kosnov motioned and the Eurasian led the man from the room. The colonel remained rigid as he studied Rone. "So this is Yorgi? How long have you known my wife?" The colonel slowly slipped on the blood-stained gloves.

"Your wife?" answered Rone. "I have no idea who you are, let alone your wife. What is all this about? What right do you have to do this to me?"

Kosnov looked down into his gloved hands and opened and closed his fists. "How long has it been going on?"

"What are you talking about? Why are you here?"

"Had she told you it was over?" Kosnov was walking slowly towards him, still staring into his hands. "Had she taunted you? Debased you?" He stopped in front of Rone and locked his arms behind his back. He jutted out his chin, but still he could not look up. "Did she force you to grovel?"

Before Rone could answer the fist smashed into his stomach. He dropped to his knees gasping for air as the boot crashed into the side of his face.

"It doesn't really matter," said Kosnov, stepping back. "She had a way of destruction about her. If you hadn't done it I suppose someone else would have – in the end it might have been me."

The colonel knelt down and jerked Rone's head up by

the hair. He spoke gently. "You see, my unfortunate friend, ultimately we must all play the dupe. Roles are cast and sides are chosen, masks and mantles donned, and logic abandoned. Emotion prevails. You are the lover; I the cuckold. You the assassin and I the avenger. I must hate and destroy you. Nothing will give me greater satisfaction."

The boot drove into Rone's face again, spinning him over on the floor. The blond bodyguard jumped down and lifted Rone to his feet. He motioned to Kosnov to look above the lab table. A small overhead crane hung from an iron rail on the ceiling. Kosnov nodded his approval.

The two bodyguards lifted Rone onto the table face down. He could hear the steel wire above him. He felt the hook lodge under his handcuffs. Rone tensed his arms and shoulders as the crane began to lift him upwards. He felt his body rise in space and slowly revolve. He was lowered into a sitting position. The line was kept too taut for him to sit upright. He remained leaning forward.

"It's a shame you didn't have this little gadget at the apartment," said Kosnov. "Shall we continue?"

A fist crashed into his face, splitting his nose and tearing his gums. The force of the blow snapped his head into the metal chain at his back. He could feel blood trickling down his neck and under his collar.

Another blow jabbed his cheek and another into his jaw. He batted his eyes to keep them in focus. The pain of the punches and the ache of his suspended shoulder muscles was starting to mount. He prayed for unconsciousness.

"Little by little I will mangle your body until it looks like hers did. I will not leave a bone unbroken – not one."

Kosnov cocked his arm back and shot it forward into Rone's Adam's apple. He felt the air rush out of him again and he began to suffocate. Nausea rose, his eyes and chest burned, tears streaked down his face as a fist jolted into his lips and teeth. A moment later Kosnov's knuckles slammed into his right eye. Rone fought for breath. He felt his eye swell shut. He was wet with perspiration and blood. His body burned with pain.

A stinging ache tore through his ribs and surged into his fingers and toes.

"Lower him," shouted Kosnov. "Lower him so we can kick his insides out through his ears."

Rone hardly felt falling on the floor or Kosnov's foot thundering into his stomach. Consciousness was slipping. He wondered why it took so long. He lay on his side, his head resting on the floor. He could see Kosnov's feet only inches away. He saw the right foot move back. He knew it would catch him full in the mouth.

He tried to scream, but nothing came. The foot shot towards him. He jerked his head; it grazed by. Once again he tried to talk, to beg, to motion. He couldn't. He knew that he could not take much more. He realised that soon he would be dying. He cursed his endurance, his stamina. What did it take to knock him into senselessness? Why must he witness his own execution?

The heel stomped down on the side of his face. He heard something crack or shatter, but he felt nothing. This was the first sign, the numbness, the painlessness was beginning to take hold – or was it death? With his open eye Rone could see the colonel's foot swing back again, farther than before. He was measuring, aiming. This might do it, Rone thought to himself. Then he heard the voice.

"I think that's just about all the exercise you need, colonel." Kosnov spun around. The tall blond man slid off the table to his feet and grabbed for his gun. Rone strained his head backwards and squinted through his bloodied eye. Ward was walking slowly towards them with his arms at his side.

"I don't know what the world is coming to. I stroll down the street for a breath of air and you fellows come running in here and beat my roomie half to death."

"Stay where you are," warned Kosnov.

"Now why don't you fellows just apologise, help my friend to his feet and get your asses out of here?" said Ward without stopping.

Kosnov stepped back and drew his automatic. He fired twice. Ward continued walking. He fired again. Ward shook his head and smiled. The colonel looked down at his gun as a shot rang out behind him. Rone brought his head forward. The blond bodyguard slumped forward dead. He looked over to the expressionless Eurasian. Slight traces of smoke rose from the pistol in his hand.

Kosnov took another step backwards. "Who are you?" he demanded.

"An old fan of yours. A very old fan."

Kosnov raced to the door. It was locked. He pounded on it and shouted for his men. No one answered. He shouted again.

"Won't do any good, colonel. I sent them all home."

"Grodin? Grodin is behind this, isn't he?" Kosnov demanded venomously.

"This is just between you and me."

"Why?"

Rone had slowly eased himself into a sitting position. He was dizzy and weak. He had to squint to see. The numbness was leaving. Spasms of pain were mounting. He saw the colonel staring quizzically at Ward.

"I know you, don't I?" he said almost pleasantly.

"Our paths might have crossed," answered Ward.

"I would assume there is no way of reaching an agreement with you?" Kosnov asked, gaining more composure.

"Not a chance."

Kosnov nodded to himself. "You went to great lengths. Was it necessary to involve the girl?"

"You're a hard man to get alone. You're too cautious. I needed you a little bit off balance."

"The rape and murder of a man's wife often has just that effect."

"I was hoping it would."

The colonel relaxed. He threw away his gun and looked down at Rone and the dead bodyguard. "And which one of these candidates will be the lover I fought to the death?"

"Take your pick."

"Who did the clothes in the apartment belong to?"

"The dead one," answered Ward.

"Then ultimately I am to be assassinated with his gun?"

"Ultimately," Ward agreed, "but that might be a while in coming. You see, colonel, you and I have a lot of grievances to talk over, a lot of old corpses to dig up and chat about. We had a lot of mutual friends – once. I don't suppose you remember Vedder?"

"The Pole?"

"That's one of them. Then there was Gustav Zeiff, and Marcel Mara. Hallaren, the British agent you interviewed. It was two weeks for him, wasn't it?"

Kosnov frowned and pinched his lips between his thumb and forefinger. He closed his eyes and listened.

"It's an endless list, colonel old buddy. Da Silva, Gottlieb, Korda, Julian and of course your latest piece of handiwork, Polakov."

"I know you from somewhere."

Ward's face tightened into a scowl. He picked up the blond bodyguard's gun. "I know everything you did to every one of those men. I've tried to imagine the pain, the torment you put each one through. If it is possible for one man to make retribution for the misery of many it will happen now."

Ward fired. Kosnov's left knee shattered back under him and he plummeted forward onto the floor.

"That's how you began with Korda, if I'm not mistaken," said Ward.

Rone's head was spinning. His body throbbed and burned. His pain was intolerable. His breath came hard. He tried to clutch to consciousness. He tried to see. He tried to listen. Ward was still visible to him. He stood above the writhing form of Kosnov.

"Remember Zeiff?" he heard Ward say. "Remember how you forced acid down his throat? Not enough to kill him, but enough to make him scream. You like to make people scream, colonel. Well, I've got a little something for you."

Rone slipped sideways to the floor. The pain and throbbing seemed to disappear. He had the feeling of coolness, of peace, of rest. He could faintly remember the sensation of being lifted by his shoulder and legs. He thought he remembered Kosnov crying. "No, no, it isn't! It can't be!" He half knew he was being taken down a flight of stairs. Then he heard the scream. He remembered that. It was Kosnov's scream. Even in his stupor it was the most terrifying sound he had ever heard.

CHAPTER THIRTY-EIGHT

SANCTUARY

RONE was lying in the back seat of the car when he regained consciousness. One eye was swollen shut. Through the other he could see the back of a bald head and skullcap – the driver. The car swerved. Rone fell forward onto the body of Kosnov. Little was left of the face. The Eurasian did not turn around as Rone pushed himself back onto the seat. He tried to muster his strength. He opened and closed his hands. They were weak. His arms felt limp.

He reached down and searched Kosnov's clothes. He jerked his hand back as the Eurasian turned and glanced at him.

"Is there much pain?" he asked impassively.

"I'll get by," answered Rone.

"Someone will look after you when we get there," he told him over his shoulder.

Rone reached down and continued searching Kosnov. What he had hoped for was not there. The Eurasian's gun had not been planted on the corpse. He continued going through the clothing.

The car came to a stop. The back door opened and two men pulled out Kosnov's body. Rone tried to raise himself up.

"Just stay where you are," Ward told him, sticking his head into the car. "The less you see, Nephew, the better off you'll be." He slammed the door. "Go on ahead with him," he told the Eurasian.

They had driven several minutes before Rone managed to sit up in the seat. He took long, deep breaths. The Eurasian kept his eyes on the road. Rone could see they were in the area of Nikolayev Square heading towards the Kremlin.

Rone slipped off his belt and held it in his lap. He exercised his fingers and rubbed his arms to increase the circulation. He tried to watch both the road and the driver with his one open eye. He took short breaths to ease the pain in his ribs and side. They were nearing a construction site. Rone knew exactly where he was now.

He reached down and tied a knot in the belt. He pulled it as taut as he could. The effort weakened him. He slid towards the door until he was directly behind the driver. He lunged forward, looped the belt over the Eurasian's head, and jerked it back against his neck. Rone pushed his feet against the back of the seat and pulled the belt with all his strength. The driver's head snapped back. His hands left the wheel and reached for the belt. Rone continued pulling. The car ran off the road and down along a culvert. Rone was thrown against the door as it tipped over.

The Eurasian was motionless. Rone reached over the front seat and took his gun. The car was on its side. He stood up and opened the door. Slowly he eased himself out of the car and started running as best he could into the construction site.

He slid down an excavation and stumbled along a water-filled ditch. He stopped and listened. There was no sound. He splashed forward until he reached a wooden ladder, arduously clambered up and crawled over a pile of fresh earth. He lay prone, twisted his body around and peered over the top towards the boulevard. He could see dark forms. Another car had stopped on the road.

Rone scrambled down the embankment. He made his way through the cement skeleton of a new building, crossed an unpaved road and staggered behind a wooden construction shack. His legs were giving out. His breath came in short, painful gasps. His nose had begun to bleed, and a cut on his neck had opened. He clung to a wooden window-sill for balance. He looked around. He saw the outline of several large gravel vans through the darkness. He started unsteadily for them. One leg buckled, toppling him over. He picked himself up and forced his body forward. He fell twice more before he reached them. He hid between two vehicles. He slid himself along a fender and reached up to the handle of the cab door. He raised himself onto the narrow running board. His arms were heavy with pain as he pulled himself over the cab. He knew he had little strength or consciousnss left. He fell into the open van body, landing face first in a pile of moist clay and dirt.

He stopped to listen. He heard a voice calling in the night. It was far away from him now. He burrowed weakly into the dirt, scooping it over his arms and legs. Then he collapsed.

Wet mud showered down over him. Rone wiped his face clean and looked up into the dangling jaws of a dirt scoop. It swung away. His body was almost completely buried. He dug his hands free and cleared breathing space between his face and the side of the van. He heard the crane swing back over him and the bucket door squeak open. Once again mud thundered down.

He heard shouts. The Diesel engine of the van whined to a start. The van lumbered forward and turned onto a dirt road. Rone knew where he was going now. He had passed the vans on his walks. He dug himself free and crawled to the opposite side of the van. He raised himself upright. The van turned again. They were on the pavement. It wouldn't be far. Just one more turn. Rone tried twice to pull himself onto the edge. The third time he made it. The van turned. He fell to the street, got up and began running towards the gates. Anyone would do. He passed the startled guard, climbed the steps to the front door, burst into the embassy and once again collapsed.

The room was cheerful. Rone sat up in bed sipping the rich Italian coffee.

"How long did I sleep?" he asked.

Amadeo Grano, vice-consul, moved one leg over the other, brushed a piece of lint from his black pinstripe, hooked his thumbs in his vest pocket and sat back in the winged chair.

"The better part of two days," he answered in Oxford English. "How do you feel?"

"Stiff."

"The doctors say it is nothing serious. If you consider two cracked ribs and a fractured cheekbone trivia, then you can agree with them."

264

"Did you contact the American Embassy?"

"The day you arrived," answered Grano. "You were barely conscious. Perhaps the information you gave us was, shall we say, confused?"

Rone paused. "What did the embassy say?"

"They have never heard of a Charles Rone."

"Well, have them contact the United States Navy."

"They have apparently contacted everyone they feel obliged to. There never was a Charles Rone in the Navy, nor do they have a record of issuing such a person a passport."

"The idiots," Rone snapped.

"I suggested that they send someone over to talk to you. They were rather curt in their refusal."

"When can I go over there?"

"Once you leave us you are free to go wherever you like, but I doubt if the Americans will be of much help. They maintain that Charles Rone does not exist. From their attitude I must infer that you are an impostor – or at least not an American."

"You hear my English – does that sound counterfeit?"

Grano stood up and brushed his fingertips quickly along his lapels. "While you were delirious you spoke in Russian," he told Rone as he began pacing the room. "What is more, you were carrying a French passport. We have consulted the French Embassy and they tell us that even though the passport itself is authentic, one was never issued with the name or number yours bears."

Grano stopped at the foot of the bed and turned towards Rone. He slapped his hands against his jacket pockets and then held them, palms up, as he spoke. "My dear friend, what am I to say? We even spoke with the British. No one seems to claim you. In fact, it is my impression that the Americans and British have gone out of their way to ignore you, but then again I have a tendency for the melodramatic. And we here also have a problem."

Rone looked up at him.

"Try to understand the condition in Moscow. We are never sure. Asylum is the constant ruse of the infiltrator. It has been used from time immemorial."

"What you're saying," Rone interrupted, "is that you want me to go."

"My dear friend," Grano said, returning to the chair and crossing his legs. "You create an embarrassment. I do not know who you are or what it is you have to say, but I am aware that no one wants to listen. At least not in Moscow."

"Is that what the American Embassy said?"

"The American Embassy said nothing; it is my interpretation of their silence you are hearing. If you are not an impostor, and there is every indication you are, then obviously you represent something they would rather forget. That is the way of diplomacy. Many things must be expendable to maintain one's façade. I have a feeling you have been placed in that category."

"If you give me my things I'll go."

"To where?"

"Obviously not to the British or American embassies."

"We believe certain elements in Moscow are looking for you."

"I wouldn't be surprised."

"Were you connected with the Kosnov murder?"

"Never heard of the man. Just give me my clothes and I'll go."

"They are in the cupboard. We had them cleaned."

Grano sat calmly in his chair lacing his fingers as Rone got out of bed and walked unsteadily across the room. He watched him begin dressing.

"You realise," said Grano, "that you will never make it out of Moscow."

"Maybe I like it here." Rone's shoulders and arms were stiff. His right knee bent with difficulty.

"Perhaps if you gave me the information, I could pass it on to the Americans."

Rone turned towards him.

"It would save everyone embarrassment," Grano pointed out.

"Which embassy suggested that?"

"None. It is a thought I have come up with completely on my own."

"Forget it." Rone eased himself into a chair and painfully bent down to put on his shoes. A new pair had been provided.

"If you are who I think you are, then bravery and integrity should come second to practicality. The facts are simple. You will never make it through Moscow. Someone is obviously looking for you. We know it, you know it and three other embassies know it. They will do nothing. You are the sacrificial calf for their pretensions. If you like, we will work a deal with you."

"And what do I get out of it?"

"Delivery to the West."

"Why?"

"My country is not as obsessed with the ridiculous war of information and deceit as are many others. At the same time we are not unaware of its importance. We, like the others, have a certain degree of prestige we prefer to maintain in such matters. Also our position with the Russians is not so sensitive as those of certain of our neighbours and so-called allies. We can gamble. I am willing to gamble with you. Tell me who you are and what it is you wanted to relay to the Americans and we will get you out of Moscow and into the West."

Rone was fully clothed. "What if I'm an impostor? What if I'm not, but don't know anything?"

"That is the risk we take. It will not be the first time I have played the fool."

Rone searched through his pockets. They were empty. Grano pointed to a dresser drawer. Rone opened it and found his personal possessions.

"I'll save you the embarrassment of my being taken," he told the Italian. "I know nothing."

"We could also arrange for money," Grano added.

Rone went through his things. He flattened out a slip of crumpled paper. On it was the address Erika had given him.

"Yes," Grano said, "a sizable amount of money could be arranged."

"I'm a French embryologist," Rone told him. "How much is that worth to you?"

"And how much is your own life worth to you?"

"I'll be going now," Rone told him. "Which way out?"

Grano stood up and slapped his arms against his sides. "Wait until dark. We don't want bloodstains on our marble. We can get you a few streets away. In the meantime, think about what I have said."

SECTION SIX

CHAPTER THIRTY-NINE

THE ESCAPE ROUTE

THE waiter paid no attention to him. Nor did the students at the adjoining table. All were watching the exotic girl with black braided hair mimic her internal-medicine instructor. Rone also smiled. He could not tell if she was Chinese or Mongolian. He finished his dish of sweet cream and sipped the glass of hot tea.

Rone looked at the address and instructions again. Erika had told him this was Polakov's escape route. Rone wondered why Polakov had never used it. Maybe he had been caught before he could. Rone could not question it. It was his only chance. Ward and the others would be looking for him. As Grano had warned him, the others were Russians.

The Oriental girl's impersonations had put the next table into hysterics. Rone paid his bill and trudged slowly out to the street. He did not have far to go.

The shadows of the University buildings loomed ahead of him. The stiffness was leaving. He still ached, but he could walk with more authority. He turned the corner and saw the building described in the instructions. The main structure went up ten stories. Two wings spread from either side. In the middle was the passageway.

Rone walked through and came out into a courtyard. He followed the diagonal path until he reached the iron fence. He turned in at the third gate, eased himself down the five steps, passed the infirmary entrance and went to the back of the building. He knocked on the grey metal door three times. He waited exactly a minute and knocked three more times. He heard footsteps approach from within, then stop. Another minute elapsed. He knocked again. The footsteps began once more. Rone automatically put his hand in his pocket and gripped the gun.

The door slowly swung open. The figure of a large man was outlined in the entranceway.

"I was told you could help me," said Rone.

"Who told you?" asked the figure in perfect Russian.

:"A friend of Polakov's." Rone could see two more figures standing farther down the hallway.

"You knew him?"

"I knew his wife."

"Come in."

The door closed behind him and the lights snapped on.

"We have been waiting for you, Yorgi," said the Kitai, revealing his two metal front teeth.

Charles Rone did not hesitate. He pulled the gun from his pocket and fired point-blank. The Kitai spun back against the wall and slid, arms outstretched, to the floor. The two Chinese down the hall turned and began running. Rone hit them both. He threw open the door and ran into the courtyard. He did not stop until he was back near the restaurant. He leaned against the tree to catch his breath.

"That bitch," he told himself. "That damn bitch tried to have me killed."

He walked five blocks before he found a phone box. Rone remembered the number. He put in the coins and dialled.

"Comrade Bresnavitch," he demanded.

"He is sleeping," replied the voice on the other end.

"Wake him," said Rone.

"That's impossible."

"Wake him. Tell him that a French embryologist wants to talk to him – a friend of Colonel Kosnov's."

There was a pause. Rone heard the phone being set down.

"This is Comrade Bresnavitch," announced a voice several moments later.

"This is Yorgi," said Rone. "I know that the merchandise was intended for you. I also know where it is and whose name is on it. I know where the money is."

"What are you talking about?"

"You have twenty minutes to meet me by the statue in

the square. If you are not there I will pass the information on to other parties."

"What statue?" Bresnavitch demanded.

"You have twenty minutes. Come by yourself. Just twenty minutes." Rone hung up.

The Zim pulled alongside Nikolayev Square and parked. Bresnavitch sat behind the wheel. Rone watched from the shrubbery. He waited another ten minutes. No other cars came into the area. He saw no one on the street. He walked to the car and got into the back seat. He pressed the gun against the back of Bresnavitch's head and said, "Drive. Keep both hands on the wheel."

Rone picked the route. Bresnavitch said nothing.

"You were Polakov's contact," Rone told him as they drove. "The two of you cooked up the letter idea together. It was intended for you, but not for the reasons Polakov told the West. You had no intention of gaining anti-Chinese support with it. You wanted it to black-mail Khrushchev. It was addressed to him. Only the letter was never delivered to you."

Bresnavitch remained silent.

"I know who has it and what happened. I've written the whole thing down. There are four copies. Two are in Moscow. If I don't pick them up within a day they will be forwarded to two members of the Central Committee. Two men you are not exactly on the best of terms with. Two other letters are already in the West. I have a week to pick those up or they become common knowledge. So if anything happens to me it also happens to you.

"Here is what I want. Passage out of Russia for me and the other American, Ward. If you don't already know where he is, you'd better find him by ten o'clock tomor-row morning. I want all arrangements made by then. You wait at your house. I'll telephone and tell you where to meet me.

"Until then I want free movement in Moscow. I'm going to move around openly. If I'm picked up, that's your problem. If I'm killed the letters go on their way."

"Can you recover the document?" Bresnavitch finally asked.

"You'll find out tomorrow. Now drive towards your house. I'm keeping the car. When you get home call the

Ukrayna Hotel and make a reservation under the name of my French passport, the passports you arranged for Ward and myself. I'll stay there – at your expense."

A few minutes later Aleksei I. Bresnavitch stopped the car and got out.

CHAPTER FORTY

CONFIRMATION

IT took Rone twenty minutes to reach the Ukrayna Hotel on Dorogomilovskaya Quai.

"Ah yes," said the delighted clerk. "Comrade Bresnavitch has just talked to us about you. Everything is ready."

The man reached under the desk and Rone automatically put his hand on the gun in his pocket. The clerk pushed a booklet in his direction.

"This tells you all about the Ukrayna," he explained proudly. "We have twenty-eight storeys, you know."

"Do you have a room with a telephone and bath?" Rone demanded.

"We have one thousand and twenty-six rooms, and every one not only has a bath and telephone, but a radio as well. We also have automatic shoe-shining machines. It's all in the booklet."

Rone slept soundly. His nine-o'-clock alarm call came at nine-fifteen. He soaked in the bath until nine-thirty, shaved with a razor provided by the hotel, dressed, placed the Intourist vouchers the clerk had given him in his pocket, and went downstairs for breakfast.

He was back in the suite at ten to call Bresnavitch.

"Let me talk to the American," he demanded.

"Certainly," Bresnavitch answered at the other end.

There was a pause before Rone heard Ward's voice. "Nephew, I hear tell you're living like you was on foreign aid."

"Stop the clowning," Rone ordered. "Now listen carefully. I owe you an apology, so I'm giving it to you now. I thought you had been working with them from the beginning. I know that I was wrong. They picked you up in the raid and you did what you had to to stay alive. Bresnavitch doesn't have the letter. I know where it is. I think I can get us out of this alive."

"I sure as hell hope so. The climate's a little thick where I'm sitting."

"Do you know if they made our travel arrangements?"

"I saw the tickets."

"I have several things to do," Rone confided. "Tell Bresnavitch to stay where he is. I'll call again in an hour and tell you where to meet me."

"Anything you say, Nephew. You're running the show now."

Rone hung up. He went to the bed, lay down, turned on the radio and lit a cigarette. Forty minutes later he took the lift to the lobby, got into the Zim and drove to Bresnavitch's house.

Rone was led to the upstairs study. Bresnavitch, Grodin and Ward were waiting.

"Now, my audacious Yorgi," Bresnavitch glowered, "let us hear what it is you have to say."

Rone eased back into the leather armchair.

"I'll start by telling you what was in the four letters I wrote." He spoke directly to Bresnavitch. "I began by tracing your association with Polakov. How the two of you unloaded certain of the paintings that were in your custody. From there I go to the evolution of the idea to destroy Khrushchev with the trumped-up letter. I follow each step. How Polakov came up with the idea of leaking out information to the West for money. This got their confidence. They began relying on it. Then it was shut off temporarily, which whetted their appetites even more. Next Polakov approached them with the plan to provide written evidence of your strength with them. You did a good job. At least one high Western official was convinced you not only planned to take over the Kremlin, but attack Lop Nor as well. Anyway, you got the letter – I mean, Polakov got the letter."

"Is that all?" asked Bresnavitch.

"I think it will be enough to hold your enemies. I did, of course, point out in detail that your intention had always been blackmail rather than action."

"And just how did you arrive at that conclusion?"

"You have always been anti-Chinese. You openly challenged Red China years ago. Having that opinion verified through the Lop Nor agreement was ridiculous. What would it gain you? The other anti-Chinese politicians were already in your camp. No, Comrade Bresnavitch, what you had to do was shake up the pro-

Chinese elements. Once they thought Khrushchev was planning an attack they would do your dirty work for you. Nikita would be out, and in the confusion you felt that your group could get in. Time worked against you. Khrushchev was deposed sooner than you had thought, and by a middle-of-the-road group. This all happened while you were waiting for Polakov to arrive with the letter.

"Your concern, comrade, was not so much who had the letter as it was who *knew* about it. You thought it was Kosnov, but it wasn't until you caught Ward that you found what we had already learned: the colonel had no part of it. The danger was that he might find out. So you eliminated that danger – both he and Erika were killed. Theoretically that should have cleaned your skirts, but then I came along. Now you have to deal with me. You have to make sure you get what I have written down."

"You appear very confident," said Bresnavitch.

"I am. I know who the Bellman is. That's what I'm trading you for our freedom."

"I want the document itself."

"You'll get the identity of the Bellman and where the letter is. That's all I'm offering."

"Even if I agree, what assurance do you have that I'll keep my word?"

"When I explain what I have to, there will be no reason for you not to."

"You're asking me to buy a pig in a poke."

"Then refuse me," Rone said calmly. He could see Ward shifting restlessly in his seat.

Bresnavitch and Grodin exchanged glances. Bresnavitch got up and walked to the desk. He returned with an envelope.

"Here are tickets, passports and all the papers you need." He flashed a smile. "You have my word as well. It's worth it just to watch your performance."

"When can we leave?"

"The plane departs from Moscow in five hours."

"Do you want the long or short version?"

"The unabridged edition, by all means. You must admit I've paid handsomely for it."

"The Bellman was Polakov himself," Rone began.

"Originally you and Polakov had agreed to charge the

West for information. Your motive was to gain their confidence. Polakov was to receive the lion's share of the money to handle the transaction. Not that the money didn't have interest for you. If the scheme backfired you might have to leave Russia on short notice. That's why part of the payments went to you.

"For Polakov it was a matter of professional reimbursement until he met Erika and fell in love. You see, the Pepper Pot had decided to retire. This took money. As time passed, his motivation changed. He wanted to milk all he could out of the operation."

"How do you know?" asked Ward.

"Uncle Morris paid me a visit just before the raid. They found Polakov's bank accounts. What happened was rather simple. At first Polakov started dividing the money unevenly in his favour. There would be no way to check on him. Since he made the deposits and reported the total price to Comrade Bresnavitch here. At the beginning all the payments were deposited in a Swiss Bank."

Rone turned to Bresnavitch. "Did the West demand that you continue supplying them with information after they had agreed to write the letter?"

Bresnavitch blanched.

"It was our understanding," Grodin broke in. "that Polakov's contact was to continue supplying information."

"But Polakov had told the West that once they agreed to writing the agreement the information would stop. It did. They received no more from that time on. However, five more parcels were delivered from the Moscow contact to Polakov, if I'm not mistaken."

"We believe that five is the number," Grodin concurred.

"You see," Rone began, "the turning point came when Polakov bumped into an old associate from his narcotics-peddling days, Chu Chang. Chang explained that Red China was interested in information. Admittedly they were new to cash-and-carry espionage, but they had money and that was exactly what Polakov was after. He began selling the same information to the Chinese that he was supplying to the West. He opened a special account in Tangier to bank the Peking money.

"It was no mistake that he cut the West off from those last parcels of information and gave them only to China. He was setting them up. Polakov had decided to peddle the letter to the highest bidder – and he had another new customer in mind: Kosnov.

"The colonel met with him in Paris and Moscow. Polakov was cautious. All he would let Kosnov know was that the Chinese wanted it and, of course, that it was a very explosive document.

"You see, Comrade Bresnavitch, Polakov held that letter for almost ten days before selling it. He was pushing the price and stalling you. In the end he would probably have told you that the West had refused to write it at the last minute. You would have had no way of knowing they hadn't."

"Who bought it?" demanded Bresnavitch.

"The Chinese."

Bresnavitch sat frozen. Slowly his lips began to twitch. Then he roared with laughter. "It is too funny. It is just too funny."

"Because they paid for it and now Khrushchev is out?" asked Rone.

"Not at all, not at all," said Bresnavitch, tears streaming down his face. "You must understand the Chinese mind. They will never trust any of us again. It is the first step. Don't you see? I've got what I wanted all along, but it happened by mistake. It's too funny. They will do my work for me."

"It could also start a war," Rone reminded him.

Bresnavitch laughed. "The sooner it comes, the better off Russia will be – and the rest of the world, for that matter."

CHAPTER FORTY-ONE

THE PRICE OF SILENCE

"YOU mean to tell me, Nephew," said Ward as he was shaving in Rone's bathroom at the Ukrayna Hotel, "that all that money is just *sitting* in some African bank?"

"It could be more than two million dollars."

"Two million dollars," Ward yelled. "There must be some damn way to get our hands on it."

"You shouldn't have killed Erika."

Ward came out of the bathroom half shaven. "You gotta believe me, Nephew, it was a mistake."

"It was a costly one."

Ward nodded and then went back to shaving. "What tipped you off?"

"Polakov didn't seem much concerned when the first two agents were sent in to get the letter and were killed. That's because he expected them to be. It was he who tipped off the Chinese. He had assumed they had taken the agents out. When he got into Moscow he learned that it was Kosnov who caught them. He realised that they wanted Kosnov to know exactly what was in the letter. They were trying to force an incident. They obviously didn't know Khrushchev's days were numbered.

"But Polakov had a good idea his might be. That's why he contacted Rudolf and asked if he could stay there. He couldn't go to Bresnavitch. His escape route was through the Chinese themselves, so he couldn't go there. And Kosnov was already hot on his trail."

"And the man in the car?" Ward asked, coming into the room.

"Chinese. Probably the Kitai."

"All seems kinda easy now, doesn't it?"

"And worthless."

"Whatya mean, worthless? We're each getting paid."

"How many lives did it cost?"

"Well, let me count. Polakov, the two agents, Kosnov and the German broad, Janis—"

"Never mind," snapped Rone.

"I told you once, Nephew, and I'll say it again – I'm sorry about that little girl of yours."

"Forget it."

Ward slipped on his jacket and looked at his watch. "We leave for the airport in about an hour. I got a little shopping I'd like to do first."

"Be careful."

"Of what?"

"Don't get into any trouble. An accident or the like."

"And miss the plane? Not a chance. I can't wait to get out of this town."

"Sure," said Rone.

Rone and Ward sat in the back seat of Bresnavitch's Zim.

"I can't get over it, Nephew, your first time across and you figure out the whole thing. It's really a hoot."

"Why did you let the Highwayman die like that?" asked Rone.

"That's the way he wanted it. He didn't have much longer to go on, no matter what, and he wanted to help. It was useless to everyone – except a dying old man."

"And who was that with him in the car, the man who was supposed to be me?"

"A corpse we bought from the city morgue. Hey, Nephew, whatya say we skip London and spend a few days in Rome first?"

"Why not just skip the trip altogether?"

"Now what the hell are you talking about?" asked Ward.

"You're staying here."

"In Russia?"

"That's right."

"Now why the hell would I do a thing like that?"

"Because you're Sturdevant."

"Nephew, you're having delirium."

"You're still Sturdevant."

"All right, let's hear how you came up with this wild one."

"It started when we first met, with the plastic surgery, but I let it slip by. What triggered it was the realisation that you were the man who took the message from the statue. I had only one simple question: why would the Russians do business with you? Why you in particular? I worked backward from there.

"First of all, you were the active head of the operation. You made the decisions and carried the Highwayman."

"He was sick."

"The way all of you operate, he would be in command as long as he could crawl, but he wasn't. You were. The thing that threw me off the track was that none of the others, men who had worked with Sturdevant in the past, knew you. You had changed your voice as well as your face."

"And when did this revelation strike you?"

"When Kosnov recognised you. Not your face – but your voice. That's what he was trying to pinpoint when he closed his eyes. He had done it just as I passed out. I kept wondering why he would recognise your voice but your own men wouldn't. It took a while, but as usual the answer was simple. You took great pains to alter your voice and speech pattern, but only for English. You never thought of doing it with your foreign languages. To Kosnov you sounded just the same as you did years ago – your Russian hadn't changed.

"Whether Bresnavitch recognised you or whether you told him who you are is immaterial. Years ago, Bresnavitch wanted you to replace Kosnov. For him, the timing is perfect. He has a big hold over you – your life. But you got something else you've waited a long time for – Kosnov."

Ward's smile was gone. He leaned back against the door and stared coldly at Rone. His lips tightened back over his teeth.

"If that were the case, Nephew, I wouldn't want anyone to know it. I wouldn't want you out of the country."

"You need me to go out. You need me to collect your money and to tell a story."

"It could be arranged some other way."

"But even more," Rone continued, "you need an insurance policy. I'm it. I realise now I had nothing to fear from Bresnavitch once the two of you had reached an agreement. In fact, I've been running around playing hero for no particular reason. One way or another I would have been let out of the country, because as long as I'm alive on the outside I can always reveal who he is. I'm sure you will convince him later I have detrimental evidence. For once the tables are turned. You need me to protect your Russian job."

"Nephew Yorgi," said Sturdevant, "you're a downright scoundrel."

"I have a few names for you."

"Now let's not end our friendship with sticky sentiment. I may be whatever you want to think, but you're smart in my book. You crowded me right into the corner. Yes sir, Nephew, you short-haired me. You short-haired me good."

The car pulled up to the airline terminal.

"Come on," said Ward. "I got you a little going away present."

Rone followed him down the hall into a side office. The Eurasian, throat bandaged, was standing against the wall.

"Let him see," said Sturdevant.

A side door was unlocked.

"Go on. Take a look."

Rone peered in. B.A. was lying on an ambulance cot smiling up at him. Her lips moved, but no words were audible.

The Eurasian pulled the door shut in his face and locked it.

"We had one hell of a time saving her,' Sturdevant said. "Only part of the poison got down. She's sorta paralysed. Can't talk as yet, but the doctors think she'll get better."

"What are you going to do with her?"

"That depends on you. You see, Nephew, as long as I got that girl where I can watch her I kinda have a feeling you'll use a little discretion in what you tell people about me. Like for instance how valiantly I died. I mean how valiantly Ward died."

"I'll get her out of here," Rone threatened. "Somehow I'll get her out."

"Ain't nothing wrong with trying."

Rone and Sturdevant sat silently in the private waiting room for some time. Finally Sturdevant spoke.

"You see, Nephew, there's not much place left for an old fellow like me to go. The world's passed me by. I have to play my own tune my own way. Not too much chance of that back West. Right now, Bresnavitch likes

281

my style. He'll let me do things my way. Now you may call that double-dealing or even treason – and it may be, but I risked my neck for better than twenty-five years back on our side, and all I got for it was a boot in the tail. Maybe I just couldn't make the grade the way things was turning. Well, here it's different, or so they tell me. They need a man with my talents, Charlie boy. I got nowhere else to go. I need action – and this is the only offer I've had."

Rone tried not to listen but he did. He was angry and disgusted with himself. He was embarrassed. Even at the last, Sturdevant had out-manoeuvred him. That in itself wasn't too bad, but the price was what hurt. B.A. would stay in Russia. There was nothing he could do right now to help her. He blamed no one but himself.

"I know you're kicking yourself in the back of the head because you think I put one over on you," Sturdevant said passively. "Well, maybe I did – and maybe I didn't. Maybe it was just a matter of minutes, a matter of time. Way back when we first met I told you it wasn't what you found out or did, it was how *fast* you found it or did it. You were almost as quick as me, Nephew. All you missed was that last little wrinkle, and who knows – with a day or two more you might have pegged it. Now that ain't so bad considering I got a dozen or two years of experience on you. It stands to reason I know a few tricks you don't. Even so, there's no one else living who could have come as close as you did."

Rone crossed the room and stared out at the airfield. A four-engine jet was touching down at the far end of the runway.

"It's a funny thing, Nephew, but I'm kinda proud of you, sorta like a father that brung up his kid right. You're a good operator, Charlie Rone, as good as there is. But there's always a little more to learn – most of all, about yourself. You have to know where you're weak. You see you care a little too much about other people's feelings. That ain't exactly an asset in our line of work.

"Kill the emotions, Charlie boy. Drag them out and stomp them into the dust. Look at the world for what it is.

"If there's anything to be learned from this little exercise we just been through it's exactly that. Potkin broke because of his wife and kids, and Kosnov got careless because of a woman, the same woman that made Polakov reach too far. And Nephew, it don't take much figuring to see why I got you in the corner right now either.

"You've just about finished kindergarten with flying colours, but before you get your diploma and gotta turn in a last little bit of homework, Do it well and I'll give you back the girl as a graduation present. Not right away, but in a year or so.

"This is the homework," Sturdevant said, handing him an envelope, "and that over there" – he pointed to a square, flat package on the table – "is a little something I picked up for your trophy room."

The scream of the jet taxiing to a stop almost drowned Sturdevant out, but he raised his voice and shouted at Rone. "Any time you're in doubt, think about Polakov and Kosnov and what ultimately killed them. Don't let yourself get caught, short like this again. As long as you don't need nothing from nobody, you'll be okay."

Rone took a window seat and looked out at Sturdevant. He was standing by the entrance shaking his clasped hands over his head.

Rone unwrapped the package and looked down at his own security file, the file that had been sent to Kosnov by Potkin. The photograph was of a man Rone had never seen – the corpse that accompanied the Highwayman to Siberia.

He opened the envelope and found a typewritten note and a pass book from a Swiss bank. He began reading:

Commencement Assignment
for Nephew Charlie

1. Deposit my share of money in account specified by bank-book.
2. Close up Tillinger house and send them all home. Don't overdo how valiantly I died.
3. Kill Potkin's wife and daughters, or I kill the girl.

A SELECTION OF FINE READING
AVAILABLE IN CORGI BOOKS

NOVELS

☐ FN7763	ANOTHER COUNTRY	*James Baldwin*	5/–
☐ FN7637	NINA'S BOOK	*Eugene Burdick*	5/–
☐ 552 07850 6	THE MAGICIAN'S WIFE	*James M. Cain*	3/6
☐ FN7317	THE CHINESE ROOM	*Vivian Connell*	5/–
☐ FN7777	THE WAR BABIES	*Gwen Davies*	5/–
☐ FN1278	THE GINGER MAN	*J. P. Donleavy*	5/–
☐ EN7488	BOYS AND GIRLS TOGETHER	*William Goldman*	7/6
☐ FN1500	CATCH-22	*Joseph Heller*	5/–
☐ FN7656	PINKTOES	*Chester Himes*	5/–
☐ EN7193	MOTHERS AND DAUGHTERS	*Evan Hunter*	7/6
☐ GN7774	THE MOGUL MEN	*Peter Leslie*	3/6
☐ FN7824	BLESS THIS HOUSE	*Norah Lofts*	5/–
☐ FN7779	THE DEER PARK	*Norman Mailer*	5/–
☐ 552 07852 2	NOW BARABBAS WAS A ROBBER		
		Deborah Mann	5/–
☐ FN7301	WEEP NOT, MY WANTON	*Nan Maynard*	5/–
☐ DN7594	HAWAII (colour illus.)	*James A. Michener*	10/6
☐ CN7500	THE SOURCE	*James A. Michener*	12/6
☐ 552 07849 2	CARAVANS	*James A. Michener*	6/–
☐ GN7727	THAT COLD DAY IN THE PARK	*Richard Miles*	3/6
☐ FN7322	UNTAMED	*Helga Moray*	5/–
☐ EN7823	THOMAS	*Shelley Mydans*	7/6
☐ FN1066	LOLITA	*Vladimir Nabokov*	5/–
☐ FN7684	ELIZABETH APPLETON	*John O'Hara*	5/–
☐ FN7766	APPOINTMENT IN SAMARRA	*John O'Hara*	5/–
☐ FN1162	A STONE FOR DANNY FISHER	*Harold Robbins*	5/–
☐ EN7749	OATH OF DISHONOUR	*Garet Rogers*	7/6
☐ EN7655	THE HONEY BADGER	*Robert Ruark*	7/6
☐ FN7670	HOW I WON THE WAR	*Patrick Ryan*	5/–
☐ EN7578	THE DEVIL IN BUCK'S COUNTY	*Edmund Schiddel*	7/6
☐ EN7567	THE DEVIL'S SUMMER	*Edmund Schiddel*	7/6
☐ FN7808	MOUNTAIN OF WINTER	*Shirley Schoonover*	5/–
☐ GN7810	THE PASTURES OF HEAVEN	*John Steinbeck*	3/6
☐ GN7600	THE RUNNING FOXES	*Joyce Stranger*	3/6
☐ 552 07848 4	BREED OF GIANTS	*Joyce Stranger*	3/6
☐ EN7807	VALLEY OF THE DOLLS	*Jacqueline Susann*	7/6
☐ FN1133	THE CARETAKERS	*Dariel Telfer*	5/–
☐ EN7352	EXODUS	*Leon Uris*	7/6
☐ 552 07851 4	THE PASSIONATE FRIENDS	*H. G. Wells*	5/–
☐ GN7672	SQUIRREL'S CAGE	*Godfrey Winn*	3/6
☐ FN7116	FOREVER AMBER Vol. I	*Kathleen Winsor*	5/–
☐ FN7117	FOREVER AMBER Vol. II	*Kathleen Winsor*	5/–
☐ EN7790	THE BEFORE MIDNIGHT SCHOLAR		
		Li Yu	7/6

WAR

☐ FB7813	THE VALLEY OF HANOI	*Irwin R. Blacker*	5/–
☐ EB7829	THE WAR LOVER	*John Hersey*	7/6
☐ FB7735	THE PAINTED BIRD	*Jerzy Kosinski*	5/–
☐ 552 07853 0	THE BEARDLESS WARRIORS	*Richard Matheson*	5/–
☐ FB7795	I SHALL FEAR NO EVIL	*R. J. Minney*	5/–
☐ EN7726	THE DIRTY DOZEN	*E. M. Nathanson*	7/6
☐ FB7476	THE SCOURGE OF THE SWASTIKA (illustrated)		
		Lord Russell of Liverpool	5/–
☐ FB7477	THE KNIGHTS OF BUSHIDO (illus.)		
		Lord Russell of Liverpool	5/–
☐ FB7703	THE DEATHMAKERS	*Glen Sire*	5/–
☐ GB7830	THE ANGRY HILLS	*Leon Uris*	3/6
☐ FB7752	THE ENEMY	*Wirt Williams*	5/–

ROMANCE

☐ 552 07858 1	HIGHLAND MASQUERADE	*Mary Elgin*	3/6
☐ GR7835	A FEW DAYS IN ENDEL	*Diana Gordon*	3/6
☐ GR7817	THE LOOM OF TANCRED	*Diane Pearson*	3/6
☐ 552 07859 X	THE TEST OF LOVE	*Jean Ure*	3/6

SCIENCE FICTION

☐ GS7742	THE HALO HIGHWAY (The Invaders)		
		Rafe Bernard	3/6
☐ GS7654	FAHRENHEIT 451	*Ray Bradbury*	3/6
☐ GS7803	NEW WRITINGS IN S.F.11	*John Carnell*	3/6
☐ GS7819	THE LOST PERCEPTION	*Daniel F. Galouye*	3/6
☐ 552 07860 3	THE MENACE FROM EARTH	*Robert Heinlein*	3/6
☐ GS7836	THE METEOR MEN	*Anthony LeBaron*	3/6
☐ ES7682	THE SHAPE OF THINGS TO COME		
		H. G. Wells	7/6

GENERAL

☐ FG7704	THE VIRILITY DIET	*Dr. George Belham*	5/–
☐ LG7566	SEXUAL LIFE IN ENGLAND	*Dr. Ivan Bloch*	9/6
☐ GC7382	THE BRIDAL BED	*Joseph Braddock*	3/6
☐ GG7296	KNOW YOURSELF	*Dr. Eustace Chesser*	3/6
☐ FG7593	UNMARRIED LOVE	*Dr. Eustace Chesser*	5/–
☐ KG7633	THE NEW LONDON SPY	*edited by Hunter Davies*	10/–
☐ 6000	BARBARELLA (illustrated)	*Jean Claude Forest*	30/–
☐ EG7804	THE BIRTH CONTROLLERS	*Peter Fryer*	7/6
☐ XG7313	SEX IN AMERICA	*edited by H. A. Grunwald*	6/–
☐ CG7400	MY LIFE AND LOVES	*Frank Harris*	12/6
☐ HG7745	COWBOY KATE (illustrated)	*Sam Haskins*	21/–
☐ FG1541	MAN AND SEX	*Kaufman and Borgeson*	5/–
☐ FG7820	THE CATHOLIC MARRIAGE	*William A. Lynch*	5/–
☐ FG7652	CHAPTERS OF LIFE (illustrated)	*T. Lobsang Rampa*	5/–
☐ FG7760	THE PASSOVER PLOT	*Hugh J. Schonfield*	5/–

WESTERNS

☐ GW7834	**TORTURE TRAIL**	*Max Brand*	3/6
☐ GW7801	**THE SEVEN OF DIAMONDS**	*Max Brand*	3/6
☐ GW7756	**SUDDEN – TROUBLESHOOTER**	*Frederick H. Christian*	3/6
☐ GW7840	**THE REBEL SPY**	*J. T. Edson*	3/6
☐ GW7841	**THE BAD BUNCH**	*J. T. Edson*	3/6
☐ GW7800	**CAPTIVES OF THE DESERT**	*Zane Grey*	3/6
☐ GW7816	**STAIRS OF SAND**	*Zane Grey*	3/6
☐ 552 07856 5	**MAN OF THE FOREST**	*Zane Grey*	3/6
☐ GW7653	**MACKENNA'S GOLD**	*Will Henry*	3/6
☐ FW7757	**THE GATES OF THE MOUNTAIN**	*Will Henry*	5/–
☐ GW7815	**MATAGORDA**	*Louis L'Amour*	3/6
☐ 552 07857 3	**DEBT OF HONOUR**	*Luke Short*	3/6
☐ GW7739	**BONANZA: ONE MAN WITH COURAGE**	*Thomas Thompson*	3/6

CRIME

☐ FC7786	**THE MEANING OF MURDER**	*John Brophy*	5/–
☐ 552 07855 7	**STRIP TEASE**	*Jean Bruce*	3/6
☐ GC7833	**DOUBLE TAKE**	*Jean Bruce*	3/6
☐ GC7623	**DEADFALL**	*Desmond Cory*	3/6
☐ 552 07854 9	**DEATH IN DIAMONDS**	*John Creasey*	3/6
☐ GC7755	**A TASTE OF TREASURE**	*John Creasey*	3/6
☐ GC7798	**TERROR BY DAY**	*John Creasey*	3/6
☐ GC7832	**AN AXE TO GRIND**	*A. A. Fair*	3/6
☐ GC7716	**AMBER NINE**	*John Gardner*	3/6
☐ GC7224	**THE LIQUIDATOR**	*John Gardner*	3/6
☐ GC7677	**DIE RICH, DIE HAPPY**	*James Munro*	3/6
☐ GC7814	**THE TRAIL OF FU MANCHU**	*Sax Rohmer*	3/6
☐ GC7784	**RE-ENTER DR. FU MANCHU**	*Sax Rohmer*	3/6
☐ GC7645	**THE DEATH DEALERS**	*Mickey Spillane*	3/6
☐ GC7753	**THE TWISTED THING**	*Mickey Spillane*	3/6
☐ GC7831	**THE BY-PASS CONTROL**	*Mickey Spillane*	3/6

All these great books are available at your local bookshop or newsagent; or can be ordered direct from the publisher. Just tick the titles you want and fill in the form below.

— — — — — — — — — — — — — —

CORGI BOOKS, Cash Sales Dept., J. Barnicoat (Falmouth) Ltd., P.O. Box 11, Falmouth Cornwall. Please send cheque or postal order. No currency, PLEASE. Allow 6d. per book to cover the cost of postage on orders of less than 6 books.

NAME ....

ADDRESS ....

(MAR. 68) ....